DEMIGODS
OF PENDILOR

DEMIGODS OF PENDILOR

The Lost Soul

BOOK 1

LAWRENCE E. JAYARAJ

CONTENTS

PROLOGUE

'The world is enigmatic and ever evolving. An era did exist when mortals lived purely for the amusement of gods, but on many planets, those times have changed. Mere mortals being sole habitants of the universe ended long ago.'

Time fell away when the sun god, Suriyar, peered down in all his shining glory and viewed a woman so beautiful even he, used to deflecting the attention of goddesses, could do nothing but stare in wonder.

Ourania, dark of skin and hair, beautiful and sweet, shining from within, as he shone from without. Living a life of love and kindness. She offered her prayers to him as others did, but from her, there was more behind it: a deep love.

Suriyar would not avert his gaze from the mortal woman, and for what should have been three days and nights, the light of the sun shone its never-ending light upon her.

The mortal people remarked on the sun god's affections and argued over what to do. Priests prayed, wise men debated, battles raged. None of it made a difference, and men turned their gazes from the sun, lest their eyes burnt from their skulls.

Ourania turned her head, and this burned Suriyar's heart. His relentless glare started to burn the green of many lands, much to the despair of the mortals.

In his pain and his love, he did a thing that a god should never do. He went to her as a man, tall and golden-haired, with skin shining in the reflection of the glow within him.

He stood before her, and still her eyes cast down, plump lips pressed together, joining her fellow humans in lowering her gaze in the presence of a god.

Suriyar approached the mortal woman, the creature with whom an obsession had been held for years now. In her presence, he did not impress a god looking upon a loyal subject but an equal. His heart filled with warmth.

'Behold me, beautiful Ourania,' he said, and although so much else was his to command, he found himself begging this of the mortal woman who had captured his heart. 'Please'.

She slowly raised her eyes. To his horror, that first glance made her fall back in pain, the awesome power of his presence rendering her blind. Suriyar placed his hands gently on her eyes and healed her, much to the wonder of the surrounding humans.

When Ourania dared look again, she found gazing upon her god was without pain. He looked back at her. Plump lips, dark eyes, and natural beauty. She put the most magnificent of goddesses to shame.

He held her, speaking of the love in his heart, and to his surprise, he found himself afraid in a way he had never been before. At least until the moment when she put her hand, silk soft, over where his heart in his borrowed form was.

'I love you too,' she whispered, and the words to him sounded like sweet honey. 'When the sun did not stop, I did not dare to hope that it did so, for me. Now you are here. It is all I could wish.'

The mortals lifted their hands in praise for their god as Suriyar swept Ourania on his chariot to his regal palace among the stars, where their lives would begin together.

As time passed, the union between the sun god Suriyar and the beautiful Ourania led to the birth of two demigod children.

Demigods are born with unique powers, and some hold stronger abilities than others.

Assyri, the oldest daughter, was filled with compassion and kindness for all living creatures. A divine creature, with blonde wavy hair, blue eyes, and holding mortal beings, such as her mother, in the same esteem as demigods. She believed, all were created as equals.

Bolara, two years younger, was the opposite of his sister. From youth, he exuded a dark rage. An angry young man, with dark-brown sinewy hair and a constant broody demeanour, holding the belief that ruling with tyranny was his right. Mortals and weaker demigods existed only to serve.

A strained relationship ensued between the siblings.

Both were aware that once their father, Suriyar, determined readiness, they would both be sent to the kingdom of Pendilor on the planet Zeldigar. As the oldest sibling, Assyri would be the rightful queen.

The thought of Assyri ruling filled Bolara with rage, but he dared not challenge Suriyar's decision, in open. To do so would incur the wrath of the sun god.

Peace and harmony are maintained on Zeldigar. No one is at war.

But like most habitats, sometimes abundance and harmony are not enough. The never-ending quest to attain more wealth and power has always been a weakness for mortals and led to many a bloodied battle.

History shows this to be the case for thousands of years. Greed and the desire for conquest are never quenched.

Why should this be any different with demigods?

CHAPTER 1

———— ◎ ————

THE KINGDOM OF PENDILOR

The lush gardens of Pendilor's royal palace are certainly a marvellous thing to behold. The gardeners work hard to preserve the exotic plant life separated in their respective gardens, the charming stone walls, and carefully crafted fences.

Bushes are trimmed and fashioned into simple mazes, featuring cobblestone paths, bird feeders, and stone fountains.

Visitors to the royal palace are delighted to wander through the garden mazes, inhaling the rich scents of flowers and fruit bushes as they discuss politics and current events while they bask in the sun.

Animals often roam these gardens, some half-tamed by the palace workers, others wandering in and out, hoping for snacks from the children or staff. Friendly little dogs, bleating goats, fluffy llamas, and groomed horses roam the enormous gardens, which the workers strive to make one with Pendilor's natural habitat.

Amid this maze of colour and wildlife is the palace itself. A grand fortress rooming servants and royals alike. Boasting dozens of corridors and rooms, an enormous dining area, and a ballroom for parties, its well-maintained walls of proud, strong stone.

Several turrets thrust into the sky, its walls and colour-tinted windows gleaming in the sun god's glory.

Two generations have passed since Suriyar looked upon the world and fell in love with the mortal Ourania. Now their children, Assyri and Bolara, have married and have families of their own. They reside together in the royal palace, nestled in the kingdom of Pendilor.

Queen Assyri is married to the mortal Lord Ranay.

Arteo is Assyri's oldest, a boy of seven, holding dark chestnut hair like his father and blue eyes like the sky of a spring day. Since he was a toddler, his gentle nature has been apparent to all who encounter him; he shows respect and empathy to the servants and the people of Pendilor.

Arteo's sister, Preeya, is a year younger, with blonde hair like her mother's, rolling waves of gold charming her nurses from the day she was born. Her glowing brown eyes always exude kindness to all, including the meekest of the garden's creatures.

The palace servants quietly agree Assyri's children are much like their mother, the queen; they are kind-hearted and respectful towards all.

However, the same cannot be said of Bolara's offspring. The younger brother of Queen Assyri also has two children with his wife, the half-witch Ritani. The oldest sibling, Ristos, is older than Arteo by a few months and holds striking resemblance to his father.

Dark of hair and with defined muscles from a young age, the handsome boy has cheekbones even the most desired of bachelors envy. From toddlerhood, Bolara's son shows an aggression rivalling his father's and a temper like thunder.

Syrana is Ristos's younger sister. Though she's also six years old like Preeya, she stands several inches taller than her cousin, with black hair and sharp eyes of dark green.

The palace servants have grown used to her cantankerous behaviour, seeing her crush bugs with sticks and tear wings of insects from a young age.

Whispers abound at the love for violence the children apparently share. But who can openly criticize the nephew and niece of the queen? Bolara and his ferocious temper have dispatched many a tongue-wagging servant deep into the Kalanya jungle for voicing an opinion on his children.

The people of Pendilor thank the gods every day that Queen Assyri is their ruler and not her younger brother.

When they aren't training or studying—Bolara's children under the tyrannical instruction of General Thamios, and Assyri's children under the tutelage of their own father—the boys and girls busy themselves with exploring the gardens, feeding the animals, and entertaining themselves as children do. Though the princesses and princes play together, their dynamics are often less than equal.

'Leave it alone, Syrana!' Preeya squeals, her blonde hair streaming behind her as she runs along the grass towards her cousin. Syrana is kneeling, the folds of her pink dress muddy, poking at an innocent beetle with a stick and blocking its escape when it tries to scuttle away. The little girl giggles, her tongue between her teeth, as she torments the poor creature.

'I said leave it alone!' Preeya reaches her cousin, trying to snatch the stick from her hands. Syrana stands to her full height, towering above her cousin.

'Mind your own business?' she yells, shoving Preeya hard. The girl falls with a gasp, crashing into the nearby bushes. Thorns scrape and cut into her skin, and the girl wails loud. Arteo comes running. Ristos, hearing the commotion, comes up beside his sister, hands on his hips.

'Preeya?' asks Arteo, reaching out a hand and pulling his little sister from the bush. Preeya whimpers, cuts on her bare arms and legs, twigs and leaves stuck in her hair. She brushes at the tears springing in her eyes, her lip trembling as she glances up to where her brother hovers over her with concern.

'What happened?' he asks.

'I . . .' Preeya glances over Arteo's shoulder at her cousins. Syrana folds her arms, green eyes glittering as she smirks, silently daring her to tell. Preeya's gaze slides to Ristos. She's seen him train with the scary General Thamios, how they spar day and night with wooden swords, practicing with bow and arrow.

Ristos is taught every day to never show pain or fear. If she tells on Syrana, Ristos might intervene and hurt Arteo.

'I fell over,' she says, casting her gaze to her feet, wincing at the sharp thorns pressing through her dress. In the corner of her eye, the beetle appears to flap its wings in thanks as it scuttles into the bushes. At least it got away.

'You fell, huh?' Arteo raises an eyebrow, as if knowing his little sister is lying. 'Come on, Preeya. Let's go inside. The nurse will tend to your cuts.'

Sniffling, Preeya follows him towards the palace. All around them are servants, gardeners, and caretakers, who nod respectfully to the young royals as they pass. None of them are fooled. Several of them likely saw what happened.

A passing guard, Galdin, gives Preeya an encouraging smile, and her heart lifts a little. Galdin is a close ally of Lord Ranay and has witnessed the early years of bullying received by the children.

⚑ ⚑ ⚑

'And then she went sprawling into the bushes,' Syrana giggles, scraping at the grass with her stick until she's pulling up soil. 'Did you see the cuts from the thorns? She didn't dare tell Arteo I pushed her. They're such cowards.'

'Both of them are weak,' Ristos agrees, caressing the wooden sword he's taken to carrying everywhere with him when he isn't sparring with General Thamios. 'Laughable that *they're* next in line for the throne and not us.' At age seven, he begins to sound like his father. 'They're weak, just like Aunt Assyri.'

Syrana half-listens, scraping hard at the soil, creating ugly lines. Fat worms squirm in the undergrowth, further victims of the little girl's incessant poking and prodding. She's too young to appreciate the unfairness of the royal line, more entertained with harming things smaller than herself.

'Princess Syrana,' says an old woman, one of the cooks who's been working at the palace forever, at least in the children's eyes. 'You shouldn't scrape at the soil like that, young lady. The gardeners work hard to preserve this garden to make such a lovely place for you to play in.'

The cook has grey hair tied in a neat bun, her leathery skin holding more wrinkles than the children can count. Piercing brown eyes sweep over them both, to where Syrana is kneeling on the grass with her stick, black hair over her face like a dark curtain, her brother standing beside her.

'Buzz off, you crusty old crone,' snaps Ristos, his fingers curling around the wooden sword. The cook shakes her head, wrapping her shawl tight around her shoulders as she ambles off, muttering something under her breath.

'And keep your mouth shut too, unless you want my father to turf you into the jungle,' Syrana yells after her. The cook doesn't answer, ambling back to the palace.

It might be Ristos's imagination, but she does appear to be walking more bent over than usual, as though the verbal lashing caused her physical harm. The thought brings him satisfaction. How dare a servant tell them what to do.

Ristos flinches when something touches his bare leg. He jumps away, turning to a small dog sniffing interestedly at his ankles. A stray, but someone has cleaned up its fur, a soft light brown.

The curious thing has floppy ears and bulging eyes, a long nose, and a pink tongue hanging out as it sits on its haunches, tail wagging, panting, and giving what can almost be described as a person-like smile.

'Get away, you stupid mongrel,' Ristos growls. The dog cocks its head, not understanding. 'I said get away!' Ristos delivers a harsh kick to the dog's side, and the animal gives a pained whimper, backing away with its tail down.

Syrana raises her stick, and the dog scampers off, a dirty footprint on its fur. Most of the animals know not to go near the siblings, for they'll never receive food or be petted. The dog, however, was a recent stray and, curious, and didn't know of the cruel nature of Bolara's children. That mistake will not be made again.

❈ ❈ ❈

'There, there, sweet girl. It's okay,' says a gardener later, out of sight of Ristos and Syrana. He brushes the dog's fur and feeds her some meat scraps from the kitchens. The dog munches gratefully, gulping down the food as she shivers under the gardener's warm hand.

'A hard kick, but nothing some rest won't fix,' he mutters to himself, examining the ugly mud print. 'Be sure to say hello to Assyri's children next time, girl. Don't bother yourself with Bolara's . . .' he lowers his voice to such a quiet whisper he can barely hear himself, 'Bolara's brats.'

⚹ ⚹ ⚹

Sunlight streams through the window of the council room. A long table of polished oak dominates the space on the flagstones. Around the walls are lanterns, not currently lit, and a large fireplace at the edge for winter.

Queen Assyri sits at the head of the table, looking radiant in an intricate gown of pale green, the sunlight from outside illuminating her hair and crown like a golden halo.

She inherited the dainty beauty of her mortal mother and the tanned colouring of her sun god father. Her eyes are blue like the sea on a summer's day, her blonde hair like woven gold, now tied up in an intricate style of braids and curls. Her caramel-toned hands sit folded in her lap as she speaks, her voice calm and clear.

Her committee of advisers sits around her, all dressed in noble clothing, watching their queen with serious interest. Assyri's brother, Bolara, sits at the other end of the table, smartly dressed in a black tunic with gold buttons, jaw tight as he listens to the queen.

His wife, the half-witch Ritani, has no place on the council but sits in the background, legs crossed on a chair. Her black hair is tied up, resting on her shoulder. She sits in silence.

Opposite her is Queen Assyri's husband, Ranay. In accordance with equality, the queen's husband has no say in the committee either, allowed only to attend and offer advice to his wife in the privacy of their chambers. His demeanour is calm, shoulders relaxed, as he stares proudly at Assyri.

'More food must be provided for the poor in the surrounding villages,' says the queen. 'We have more than enough here in the palace. Why should innocents starve just because they were born on the wrong side of the walls or have had a bad harvest?

'We can spare some wheat and barley at the very least. Macara, how much will it cost us to lower taxes for six months?'

'It will put a dent in our income for certain, Your Grace,' Macara replies. He has a goatee that he has a habit of tugging on, the feather in his felt hat bobbing as he speaks.

'So we live without jewels in our gowns and lavish new clothing for a couple of months,' says Assyri. 'I don't want a single person, old or young, rich or poor, starving to death whilst I rule.'

Ritani makes a noise, somewhere between a laugh and a cough, but says nothing. Queen Assyri ignores her.

'So we're just going to feed the entirety of Pendilor with our own coin?' Bolara scoffs, as though voicing his wife's unspoken opinion. 'This is ridiculous, sister. We cannot pander to every need of the common folk. It will make them lazy and too reliant on the crown. We might as well allow them to live in our gardens and dine on the food from our kitchens while we're at it.'

A faint murmur spreads around the table.

'Show weakness as queen, and you show our enemies that we're an easy target,' says Ritani, a small smirk on her face.

'What enemies?' asks Assyri, a thread of annoyance running through her. The queen is slow to anger, but Ritani has spoken out of line, something she has little patience with. 'The world has been at peace for years. Showing kindness to our subjects is *not* weakness. Speak out of line again, sister-in- law, and you will be unwelcomed to future meetings.'

Scowling, Ritani regains her composure, acknowledging the Queen's warning with a small nod.

Bolara glares at Assyri, tapping his knuckles on the table. 'Enough of this,' he rumbles, getting to his feet. He and his wife storm out of the room, and the slamming of doors echoes down the corridor. The council is silent in their wake.

Assyri closes her eyes, wrestling her patience. 'That's enough for today,' she says, somewhat tired as she dismisses her council. 'Thank you, everyone. We will discuss other matters tomorrow.'

With murmurs of 'Yes, Your Grace,' and 'Thank you, Your Grace,' the council disperses with scraping of wood and rustle of cloth. The setting sun shines its glory on the queen and her husband.

The sun, power, and protection from her father usually give Assyri comfort, but anxiety swirls in her stomach. Ritani speaking against her in front of the council shall not go unchecked.

Later that day, the queen heads to her chambers alone. Ritani appears at the end of the corridor. She's wearing a sweeping gown of dark red, her dark-brown eyes glinting as she makes a beeline for the queen.

'Ritani,' says Assyri calmly, privately wanting nothing more than to avoid the half-witch and head for her room. 'What can I do for you?'

'I don't appreciate you scolding me in front of the council,' Ritani snarls, jabbing her finger in the queen's direction. 'Especially when it is up to us all to ensure our rule is not weak.'

'And I don't appreciate you offering your opinion where it isn't permitted,' says Assyri. 'Nor your demeaning remarks on *my* rule. You know the protocol. Discuss things with your husband in private, and he can put forward ideas from you both.'

Ritani's eyes light up, not with emotion but with power. They glow emerald as her face twists into a snarl, magic crackling through the air like the thick air of a storm right before lightning strikes.

Assyri's hands glow with energy, defensive retaliation, and the two women glare at each other, rage building between the two powerful forces as their disdain grows.

'Assyri?' says a voice behind her. *Ranay.* At the same moment, her brother appears behind Ritani. Both men approach their wives, and the energy from them both fades. Assyri swallows, ashamed that her emotion almost got the better of her. Ritani's eyes revert to normal as Bolara takes her hand, murmuring something in her ear.

'My queen,' says Ranay, *gentle as ever.* Assyri turns to face her husband, the crease between his eyebrows, his strong jaw. She forces her lip not to tremble as guilt floods her. She cannot let her feelings for her brother and his half-witch wife interfere with her ability to rule.

'Come,' she whispers, taking his hand and sweeping towards their chambers, not sparing her sister-in-law another look.

❆ ❆ ❆

Safe in their chambers, the doors firmly closed and away from unfriendly ears, Ritani seethes to her husband. 'Your sister is a blight on this kingdom, Bolara!'

'A blight who is queen and whose palace in which we live,' Bolara reminds his wife, looking out of the window at the sprawling gardens. Down below, he can see the children playing together, oblivious to the argument that ensued between his wife and his sister. 'I don't like it any more than you do, but Suriyar's word is law. Assyri is older than me, and her first-born, Arteo, will ascend to the throne when she is gone.'

'She is not fit to rule.' Ritani folds her arms.

'Lower your voice, dear wife.'

'She'll be the ruin of this kingdom in our lifetimes, I know it.' When Bolara looks to her, her eyes light up again. They glow emerald, darkness rising as though she's sucking all the light from the room. He can sense the power building in her, yearning to be unleashed. '*You* would make a better leader, my husband . . . King Bolara.'

'And how would Suriyar react to his oldest child's throne being stolen, and by her younger brother no less?' Bolara scoffs. He would be lying if he denied ever fantasizing about being on the throne, about Assyri being gone and *he* ruling Pendilor, but it is a fool's dream. Even if Assyri somehow could be ousted, the throne would immediately go to Arteo, then to Preeya, or Arteo's eldest child.

'Why is it not possible, Bolara?' asks Ritani, her rage fading as she slides an arm around her husband's waist, joining him to gaze out of the window.

The sun has nearly set, casting orange on the gardens. Somewhere outside, a servant calls to the children. Syrana throws away her stick and runs towards the palace, skirt and black hair streaming behind her. Ristos follows behind, his wooden sword bouncing against his thigh.

'Perhaps, with our combined powers, we may be strong enough to take the throne,' murmurs Ritani. 'The children will grow into lethal forces. They both already show promise in their training. We also have the formidable Thamios at our side. What's to say we can't take the kingdom by force, sometime in the future?'

Bolara shifts, listening to his wife. The idea is ludicrous, insane. However . . .

'We are a supreme force, Bolara. To sit back and let Assyri rule would be a terrible waste of those powers,' she whispers, her breath tickling his ear, sending heat through him. She kisses his neck, like fire on his skin. 'One day, Suriyar will not be concerned with this place any more,' whispers Ritani. 'We may even become too much of a force for him to contain.'

Bolara says nothing, watching the sunset. His wife's words have struck a chord with him, however, and he finds himself pondering.... wondering.

CHAPTER 2

SHAKTI POWERS

'You're late,' says Master Chirok as Preeya, now thirteen years old, emerges from a cherry bush to join the class. The years have turned her chubby childishness into youthful beauty, favouring her mother's blonde locks. She swallows, wilting under her teacher's stern gaze.

She tends to go wandering around before class, inhaling the sweet scent of the palace garden flowers, watching butterflies or birds flittering between the branches. Much more interesting than being tormented by her cousins. Often, she loses track of time and ends up late for class.

'I'm sorry, Master Chirok,' she murmurs. Their lessons are held in the gardens, surrounded by nature and under the sun. A beautiful place to learn, with its rolling green hills like gentle waves on the ocean, surrounded by exotic wildlife. Some trees are so tall they almost touch the heavens. Rivers carve their own pathways as though they have minds of their own.

'Stop daydreaming. You're wasting everyone's time.' Ristos smirks at her. The years have broadened his shoulders and developed his handsome chiselled features. But when he glances at her like that, Preeya's stomach churns in fear.

'Sit down, Preeya, or I'll make you sit down,' Syrana threatens, green eyes glinting as they fix on Preeya like a bird of prey upon a mouse.

Bolara's offspring do not particularly favour Master Chirok; Preeya being scolded is just another reason to torment and humiliate her. Though the girls are the same age, Syrana is two inches taller.

Preeya sinks into her chair, a hot blush creeping up her neck, her demigod cousin's threat beating in her ears like battle drums. She has endured Syrana's and Ristos's physical and emotional bullying for years. It's one of the reasons she prefers exploring the palace gardens to sitting with them in class.

She often goes back to the palace many times with a new bruise or cut, mumbling some excuse when a servant or her mother enquire about it.

'I had a fall.'

'Um . . . I ran into a tree.' 'I was clumsy today.'

The lies spill from her mouth easily, and her mother simply nods, nothing but love in her eyes as she says in her soothing voice, 'Be more careful next time, my beautiful princess.' Perhaps she is aware of the endless bullying, but it's not like talking to her brother, Bolara, about it will change anything. Perhaps the queen hopes that the children will grow out of it and learn to vent their energy elsewhere.

Preeya's brother, Arteo, stares straight ahead, ignoring the banter going on around him. He's looking more and more like their father, Ranay, with each passing day. Rich chestnut-brown hair and eyes the colour of a spring sky. His handsome features, the envy of the whole kingdom.

'Go on, master,' he blurts as their cousins snicker. 'Please explain the Shakti levels.'

Master Chirok eyes them all with his dark-blue stare. He's short for an adult man, slim with a long beard the colour of freshly fallen snow, matching the robe that grazes his boot-cladded ankles. Syrana mumbles to Ristos, 'Does the old man have a wardrobe full of identical robes, or does he wear the same one, over and over?'

The elderly master carries a wooden cane around everywhere he goes, which he likes to rap on the boys' backsides if they aren't paying attention. The girls are spared from this punishment, but his sharp glare can cut glass and is generally enough to keep them in line. He's fixing them all with that intense gaze now, silently goading them to settle down.

'As demigods, you all have Shakti abilities,' replies Master Chirok, walking between the students with his gnarled hands behind his back, gripping his cane. 'Whether you have one mortal parent or not is irrelevant as you still hold divine blood,' he continues. 'Each level is an enhancement of the previous. Shakti 1 is superhuman strength and agility, and most demigods have at least this at their disposal. Shakti 2 adds the ability to move at breakneck speed.'

'Arteo's got to be a Shakti negative,' whispers Ristos, snorting with laughter at his own joke.

'Then Preeya must be a puny mortal,' Syrana remarks, reaching over to yank a chunk of Preeya's blonde hair.

'Yeowch!' the girl yelps.

'Leave her alone!' Arteo snaps, getting up.

'What are you going to do about it?' Ristos jumps to his feet so fast his chair nearly topples over, his fists curling. He is always ready for a fight, any excuse to throw punches. He taunts Arteo all the time, hoping he'll snap. His superior training from General Thamios, who encourages the boy to be merciless, has shaped the fourteen-year-old into a bloodthirsty youth.

Arteo, however, takes after his parents, sharing his sister's passion for nature and academics, not physical contests, although he has the physique of a young warrior.

Preeya pulls herself from Syrana's grip. 'I'm okay,' she says, getting up to lay a hand on her brother's shoulder. He is shaking with rage. 'Please, Arteo, let it go.'

Anger swims in Arteo's eyes as he looks at her, jaw tight. He slowly sits back down.

'Yeah, sit back down, you weakling, before I kick your ass.'

Crack. The cane slams on the desk like thunder, sending a shock wave that blasts through the palace gardens and knocking Ristos back into his seat. They all sit up to see Master Chirok glaring down at them all.

'Enough!' he rasps. 'Or you will enjoy my cane against your royal backsides.' He pauses. 'That goes for all of you.'

His threat is real. Master Chirok has been teaching princes and princesses for years, even tutoring their parents, Assyri and Bolara. He is not afraid to dish out punishments, and he does not make idle threats. In a past life, he had held the battlefield with the mighty Suriyar and was revered and respected by all. Though he has aged, he is still a capable fighter and held in high esteem.

The teacher continues as if no interruption occurred. 'Shakti 3 allows for superior agility and releasing low-level energy bolts. Those with this level can use the vitality of the sun for their power. Shakti 4 allows you to place a protective cosmic shield around yourself in times of need.'

Preeya and the others listen intently, all wondering the same thing. *What Shakti level am I?*

'Shakti 5 is the most gifted of all,' continues Master Chirok, looking pleased that he has captured the students' attention. 'Simultaneously being able to attack and defend with cosmic energy at the same time.' He pauses. 'But bear in mind, using too much cosmic force in a defensive or attacking strategy drains the individual of vital energy and can make them an easy target for someone armed with a weapon.'

Chirok scratches his chin, then continues, 'Time is required to recoup. The strongest warriors will balance cosmic weaponry with skilled archery and swordsmanship. A necessary balance is required.'

'Who in our kingdom has these powers, master?' Preeya asks meekly, in her gentle voice.

Before their teacher can respond, Arteo blurts, 'Would a Shakti 2 be able to beat a Shakti 4?'

Master Chirok raises a bushy, white eyebrow in Preeya's direction. 'I believe the queen and her brother hold these abilities. General Thamios has also shown Shakti 5 traits.'

Ristos slowly glances skyward and wonders, *What destructive capabilities would I have as a Shakti 5?*

'Sometimes these powers are only released under some type of duress . . . like when the user's life is in peril.' Master Chirok gazes into the distance, blue eyes narrowed in thought. 'Some thought to have lower abilities have shown increased levels when cornered in battle, for example.'

The teacher turns to Arteo. 'In answer to your question, young prince, it has not yet occurred. A lower-level Shakti can battle one of a higher level, of course, but without assistance, they usually cannot defeat a more gifted demigod without the gods on their side.'

'What level will I be?' demands Ristos, a grin splitting his handsome face in anticipation. He wants to be a Shakti 5 more than anything else in the world. Preeya could not think of anything worse than he holding such power, maybe perhaps, his sister being as powerful might be worse.

'It is yet unknown,' Master Chirok replies. 'You are simply still too young. Whilst you may all show some minor abilities while you mature, your real capabilities won't be uncovered until you reach eighteen. We call this the *age of reveal.*' He gazes at them all with a rare smile. 'You will continue to train and learn the arts of warfare . . . and rule.'

Maybe it was Preeya's imagination, but it seemed their teacher's eyes swept to her cousins at the mention of war and to herself and Arteo when he said rule. 'Remember, as I mentioned earlier, greater powers manifest under extreme battle conditions.'

Preeya suppresses a shudder. She hopes she'll never be in such a dire situation.

'Are there any Shakti levels higher than 5?' blurts Syrana.

Master Chirok gazes skywards towards the sun, as if talking to his old friend, Suriyar. 'Well, there is a myth about a demigod who has level 6 Shakti powers. Formidable enough to challenge the very gods themselves. Superior cosmic blasts and the ability to hover in the air. However, there are none in the kingdom that have shown such prowess. It is unlikely they exist, and it is a fanciful tale for bedtime stories, nothing more.'

There is a pause as everyone ponders the implications of Shakti 6 abilities.

'And what level are you, old man?' Ristos asks arrogantly.

Without blinking, Master Chirok holds out his hand. He closes his gnarled fingers, and when he opens them to reveal his palm, it is glowing with a soft, amber light. The children stare as the glow turns to bright yellow. Without warning, he jabs his palm towards Ristos's chair, and its leg shatters in an instant.

The youth gives a cry, arms flailing like an octopus trapped in a bucket, as he falls to the ground with a loud crash. Preeya and Arteo roar with laughter.

'You will refer to me as master, *young* man,' says Master Chirok, voice dry as desert air. 'That is the end of the lesson for today.' He gathers his books from the desk, and Preeya swears she sees him turn to give the tiniest of winks.

Ristos scrambles to his feet, face flushed with anger as Preeya and Arteo catch each other's gazes, falling into fresh giggles. Preeya catches him mumbling to Syrana, 'The old man will pay for that one day.'

Arteo and Preeya chatter and laugh about the incident, satchels hoisted on to shoulders as they head to the royal animal enclosure next to the training arena. The palace wildlife staff keep wounded animals from the nearby jungle here, nursing them back to health until the royal animal keeper, Tarap, believes they can survive on their own.

Tarap is a middle-aged man, holding a strong bond with animals, his short brown hair and slight build belying his ability to hold no fear in nursing ferocious animals back to good health.

He holds many scars from head to toe, courtesy of sharp claws and the odd set of teeth. *Nursing wild animals does have its challenges.* The queen has allowed him to care for injured wildlife, and her children spend many hours visiting the animals on a regular basis.

Preeya inhales the ruffled fur, feed, and manure as they pass massive enclosures of lions, tigers, exotic birds, and Tolverines. Most are wrapped in bandages or lying quietly, glancing at the young royals before lapping water from bowls or closing their eyes to rest.

Preeya and Arteo are particularly fond of two baby Tolverines, abandoned by their mother somewhere in the jungle and rescued from a wild Burrintot. These rhinoceros-like brutes love to feast on abandoned wildlife, but the baby Tolverines made it to the enclosure with non-fatal injuries, their mother nowhere to be found.

Though still babies, they're already huge, the size of fully grown lions. The princess adores their big eyes and soft fur.

'Hello,' coos Preeya to the pups, admiring their bright-brown eyes and cute little snouts. They're recovering from their injuries, stitches visible on their fur. The nearest comes to sniff Preeya's fingers through the cage bars.

Syrana and Ristos, who have no interest in wildlife or anything they consider weaker than them, watch from afar, glaring daggers at the children.

They consider taking care of defenceless animals a terrible waste of time and much prefer hunting trips with their father, Lord Bolara, chasing down wild animals and slaughtering them for fun.

Ahead, General Thamios waits for them, his burly arms folded, always wearing his glinting black armour like it's a part of him. It is time for their second lesson of the day: war craft, under their father's supervision.

General Thamios is a brute of a man. Dark black hair, brown eyes, and a huge scar running down the left side of his face. Built like a tank, but with amazing agility for such a huge demigod. Having fought many battles over the years, he is well versed in all arts of warfare and is a formidable warrior.

He is feared by all as a supreme demigod, perhaps only matched by Bolara and Assyri in abilities. He taught Bolara from a young age and is a loyal ally to the queen's brother, sharing many of his philosophies. The kind rule of Assyri is one he views as weak.

✄ ✄ ✄

The training arena is a sight to behold. Battered targets take up most of the surrounding space, all varying heights and distances for keen archers to test their skills. Obstacle courses of rope ladders and timber bridges hang on the surrounding trees, challenging the fittest of demigods to swing and climb and jump from great heights, if they so dare.

Swords, arrows, shields, and lances, all crafted from rungan steel, the hardest metal in the universe, wait for demigod warriors in training to spar with. Other weapons made from timber are used for light training and practicing battle techniques.

Syrana and Ristos eagerly approach the waiting armour, glinting in the sunlight, tailored perfectly to the teens' measurements.

Fifteen minutes later, there's a *thwack* as Ristos fires an arrow, hitting a target in the bullseye fifty feet away. He tosses his hair, a smile curling on his lips. He has immense skill with a bow, and he knows it.

'Super shot!' Syrana calls.

General Thamios, enormous and regal in his armour, growls. 'Hit the target one hundred feet away, boy, not the near one.'

That is the way of the surly general. He doesn't praise them, only grunts, and offers more challenges, always pushing the children to their limits. Not that Ristos cares about encouragement. He's being trained to be an elite killing machine, not to be showered in praise.

Ristos nocks a new arrow, pointing with precision, pulling the string tight with his strong fingers. He lets it fly, and it cracks through the air. It pierces the target several inches from the bullseye.

'Again,' General Thamios snaps.

His smile vanishes. Ristos releases a third arrow, which narrowly misses the bullseye again. Syrana groans behind him. It is a shot any mortal, or demigod, would be pleased with, but not General Thamios. He expects perfection, even when his student is only fourteen years old.

'Again,' he mutters. His voice rumbles like thunder on the horizon before a storm.

Ristos practices and shoots at the target one hundred feet away, but with the scrutiny of his teacher, the pressure to hit a perfect bullseye every time starts to show.

Though he has hit many, Thamios expects him to hit all. After hours, the boy's fingers are bloody. Ristos keeps his jaw tight, not betraying the slightest hint of pain.

With General Thamios's blessing, he finally throws down his bow and starts the obstacle course, lunging, jumping, climbing, somersaulting. He doesn't bother wiping his calloused, bloody hands, instead smearing all the obstacles with crimson, as though the equipment is privileged to receive such a gift.

He finishes the last rope with an athletic swing and a mighty somersault, landing perfectly on his feet, crouched at ground level, arms extended to his side.

General Thamios grunts. 'Faster next time.'

Ristos, sweating with perspiration and breathing hard, nods to the general and starts removing his armour. He glances at where his father is watching, waiting for any sort of acknowledgement. Bolara watches, his expression blank, before shifting his gaze to his daughter.

Ristos snatches up a jug of water, leaving the training arena behind to a lush, green hill overlooking the gardens. Syrana is still training, dark hair flying around her beautiful face as she clacks her wooden sword with a guard in training, her teeth bared like a wild animal.

She gives a crazed scream as she ducks, dodging a blow aimed at her side. She leaps over a clumsy sweep, landing on her feet with the reflexes of an alley cat.

Like her brother, Syrana wields her sword with dexterity and power. She lands a blow to the trainer's leg, pivots, and jumps, landing a strong blow to the side of his helmet with a metallic clang. Speed and agility are her forte, too fast for the guard in training General Thamios has pitted her against. The man glances at the royals' teacher as if silently pleading for mercy.

'Finish him!' roars General Thamios.

Syrana displays her acrobatics like a seasoned gymnast. With each weave and jump, she lands blow after blow. More guards in training approach her, some looking nervous as the girl appears to have a crazed look about her.

She cuts and pounds and smashes with skill, the years of training evident in her wiry frame, face contorted with determination, until the guards yield and beg, clutching bloodied body parts and fresh bruises.

She raises her sword at the final guard who is already lying on the ground, cowering to the incoming blow, when Thamios bellows, 'Enough!' The palace training grounds are not the place to beat opponents to death. Not with many palace dwellers watching on and news possibly reaching the queen.

There are plenty of opportunities to do that in the jungles, chasing wild animals or the jungle dwellers of Kalanya. Those people do not feel the bruise of a wooden sword but the might of rungan steel, crushing bones and spilling red.

Lord Bolara and General Thamios lead jungle sessions such as these, and they're kept secret from Queen Assyri and her husband, Ranay. According to them, they are simple hunting expeditions, essential for the children's training. But creatures of another kind are on their list, and for egotistical, narcissistic demigods, they're the height of amusement.

Syrana gives a frustrated cry and throws down her weapon. General Thamios ended her fun. She unstraps her armour and dumps it on the dirt, storming over to where her brother is watching. With a smirk, General Thamios turns to Bolara, who nods in acknowledgement, an eyebrow cocked in approval.

✂ ✂ ✂

Preeya tosses a chunky piece of meat between the cage bars to the baby Tolverines, who snarl and snap at one another as they tear into it with their sharp teeth. Even injured and in their infancy, these animals are deadly with their razor-sharp claws. They'll be the size of elephants when they hit adulthood. Not even the horses would be safe if they escaped. Once they've fully recovered, they'll be ready to be safely led back to the jungle.

'Look at the jaws on that one,' Preeya exclaims, tucking a blonde curl behind her ear. She holds a love for even the fiercest of creatures, looking upon the intimidating beasts with respectful fascination.

'I would not want to get into a tangle with one of those, sister,' Arteo remarks, watching the clamp-like jaws of the Tolverines chomp as they gobble up the meat.

In his peripheral vision, Arteo spots Ristos and Syrana training. They're talented, everyone within the kingdom and surrounds is aware, but he doesn't let it perturb him.

One of his cousins' mistakes is underestimating himself and his sister. They don't spend *all* their time taking care of animals and relaxing in the gardens. They've been doing their own secret training, under the supervision of their father, Ranay, and his trusted friend Galdin.

Galdin is the strongest of Assyri's guardsmen. He's a Shakti 4 demigod who trains the youths under Ranay's watchful eye. Queen Assyri is unaware of these training sessions, but Ranay feels it's important that their children know how to use their abilities, even if they might never have to use them.

Queen Assyri is busy running the kingdom and juggling the antics of her brother; their children's war craft training is a distraction she does not need.

CHAPTER 3

No Remorse

Queen Assyri's fists clench as she glares over at her younger brother. Bolara is standing beside the general, the corpse of a villager at their feet. They executed him without her counsel.

Lord Bolara stands regal and tall, undeniably handsome but with a cruel edge she has endured since they were children. He holds no weapon in his hand, though he doesn't need one. He has his powers, as well as the brute Thamios, beside him. He's wearing an impassive expression, as though he's just arisen from slumber, not murdered an unarmed man in cold blood.

It makes Assyri sick. She is not a cruel ruler. Her heart cleaves in two as she gazes down at the corpse. He's a simple commoner; he probably left behind a family. How could Bolara have done this?

A deafening silence hangs in the throne room. Courtiers, lining up to talk with the queen, purvey the scene, some with their hands over their mouths in shock, staring at the dead commoner at Bolara's feet. The guards stand rigid in their armour, waiting to see what the queen will do about this outrage.

Even Ranay is hanging back, though he's close enough to silently tell her she has his support if needed. As the queen, she must make the first decision.

She clasps her hands together, her rage growing in them, her power as a demigod flowing through her veins with anger, until it threatens to burst from her fingertips and obliterate the traitors before her.

'Enough,' she whispers instead. Bolara's eyebrows raise. 'Sister—'

'Your actions have undermined me,' she says, interrupting him. He doesn't deserve the chance to speak. 'And it is not the first time. Since the moment I became queen, you have treated me as if I do not lead. As if I *should* not lead.'

Her anger is like a winter breeze, the rarity of her losing control, attracting the attention of others in the throne room. A nearby aide flinches at her icy tone, or perhaps it's from the energy, brewing to be released.

Bolara appears more confused than contrite, handsome features creasing as though he's spotting an undiscovered species in the jungle. His green eyes sweep the courtiers, as though seeking their support.

They stay silent, not interfering in the siblings' argument. Assyri can see it plain as day on their faces—they fear him. Some staff nearer the doors shuffle, as though longing to escape.

Bolara gestures to the dead man. 'If you want me to treat you like a leader, dear sister, then lead,' he says. Thamios stands beside him, his blade still in hand, red dripping from it and pooling on the throne room floor. Still fresh, still warm, obscuring the intricate pattern on the mosaic tiles. His cold indifference breaks Assyri's heart.

'Killing someone for stealing fruit is not leading,' Assyri shoots back. Her brother scowls upon her with contempt, again shifting his gaze to challenge the onlookers. She glares, thinking, *Why? Why is he so cruel?*

'A real leader shows empathy,' she says.

Bolara snorts at that. 'A real leader instils fear. They are to be obeyed. They enforce their will and are swift to punish any who go against them.'

The glassy, unseeing eyes of the farmer gaze up, his throat open, the blood flow stilling. He didn't need to die.

'You went against me by ordering this man to be killed without my permission,' she says. She hates that this argument is so public, but Bolara knows exactly how to push her buttons, to make her react before they're behind the safety of closed doors.

She wrestles control of her emotions, dampening the power that's fighting to emerge. She turns to her aide and murmurs, 'Find this man's family. Explain to them all that has happened and offer them recompense.'

'Yes, my queen.'

Before the aide can leave, Bolara scoffs and steps over the body of the fallen man like he's a tree root, not a person. The royal guards dart forward at his approach. Brother of the queen or not, approaching the throne so boldly is going too far.

'A man steals from us, breaking our laws, and you want to reward that behaviour by giving money to his family?' he demands in a cold but calm voice.

'What would you do, Bolara? Kill them too? Is violence your answer to everything? Should we punish every small crime with death?'

She's being sarcastic, but to her shock, her brother pauses and tilts his head. Then he nods, gently, as if the idea is not unreasonable. It makes her stomach go cold.

'If we don't kill them,' says Bolara, 'then we show weakness as a kingdom. Remove the criminal'—he gestures to the body behind him—'and all who love him. That will make people respect us and think wisely before breaking the law.'

'Respect us or hate us,' Assyri retorts, 'I will not rule with tyranny and fear.' She glances to her aide. 'Go do as I've asked.'

The woman appears grateful to get away, almost tripping over her skirt as she all but runs from the throne room, giving Bolara a wide berth.

At Assyri's gesture, a couple of guards move forward to remove the body from the room. They leave a trail of blood as they drag the corpse away, a path of red hate for her brother's crimes. She gives orders for the body to be returned to the man's family for a proper burial.

'This is foolishness,' General Thamios murmurs. The enormous general is, as always, wrapped in black armour, his dark eyes cold and without any remorse for his part in executing the commoner. Over the years she has known him, she's seen no compassion in the large man.

The queen casts her eyes towards him, her eyes glowing with rage. He bows his head under the weight of her gaze.

'Remember your place, General,' she says, wishing that she didn't have to tolerate the brutal man's presence.

Thamios sweeps a bow of apology with the crisp efficiency of a military man. It lacks sincerity, like always, not that she can prove it. His loyalties are to Bolara and no one else.

Bolara does not bow, instead saying, 'You will regret this, sister.'

Whispers ripple through the throne room, murmurs of shock at such a defiant tone.

'Is that a threat, brother?' she asks, turning towards her brother, forcing herself not to clench her fists. Surely not. He would not dare?

He gives a smile, strained and insincere. 'I would not threaten you, dear queen. I am merely pointing out the dangers of letting criminals go unpunished. What would you have had me do? Gently chastise the man who dared steal from the palace gardens? That would only have encouraged him to do it again. This way, the thief is eliminated.'

'People can err in judgement,' Assyri insisted. 'Perhaps he was poor or his family starving.' When would her brother understand that? 'That doesn't make them evil, and it doesn't mean they deserve to die.' She sighs, rubbing the brow of her forehead. 'You are to be the one to make recompense, Bolara. The compensation will come from your personal vault.'

His green eyes flash with anger. 'It will not.'

'It most certainly will.'

She isn't going to let him get away with doing whatever he chooses, especially when it undermines her ruling. She holds the crown, not him.

'Dear sister, you've made it clear you will not punish those who wrong you or the kingdom.' He turns on his heels without bowing, Thamios at his wake, sheathing his blade without bothering to clean the blood still dripping from it.

The guards look to Assyri, but she shakes her head. Better to let Bolara storm out without confrontation from her men. Her brother is a demigod, and like it or not, the guards would be no match for him. Only she might have the ability to stop him if it comes to a real fight.

She prays it will never come to that.

Assyri turns, seeking her husband. Ranay appears as perfect to her as he always has, the last of her anger ebbing away as her heart fills with love at his gentle smile. He lets her deal with Bolara out of respect, not disregard. As Ranay reaches her side, she says softly, 'He's getting out of control.'

Her words don't reach the ears of the courtiers, who busy themselves with chattering among themselves or watching the servants as they come to clean up the blood on the tiles. Assyri is certain that Bolara wouldn't have done any of this a short time ago. Killing innocents, pushing her to use violence. *What has changed?*

'I know,' says Ranay. He takes his hands in hers, his palm warm and smooth. 'He's getting worse.'

'I'm . . . afraid.' It hurts her to say that. She shouldn't be afraid of her own brother. Of him, of what his children are becoming. 'He's getting stronger, and his children . . . with Thamios training them, they're getting more skilled by the day. Soon Ristos and Syrana's abilities will come to the fore, and then what will happen?'

Ranay nods, a crease in his eyebrows as he strokes his wife's hand with his thumb. She feels herself calming at his presence alone.

'He'll see reason,' he says.

She exhales, as though trying to blow the tension from her lips. 'I hope so.'

'Whatever happens, the gods protect us.' He gently squeezes her fingers, guiding her to her feet. 'Come, let's stop worrying about Bolara's children and see to our own.'

What a good idea; nothing gives Assyri greater joy than her children. Arteo is bright and intelligent and has his father's appearance. Preeya inherited Assyri's own bright-blonde locks and love for nature. Yes, seeing them would help wash away the turmoil swirling in her chest.

'You're dismissed,' she says to the courtiers. Some are disappointed that they aren't able to speak with the queen today; others are relieved they won't be required to take sides in the latest spat between Assyri and her brother.

'Come, my husband,' she says to Ranay.

They make their way through the palace hand in hand, servants bowing and scurrying past, the sun casting its light through the colourful windows, casting multi-coloured rays on the carpet. Courtiers and guards follow them like ducklings, but she dismisses them with a wave of her hand. She needs this time with her family.

They enjoy the beauty of the palace around them, the framed paintings, the soft carpets, and the flowers in vases the servants take care of daily. Though she appreciates it, some part of Assyri is embarrassed by the extravagance.

Each jewel, each gold-framed piece of art, can provide food for the poverty-stricken of the kingdom. Still, it is impossible to gaze upon the opulence of their wondrous palace and not feel *something*.

Statues of former rulers stand here, paintings depicting past battles with darkness and bringing order to the world, memories captured and immortalized in art. There is a statue of Suriyar, her and Bolara's sun god father. Never has he looked so handsome and regal as depicted in stone.

As well as the beauty of the palace is the scent of it. The aroma of honey and rose waft in the air, burning oil and incense reminding her of strolling through candy markets as a child.

The doors to their chambers are of marble, exquisitely balanced to open at the lightest touch. The mark of the sun, dedication to her father, is carved on to it. The doors open at her feather touch.

The first of their rooms is a high-ceilinged space with cushioned benches and smooth stone tables, black-and-white floors, and fresh fruit in golden bowls. Her stomach writhes as she gazes upon a bunch of grapes, remembering the incident in the throne room.

Rugs offering soft solace for tired feet are dotted around the chamber, sandstone pillars holding up the ceiling. Flowers are wound around each one, their fragrances reminding Assyri of the palace gardens she played in as a girl. Calm sweeps over her.

Their children are waiting for them.

Arteo comes first, though as she's noticing day by day, he is hardly a child any more.

Fifteen and handsome, he is now as tall as her, his baby fat shredded and his wiry body muscled and strong. His demeanour is pleasant and respectful, his features a perfect blend of Ranay's and her own.

'Mother, Father,' he says, nodding respectfully to them. Studying inside most of the day, the boy is restless, but it's hardly surprising. Assyri has watched both her children enjoying the palace gardens for years, talking with gardeners and servants, enjoying the fresh air.

He may be a prince and the heir to the throne, but he still treats all living things, big or small, royal or common, with respect.

Arteo hurries forward, embracing his father in a tight hug. Despite being older now, he never grows embarrassed of showing affection to his parents. His smile fades as he turns to his mother, noticing the lingering solemnness on her face.

'Is everything all right, Mother?' Her heart warms. *As empathetic as ever.*

She forces a smile. 'It's nothing for you to worry about, young prince. All is well.'

Not fooled, Arteo raises a dark eyebrow. 'Has Uncle Bolara gotten under your skin again?'

Her son has always been able to read her, no matter how much she fights to guard her expression. Can others read her heart so easily too?

Preeya joins them in their room, her blonde locks flowing like rippling sand dunes. She's wearing a dress almost identical to her mother's, fitting her slim, athletic build. Her face is angelic, reflecting her sweet and kind nature.

Assyri takes pleasure in watching her daughter gazing at butterflies and flowers, spending her time with the animals that roam their lands, her heart bursting with love and concern for all.

Assyri is grateful for her children's gentle natures, but there is more to them than many know. She can sense their power, the blood of the almighty sun god in them, the same blood that dwells in Bolara's veins, in his children's, in her very own.

She sweeps up Preeya in a hug, inhaling her flowery scent, feeling the mystic energy dwelling beneath the surface, waiting to be called upon and maybe, one day, unleashed.

❋ ❋ ❋

Ranay is a tall handsome man. Dark chestnut wavy hair, dark-brown eyes, and a physique like a warrior. A mortal, yes, but still a handy swordsman. When Assyri first arrived at Pendilor, he came to meet the new queen, as many on Zeldigar did.

He fell in love with her at first sight, and she with him. It did not take long before they courted and married.

He watches with love in his heart as his wife and daughter embrace. He glances towards his handsome son. Deep down, he is hoping that they will never have to use their powers.

The kingdom is at peace, with no conflict demanding royal children to pick up real weapons. Still, he is unsettled by the developing resentment between Bolara and his wife.

He has seen the training that Ristos and Syrana undergo under the masterful eye of General Thamios. If this continues and Bolara gathers support, he may harness enough force to overthrow the kingdom. Ranay cannot let any harm come to his family.

Maybe he's just imagining things. *They may clash sometimes, but they're still brother and sister*, he thinks to himself. Family is more important than anything else. He tries to calm his ill judgments; Assyri needs him when she has doubts. He needs to be her rock, her pillar of calm in troubled times.

Still, he is glad that the children are being trained in secrecy with his most trusted guard, the experienced Galdin. Kind green eyes, with thick black hair, belie a mighty warrior. Many cuts and bruises, of past battles, adorn Galdin. He has trained and fought under Thamios for many years but does not have the bloodthirsty nature of the general.

Instead, he supports the gentle and kind rule of Queen Assyri and is a trusted friend.

The children have been training for some time now and show great promise.

Ranay thinks to himself, *Their full potential will be unleashed, even if they are not called upon to use their powers.*

'Come,' Ranay gently says to the group. 'Let us feast in the dining hall. I believe Yackenhaus is on the menu.'

The children let out cries of 'Yummy' and 'Yes' as they have a love for tender, slowly cooked Burrintot stew, mixed with exotic vegetables and fresh spices from the palace gardens. It is always a favourite.

The aroma itself brings many palace workers to a halt as they inhale the wondrous spices wafting through the many halls and corridors.

The group heads towards the grand dining room, laughing and giggling in one another's company. Ranay is happy to see the tension has melted from his wife's face, her frustration at her brother's actions pushed aside for now. With their family around them, it is easy to remember the truth: she is the queen, and Bolara will fall into line eventually.

He hopes with all his heart that he is right.

CHAPTER 4

RUTHLESS AND EVIL

Ristos, now sixteen years of age, thrusts his sword upwards at Thamios, who repels it with an almost lazy raise of his own weapon. Despite his enormous size, the general has remarkable agility. He slams his shield into Ristos without mercy, and the teen sprawls on the ground. 'Find your footing.' Thamios growls.

Spitting dirt, the boy glares up at his teacher, scrambling for purchase. Breathing hard through clenched teeth, he somersaults over Thamios, landing a blow on the general's flank with his wooden sword.

Thamios accepts the blow but does not lose balance; instead, he sweeps at Ristos's leg, but the boy jumps out of harm's way, or so he thinks. The general wields around and slams the wooden sword into his shoulder, drawing a small amount of blood from the boy.

How could such a massive brute be so damn agile?

Ristos winces at the pain but does not let out the scream building at the back of his throat. His father, Bolara, is watching and will frown upon any act of weakness.

With a growl, he throws an energy bolt, which is deflected with his mentor's shield. Thamios returns an energy bolt, stunning Ristos and making him stagger. Anger builds inside the boy, and he launches with everything he has: energy bolts, wooden sword weaving and thrusting, all with an animalistic roar that echoes through the palace grounds.

His parents observe; Ritani leans in towards Bolara to say something in his ear. Ristos reads her lips. 'He's getting stronger.'

Noticing his distraction, Thamios delivers another energy blast, hitting Ristos in the midriff. It knocks the boy off his feet, and he darts over, pointing the sword tip to Ristos's neck.

There is no compassion or pity in the general's black eyes; they're like cold, dark tunnels, void of light or warmth. Ristos swallows hard. The man standing above him is possibly the strongest demigod in existence. Maybe even stronger than Bolara, not that he'd ever suggest it aloud. Ristos gives a hasty nod, acknowledging the lesson is over.

'He is not yet ready,' mutters Bolara to his wife.

Ritani gently puts her arms around his waist, in comfort, but says nothing.

Ristos gets to his feet, frustration rippling through him. 'I will better you one day, General.' He growls. 'When my powers are fully developed.'

Thamios does not respond, but a small smirk twitches at his mouth as he turns to Bolara and extends a small bow. Bolara nods back in appreciation.

Ristos is aware his father is approaching.

'You're almost eighteen,' Bolara rumbles, his hands behind his back and regarding his son with narrowed eyes the colour of emeralds. 'You have to perfect your abilities and be one of the strongest in the kingdom.'

'I'll keep training, sir.'

Ristos is in fear and awe of his father. He once witnessed Bolara tear a man's head off with his bare hands. The cold, calculating way he deals with Queen Assyri and her weak rule—Ristos has the same meanness inside him.

The perfect blend of Bolara and the witch Ritani. He is every bit as bloodthirsty and hungry for more conquest and power.

Bolara turns to Ristos's sister with a stern look and says, 'You too, daughter. You must be ready to unleash your full power soon.'

'I'll be ready, Father,' says Syrana, casually twirling her black hair as she speaks.

Bolara addresses his general, 'Next week, we train in the jungle, Thamios.' The general nods in acknowledgement.

⌘ ⌘ ⌘

A few weeks have passed, and regular visits to the jungle have become an integral part of the training regime for Ristos and Syrana. They are now fierce and merciless.

The jungle of Kalanya is miles and miles of thick trees filled with fierce Tolverines, angry Burrintots, lions, tigers, and many other wildlife. You can even catch a glimpse of the exceedingly rare and majestic Lawky bird. Beneath the branches is cool, dry soil and scattered leaves.

It is a peaceful place full of nature and tranquillity . . . until the young royals appear.

Ristos blends with the trunks and the leaves, crouching as he fixes his green eyes on his prey. He moves, each step gentle, careful not to crunch a drying leaf or snap a twig.

He nocks an arrow, holding the weapon with expert grace like he was trained to since he was a boy. He leans against a trunk, looking past the trees and the bushes, sighting his target.

A stone's throw away, the jungle dweller raises his head, as though sensing something other than the wind rustling the leaves above.

Thwack.

The arrow soars through the air like lightning. The jungle dweller's spine snaps upright as the arrow pierces his back, sprouting from his chest with a wet squelch. Blood spurts on to his dark skin, on the furs wrapped round his body.

He drops to his knees, his spear falling on to the dirt with a thump, gurgling and gasping as his fingers scramble at the arrow sticking out of his chest. He collapses, body shuddering before he takes his final breath.

'Nice shot, Ristos!' shouts Syrana in glee, giving a cackling laugh of delight at the fallen dweller.

The young royal jumps from her horse, her sword slicing through the air as she swings hard, cleanly chopping the head off another approaching jungle dweller. He falls to his knees, dead in an instant.

The forest erupts with activity. Birds flap into the air with panicked squawks, quick footsteps, and the sounds of slicing weapons and flying arrows filling the air. Two more of the jungle people round on Syrana, their white teeth bared in anger for their fallen brethren.

Spears are in their dark hands, furs and clothes made from leaves and vines wrapped around their lithe bodies, shocks of black curls or dreadlocks framing painted faces. Syrana doesn't regard them as people. They're simply game for her and her brother.

The jungle dwellers dash at Syrana with enraged shrieks, wielding their spears with razor-sharp points. She makes an expert leap, one she has made hundreds of times with hours and hours of practice, dark locks flying as she avoids being impaled.

She retaliates with her gleaming blade, slicing the leg off one. The blade is sharpened to a razor edge, and the jungle dweller's thigh is no match for it. He falls, screaming, and before his companion can react, Syrana swings her blade and cuts the head clean off the other. Their eyes, dark as night, stare unseeing up at the treetops in shocked horror.

Syrana wipes her sword with her sleeve, pausing for a moment, enjoying the rich crimson colour of a fresh kill, ears pricked for more enemies. All is quiet in the jungle. Her father is approaching on a bay stallion, his own colours of black and red on the saddle and his cloak.

He would never dare wear the colours of the palace, but Syrana thinks his own colours suit them more anyway. He is handsome and regal, smirking as more of the jungle dwellers flank him, snarling in their language, chittering like beasts.

Syrana isn't worried and settles in to enjoy the show. Her father, after all, is where she learned most of her tricks.

He's fast, faster than anyone she's ever seen. He sends out an energy blast from his palm, knocking the nearest two enemies off their feet. He pulls out his sword, bright and gleaming in the sunlight, coming from a gap in the leaves. He drives it deep into the chest of another approaching warrior.

Syrana folds her arms, leaning against a tree trunk. The people of the forest must be either very brave or very stupid. Bolara is a force to be reckoned with, powerful and wise, merciless and brutal.

She does not wince as he hacks the shoulder of another; the dweller falls with a scream, clutching his bleeding shoulder, until Bolara shoves his sword into his chest. He yanks it out so hard he brings a couple of ribs with it.

Syrana is fascinated, her blood pounding, excitement rising in her chest. Something about the ferocity of such a bloodthirsty kill gets her heart racing, makes her feel alive.

The more close-up and bloodier a kill is, the better. She loves to see the light leave her enemies' eyes, taste the spurt of hot blood on her skin, and whiff the metallic scent of death as she sends them to the heavens.

The other two are still stunned by the mighty demigod's blast, and Bolara approaches them almost casually, twirling the bloodied blade over in his hand.

He ends the nearest one's suffering with a clean stab right through the heart. The jungle dweller falls limp with a pained groan. Bolara stabs the second, the dweller's body shuddering into death in moments.

Just a minute earlier, they were running with spears in their hands and vengeance in their hearts. Now they're dead. Worm food. It's nothing short of thrilling.

Ristos is now almost seventeen years of age, Syrana a year his junior. Simple wooden swords are not used in the jungles; now they use real weapons. Bolara has declared that the jungle dwellers of Kalanya are perfect targets to practice on.

The jungle dwellers are peaceful people, living off the land and harmless if left alone. They are cautious towards visitors to the forest. After visits like these, where young royals hunt them for sport, who can blame them?

Ten thousand people dwell in the wilds of Kalanya, living a simple existence, growing their own food, and hunting only what they need. King Ranakin is their leader.

Syrana learned from Master Chirok that King Ranakin isn't interested in meeting with the kingdom rulers to discuss politics. 'He wants to be left alone to rule his people in peace,' her teacher said.

Syrana likes to fool around in class and bully her cousins, but she has a good memory and hasn't forgotten any of her lessons with her tutor. 'Ranakin is rumoured to have a foul temper, but he treats his people fairly.'

Syrana is snapped from her memory as General Thamios approaches the battle on his mount. He leaps off his horse with astounding grace, landing with a mighty thud that shakes nearby trees. He slashes another jungle dweller with ease, slicing him right in half as easily as though he were made of paper. The two pieces of the man's body fall separated, spilling crimson on the forest ground.

A young dweller, not much older than Syrana, runs at General Thamios with a roar like an angry animal. He's clumsy, his form terrible. A suicidal decision.

The seasoned general grabs the dweller by his neck, a vicious grin creeping across his hardened face as he squeezes. A nasty pop erupts, and the boy goes limp, his arms dropping to his sides, his spear falling from his fingers.

When two more warriors run towards him, Thamios throws the boy's body at them, and they crash to the ground in a heap of bloody limbs.

They rise to face a rungan blade wielded with dexterity and force. They don't stand a chance. Syrana's breath catches in her throat, a thrill running through her as she witnesses the general sidestep and parry with grace. She lets out a squeal of enjoyment.

A head goes flying, separated from its shoulders in one sickening swipe. The other clutches a bleeding stump where his arm used to be. Thamios swings his weapon with a mighty roar, and three corpses fall around him.

'Eyes on Ristos!' roars Bolara as he whirls around towards his son.

Syrana's gaze follows Thamios's to her brother, who's surrounded by three more of the dwellers, their painted faces twisted in rage at their kin being cut down. The general's eyes follow the boy, ready to assist if needed.

The dwellers inch towards him, acutely aware of how deadly he is, how effortlessly he cut down their friends. They're eyeing his sword, but Ristos takes them by surprise, sending a cosmic blast of energy from his hand and knocking the nearest off his feet.

Ristos turns with expert grace, after hundreds of hours of practice, each movement perfected. He slices through the torso of the next warrior like a knife through butter.

The third gives a scream and throws his spear at him. For a moment, Thamios moves, his hand on his sword hilt. But Ristos slices the spear in half with one lithe swipe. Then he throws the sword, fast and direct, straight into the jungle dweller's horrified face.

It slices through his eye. The warrior clutches his face, screaming, before crumpling to the ground. Red gushes from his eye, his body shuddering as he gargles into death.

The warrior thrown to the ground by the energy blast struggles to regain his feet, but before he can get up, Ristos reaches him. He unsheathes a dagger at his belt, kneeling beside his fallen foe with agonizing slowness, savouring his victory.

He strokes the blade across the warrior's throat. A slow gesture, almost a caress, that leaves the warrior choking and spilling crimson on to the dry leaves.

Ristos yanks his sword from the dead warrior's head, turning to grin at Syrana as she gives a cheer.

'Bravo, brother. Bravo.'

The hours flit by, the sun making its steady journey across the sky, and more and more of the brave jungle dwellers are slaughtered on their own lands. The warriors are trained well and know the forest, but they're no match for four bloodthirsty demigods.

The teens were trained from childhood to kill without mercy and hide like shadows among the trees.

Severed limbs and blood surround the group, and the forest so red it is almost unrecognizable. The once green leaves are now a splattering of thick crimson. Over a hundred corpses surround them, some with missing limbs, some cut in half, all of them covered in blood.

The survivors already fled, knowing it was suicide to face such fierce enemies. Syrana and Ristos clamber on to their mounts to chase them, eager to finish the job. Their thirst is never satiated, and they decapitate and stab and slash all the screaming survivors they can find.

The youths cheer and laugh, the murder of the jungle dwellers an excellent game to them.

When they ride back to where their father is waiting, their horses' hooves covered in sticky blood and leaves, Syrana holds her sword aloft and cries, 'What are we waiting for? Let's finish them all off right now!'

Bolara grips his horse's reins, drying blood matting his hair and skin, dark eyebrows raising in amusement at his daughter's bloodlust. 'They are ten thousand strong in their kingdom, sweet daughter. This is but a small hunting party we have toyed with.'

'We aren't afraid, Father. We'll slay them all,' Ristos says. His chest is rising and falling with quickened breaths, a wild look in his eyes and his dark hair tousled and drenched with red.

'Yes, we may be formidable, but to take on a force of ten thousand . . .' He pauses, shaking his head. 'I admire your passion, both of you, but it is wise to know your limits.'

'Yes, Father.' Ristos nods.

'Now is not the time.' He drinks from his leather waterskin as casually as though they were out for a picnic. His canteen was made recently, fresh hide from a recent Burrintot kill. 'This is training, not war.'

Syrana and Ristos glance at each other. Despite the slaughter, they still aren't satisfied. They have outgrown the need for wooden swords and training dummies. They want more.

Meaningless, bloodthirsty slaying—there is nothing quite like it. However, to question their father is not wise, and they follow him and General Thamios without any further argument.

Thamios heads back through the jungle, leaving the massacre behind and heading towards the Kalanya River.

No more birds sing in the treetops.

CHAPTER 5

———◉———

A Plan Is Hatched

The drying blood is cracking on Bolara's skin, reddish brown staining his tunic. None of it is his. There is a dull ache in his arm, and tiredness pulls at his eyelids, but he shows no weakness. His children ride behind him, both as bloodthirsty and vicious as himself. A smile curls his lips.

The Kalanya River winds from the hills, bright and curving like a giant blue snake. As they approach, the sounds of weapons clashing, and voices screaming, is evident. Bolara glances at General Thamios, whose head cocks in confusion as they lead their horses out of the tree line.

Several knights are wearing silver armour that gleam in the sun. It appears they are slaying more of the jungle dwellers.

'Well, well, well. What do we have here?' Bolara mutters to himself whilst gesturing Thamios over.

The general peers through the trees and witnesses a soldier beheading another jungle warrior who is kneeling.

A rustle in the bushes, but Bolara does not flinch. He turns. A knight in the same armour of silver with the sigil of Zartali painted on his chest plate appears. 'Who goes there?' the man bellows. Several more soldiers arrive and circle the group.

They soon find an assortment of spears and swords are pointing at them. At his side, Thamios's fingers close around the hilt of his sword.

'No, Thamios,' mutters Bolara. Amusement runs through him. These Zartali guards are clueless, unaware that this group they have stumbled upon could destroy them within moments.

'We are merely out for an afternoon stroll. We mean you no harm?' Bolara says, turning to smirk at the guard and his sword, which shines brightly in his gauntleted hand.

'You will come with us,' says another soldier.

Thamios appears annoyed and raises an unimpressed eyebrow at the knight's weapon pointed at him. He glances at Bolara, with a blank expression, in anticipation of a signal to proceed with destroying the puny idiots that surround him.

Bolara smiles at the sword holding hands, which are trembling, possibly in nervousness at the size of the general, surely wondering how they would survive if this man was to retaliate.

Syrana is not impressed by the influx of soldiers around her. Through the long strands of black hair covering her face, she snarls at a young one near her, which nearly forces him to fall from his horse. Ristos snickers as he gently releases the hold of his sword handle.

Flanked by the guards, they are led out of the trees and approach the river, which sparkles in the sunlight. The hills are on the horizon, mist caressing them like a lover's touch. The familiar stench of blood and death surrounds them. Ahead are the rest of this amusing contingent, surrounded by a dozen or so dead jungle dwellers.

'We share an interest, I see,' remarks Syrana. Ristos snorts a harsh laugh. The teens are not fazed by the interruption of their afternoon.

'Sir! My king!' calls a guard, running to greet a great beast of a man. He is shirtless, his tanned skin shining in the sun, illuminating countless white scars all over his muscles. He has a mop of black hair and a nose that's been broken so many times it's crooked in several places.

His face is scarred worse than his body, and two keen squinting brown eyes rest on a jungle dweller lying at his feet, mouth curled in a snarl.

'We found this lot sneaking around in the woods, Your Grace,' says the guard as they approach King Hirtila, Lord of the Zartali people.

The jungle dweller at Hirtila's feet is lying on his back in the grass, bleeding from a deep wound in his side, hands shaking as he begs something in his chittering, clicking language. Hirtila grins at him, showing several yellowed teeth, before slamming down his sword into the man's chest.

A cheer rises from the watching guardsmen as the dweller gives a pained scream before flopping on to the grass, dead.

'Who are those that disturb my pleasure?' the king bellows, sheathing his sword and coming to confront the newcomers. 'You're in a very dangerous pla—' His dark eyes widen as his gaze moves to Syrana, then Ristos, then to General Thamios, before finally resting on Bolara. *These are not common folk*, he muses.

'I am Bolara of Pendilor,' Bolara says, giving a mocking bow as he smirks. 'This is my head guardsman, General Thamios, and this is my son, Ristos, and my daughter, Syrana. Say hello, children.'

Ristos stares at the king unperturbed, while Syrana turns her head with a sweet smile, red streaking most of her face. Hirtila glances around, purveying their bloodstained clothes, their blood-ridden weapons, and what appears to be bits of flesh, dripping from the girl's hair.

His face is drained of colour.

'B-Bolara of Pendilor,' stutters the Zartali leader. He rounds on the nearest soldier. 'You idiot! Don't you know who this is? Stand down! Weapons *down*, I said!'

The guards hurry to lower their weapons, glancing nervously at one another.

'Good-for-nothing dogs!' Hirtila roars. 'My lord, forgive my foolish soldiers. I apologize for the insult.'

'No matter.' Bolara waves his hand, and they all dismount their horses. 'Though you must understand, we're hungry and thirsty from our recent travels. Are you able to offer some refreshments?'

'Of course, of course.' Hirtila snaps at the nearest guard, and soon they're all sitting near the river, a cool breeze on their faces as they eat and drink their fill of whatever the Zartali people can offer for the insult.

'Again, I apologize for my guards' behaviour,' says Hirtila. He sits beside Bolara, now wearing a shirt. It sticks to his sweat-soaked skin, beads of fresh perspiration on his scarred forehead. 'I should have them all executed for their ignorance.' He smiles nervously. His yellow crooked teeth bringing a curdling sensation to the stomach of the visitor. Bolara puts the piece of bread in his hand down, having lost his appetite.

'A simple mistake', says Bolara, no longer hiding his amusement. 'I see we share a pastime,' he adds, nodding to the jungle dweller corpses.

'Yes. Vermin.' Hirtila spits.

'Vermin,' Ristos agrees, nodding.

'Killed your fair share of them, son?'

'We slaughtered over a hundred this afternoon,' Ristos boasts, puffing out his chest.

'Over one hundred, with just four,' Hirtila responds, looking more nervous. 'Um . . . now then. What can I do for you, my lord?'

'Well, it appears our meeting may be fate.' Bolara takes a sip of wine from the shiny mug handed to him crafted from a Burrintot horn. He continues, keeping Hirtila on tenterhooks. 'There is something I need your assistance with. Something that could use you and your people's . . . talents.'

One of Hirtila's dark eyebrows cocks in interest. Up close, he's even uglier, with speckled skin and a face like a pig. 'Please continue, my lord.'

'It appears our queen has grown soft,' says Bolara. 'Our servants steal from us at their own leisure. The common rabble don't know their place. Filth like this'—he gestures to the dead bodies—'are free to roam around as they please. This cannot be tolerated any longer.'

He glances towards his children. Ristos and Syrana are at the water's edge washing the blood from their bodies and weapons. Syrana removes her armour and tunic top to wash her arms and shoulders more thoroughly.

The Zartali soldiers point, stare, and snicker to one another at the sight of such beauty. She may be only sixteen but already displays the body of a young goddess. Thamios, who is busy cleaning his weapons, grunts at the soldiers, causing them all to avert their gaze.

'I plan to take the throne from my sister,' continues Bolara

Hirtila, who is taking a drink from his own Burrintot mug, chokes, spilling wine down his front. 'Take over the throne? From Queen Assyri—'

'She is weak.' Bolara spits. 'She cannot run a kingdom as great as ours. My father, the sun god Suriyar, made a mistake putting her on the throne. If all we preach is peace, we'll be overrun at the first sign of rebellion.'

Hirtila gives a slow nervous nod, taking another long drink from his mug, carefully running his fingers down the spine of the beautifully crafted goblet.

'But I could do with some colleagues on my quest.'
Hirtila glances around at his guards. Bolara is aware that Hirtila is known for his bloodlust, his merciless ruling, and his love for violence. Only three dozen soldiers here, but that is only the beginning of Hirtila's impressive force.

'Join me, King Hirtila, and you'll get power as my right-hand man in Pendilor,' says Bolara, his voice quiet. 'A royal seat . . . more land . . . more riches. Just lend me your men. Ten thousand soldiers should suffice to take over the palace and the rats that dwell within.'

Hirtila's dark eyes meet his, and he gives a grim nod. They clasp hands, still brown with dried blood from their slaughters of innocent.

⚜ ⚜ ⚜

Blades clash and arrows twang, groans of excursion echoing around the training area. This one is secret, hidden from the eyes of Bolara and his followers. Given Ristos's and Syrana's disdain for nature and animals, it is unlikely they'll stumble across this place, tucked in a quiet corner outside the palace gardens.

Ranay set up this secret space for his son and daughter to train away from the eyes of Bolara and the brutal General Thamios. Most of the servants don't know about it.

Galdin runs this secret training area. Preeya knows her father is disappointed that, as a mortal, he cannot train them in demigod war craft by himself. But Preeya would rather have a kind, wonderful mortal father like the one she has than an evil father with a cruel, black heart like her uncle Bolara. She shouldn't think such ugly thoughts about her family, but she figures it's okay if she doesn't say it aloud.

Galdin is a kindly enough tutor, and extremely skilled. He is her father's most trusted guard, and the man is proud to be teaching the queen's children. He certainly doesn't hold the same merciless harshness that her cousins' tutor has and is much more patient and understanding, encouraging them both to practice the same techniques over and over until they're like second nature to them.

Queen Assyri hasn't been told about the training sessions, thinking that the children are off on wilderness walks with their father. There is enough on her mind, and Preeya is aware that Ranay believes the peace-loving queen will not be pleased to hear her children are learning how to fight.

Preeya privately agrees and continues to reluctantly train with Arteo, under her father's instructions.

Preeya holds the sword in her hand, swallowing as she takes a slow step back. The grass tickles her toes, the metal of the sword hilt cold in her palm. She inhales the scent of fresh soil and lilies, the three guards around her standing in combat stances, their own weapons raised.

'Don't be scared, my lady,' says one of the guards, his voice muffled in his visor. 'We won't harm you.'

'She isn't scared for herself.' Ranay chuckles from behind them, his arms folded.

'I'm scared of hurting *you*,' says Preeya. She's seen what demigod powers can do to mortals. She saw what Ristos did to the guards fighting him during his training. She probably isn't as strong as Ristos but still strong enough to do damage to her own soldiers.

'They're wearing armour, and they are more skilled than you think,' Ranay says, giving her an encouraging smile, his brown eyes crinkling. 'You won't learn how to use your powers unless you practice in a real setting.'

Preeya is still learning her skills, and she has been advised that the guards are trained well. But she is still cautious. She doesn't enjoy fighting and can't bear to cause harm to anyone or anything, not even the tiniest of creatures.

The guards move towards her and thrust their wooden swords at her gleaming silver armour.

She avoids the attacks easily as she moves with the guile and agility of a panther. They cannot land a blow on her as she appears to dance around the thrusts and parries with ease.

Now strike back, Preeya,' yells Ranay.

Preeya hears her father's plea but cannot bring herself to wield her sword towards the guards. She continues to defend with her sword and avoid any strikes coming her way. Somersaulting over one guard's head, sweeping beside another, leaping above swinging weapons, she cannot be touched.

Ranay observes the contest and laughs out aloud as the guards start sweating profusely. They are getting agitated and frustrated that they cannot land a single blow.

Preeya looks to her father as if pleading for him to say *enough*, but Ranay is now too busy bent over laughing that he cannot muster a word. Preeya fails to understand what the amusement is about.

Nearby, Arteo is showing his prowess with the bow, his brows knitted together in concentration as he nocks another arrow, aiming for a target one hundred feet away.

Instead of berating the boy for his misses, Galdin praises Arteo's good shots, giving gentle advice on improvement and form. The boy isn't shy like Preeya, and when he's handed a sword, he fights with grace and skill. She was watching him earlier, comparing him to their vicious cousin.

While Ristos fights with ferocity and without mercy, Arteo moves like a dancer, fighting with grace. Both styles appear effective. Preeya often wonders which of the boys might win in a fight, though she isn't sure she wants to find out.

In these secret training sessions, the intensity levels are always increasing, particularly for Arteo. Whilst Preeya cautiously improves, Arteo is surging ahead in leaps and bounds. Ranay watches his son with pride, knowing that he has made the right choice with these secretive sessions.

Galdin beats Arteo a few times, but the young prince learns quickly, practicing new combinations and dodging the bigger man's swipes.

Their teacher practices the same blows again and again until he's close to mastering them.

'When he is older, he'll be a force to be reckoned with,' Galdin is heard muttering to Ranay when having a break. 'He might develop to be stronger than Ristos.'

'I pray we never actually have to find out, my friend,' replies Ranay with a solemn expression on his handsome face.

'Come on, Preeya,' says Ranay, having picked himself up off the ground, his voice encouraging. 'You won't hurt them.'

Preeya nods to her father and throws herself into training, using some moves she's seen Arteo use, utilizing her own lithe grace to sidestep, dodge, and parry the guards' attacks.

Her sword pings off their armour, not harming them, and soon she gets into the flow of things, wooden swords cracking, the dull thuds of weapon against steel, and Preeya's own panting breaths in her ears.

Sweat trickles down her back, beading on her forehead and dampening her blonde hair. She lands a few blows which knock a guard off his feet and then surprises all when she pauses midfight to apologize and reach out with a hand to the fallen soldier.

The guard himself is unsure of what to do as he is not permitted to touch the royal princess's hand. Ranay and Arteo chuckle to themselves.

'Excellent work,' says Ranay later as they eat peaches in the shade of a large oak. 'You are both blessed with wonderful Shakti powers, I know it. Suriyar smiles on you both.'

'Just remember,' says Ranay, biting into a peach. He chews the soft flesh of the fruit, dark eyes moving from his son to his daughter, who both nibble at the peach down to the core. 'Your powers are only to be used in defence of the kingdom, never to be used as a show of one's strength. He who boasts shows real weaknesses for all his enemies, or *her* enemies,' he adds, nodding to his daughter with a smile.

Preeya nods, returning her father's grin.

'There may come a day when you need to use your powers to protect your mother and the kingdom,' says Ranay quietly, looking down at the half-eaten peach in his hand.

'It is not a desired action, but . . . anything is possible.'

'Yes, Father,' they both respond.

It is clear that Preeya does not enjoy training. She would rather be watching butterflies or playing with the animals in the enclosure. But her father is right. She and Arteo need to train. They might have to protect their kingdom someday in the future.

Though the kingdom of Pendilor is at peace, history books tell them that peace often does not last. The royal children need to be prepared in case something unforeseen happens in the future and their powers are required.

Preeya turns her head to glance through the curtain of ivy towards the palace. If there are enemies that are lurking, she has a fair idea who they might be.

CHAPTER 6

◎

CRUELTY UNLEASHES POWER

'**W**ait up!'
'Faster, they'll catch us!'

Arteo and Preeya scamper through the jungle, trampling on vines and ducking under branches, giggling hysterically as they leave the guards far behind. To try and keep up with the agility and speed of two young royals is futile for the heavily armoured protection.

The mischievous youths have done this plenty of times before, despite being counselled to be more cautious and respect the guards.

When you're a demigod teen, complying with such instructions is not so easy. A sprint, a somersault over small trees and branches, and a huge leap leave the guards well behind. The siblings can't resist such a wonderful game.

Preeya's sprint slows when she nears a tree. Beautiful and majestic, like most in the forest. Its skeletal boughs twist and glitter in the sunlight, and its great trunk curves in different directions, sprouting new branches, birthing pale-green leaves.

The noble roots of the tree are embedded deep into the hard ground. All appears well in the quiet peace of the forest save the sad squawks coming from the branches above.

The princess, now sixteen years of age, scrambles up the tree with such dexterity even her brother Arteo will struggle to match. She hides her smile as she climbs. Arteo may be older, arguably stronger, but she has the edge in gymnastics.

She leaps from limb to limb, somersaulting like a gymnast to the highest branches, blonde hair rippling behind her like a golden waterfall.

'Be careful, Preeya. Quit showing off.'

'There's something up here!' she calls, following the sad little squawks. They're different from the usual chirping of the jungle's many birds. Clearly the sound of an animal in pain.

She gently moves aside a branch, uncovering a beautiful baby Paraka. Her breath catches in her throat. The little bird has a spectacular rainbow coat, multi-coloured feathers, a short stubby beak, and bright little eyes. Head tilting this way and that, peering up at the newcomer with fear. Its wing is bent at an awkward angle, and as Preeya approaches, it trembles.

'Oh, you poor little thing,' Preeya whispers, gently reaching to take the delicate creature in her hands. The frightened bird delivers several panicked pecks to her fingers, but she pays them no heed. 'There, there, sweetie, all will be okay.' She quickly slips her way down the tree and shows the injured bird to Arteo.

'What are you doing?' her brother exclaims.

'This poor little baby is injured. Look,' she says, gently showing Arteo the bent wing. The chick trembles in her hands. 'We have to help him. He's all alone.'

'Did you see the mother at all?' Arteo says, his blue eyes flickering down to where the baby bird shivers in Preeya's hands. 'She may still be around.'

'We cannot wait. We must take it back to the palace gardens,' she snaps. 'The immense pain it must be in', she continues. 'Tarap can heal him.' She fixes her brother with such a glare he nods.

A small smile graces his handsome face. 'You always remind me of mother. Sweet and gentle on the surface but deep down burns an inner fire.'

'Well, don't let me torch you, brother,' she says but grins back.

'All right. Let's take him . . . um, her? Back to the palace gardens.'

'A boy', she responds, voice gentle as she lightly strokes the bird's feathers. She yanks off her silk scarf, wrapping the bird inside, hoping he understands that they're here to help.

'Princess Preeya! Prince Arteo!'

'Took them long enough,' Arteo remarks. It isn't long before their guards appear, panting in their heavy armour as they push aside branches, relief flooding their faces as the young royals appear in sight. They all display a level of embarrassment, blaming one another for being outrun by the teenagers.

'There you are.' The nearest guard, Allard, pants, reaching to his visor to wipe the sweat from his eyes.

As the guards pause to take a break, the two teens start heading towards the opening.

'Back to the palace,' Preeya declares.

The guards look at one another and let out a sigh, quickly jumping back to their feet.

Off they all crunch through the jungle back to the palace grounds, maintaining a slow enough pace for the *protection* to keep up. Preeya cannot control her urges though and starts sprinting her way back to the gardens. She can still feel the poor injured bird quivering in her silk scarf. Allard yells out, but to no avail; the teens disappear out of sight.

✄ ✄ ✄

As they inhale the familiar scent of straw and garden herbs, Syrana and Ristos approach, and Preeya forces herself not to groan. Despite being able to hide the bird from the guards' sight, she sees that her cousins are looking at the scarf with matching sneers.

'What's that you got there?' asks Syrana, pointing.

'What does it look like?' Preeya grumbles. 'It's a bird.' She makes to push past them, but they block the way.

'You should have left it in the jungle, where the weak die,' says Syrana, tossing her wavy black hair over her shoulder. She is a sight to behold now. Sixteen years of age and an absolute beauty.

'No one asked you,' retorts Preeya. She's sick of the bullying and taunts from her cousins.

Unfazed, Syrana moves closer, green eyes glinting. 'When will you learn, cousin, that only the strong survive? The world is not a place for weakness.'

'And when will *you* learn that the world is for all?' Preeya snaps. 'To show compassion isn't weak but a show of humanity's strength.' She turns her back on Syrana and heads towards Arteo. She can almost feel Syrana's smirk on her back. Ristos is glaring at Arteo, his jaw clenched.

Preeya's brother is slow to anger, but she senses irritation on his face, creasing his eyebrows, fire in his blue eyes. However, he turns and joins her towards their training.

'I'm sick of their bullying ways,' Preeya mutters.

'I know,' Arteo agrees. 'Forget about them. C'mon, Galdin is waiting for us.'

⌘ ⌘ ⌘

Over the next few weeks, when she isn't eating, sleeping, or training, Preeya cares for the injured Paraka chick. Syrana observes her cousin, the daughter of her weakling aunt, sneak to the palace gardens to care for the injured bird's wing. Syrana hides in the bushes or behind walls, watching the bird turn from fearful, to trusting its helper.

Slowly but surely, the wing heals, and nearly a month after Preeya brought the bird to the palace, it takes short flights around its surroundings, giving happy little chirps. It always returns to its perch, waiting for Preeya. The sight makes Syrana's stomach churn.

She grimaces as Preeya drip-feeds it and notices the baby Tolverines from their enclosure, watching with hungry eyes and panting mouths. Syrana fantasizes feeding the wretched little bird to them, if only to make Preeya squirm. Why is her cousin wasting time with this pathetic little animal?

Syrana continues sharpening her arrow tips until they glint like blades. Glistening steel capable of shattering bone. She places them beside a quiver of cosmic arrows: a weapon that unleashes a burst of energy, stunning larger opponents, or other demigods. Arsenal not able to be wielded by mortals.

⌘ ⌘ ⌘

The next few weeks pass quickly. Preeya spends her free time with the baby Paraka. By the time spring is warming to summer, she's delighted. The little bird's wing is much better, and he flies and chirps so happily. No one can tell if he was ever hurt at all.

'Let's release him now, Arteo,' she says with excitement. It warms Arteo's heart to see the bird, once so pitiful and weak, now fluttering from perch to perch with ease. 'He needs to join his own kind, back in the jungle.'

'All right, slow down.' Arteo laughs. His sister is practically bouncing up and down, her eyes sparkling. He watches as she gathers the bird up in her hands. It no longer pecks her but gives a nervous chirp as she talks to it in quiet, soothing tones. Its multicoloured feathers shimmer in the sunlight.

'You're going home, sweet boy. Yes, you are.'

Arteo opens the gate. Preeya spreads her palms; they smile as the Paraka takes flight, twittering as it soars into the air. They watch as it lands on a nearby branch, looking back as if to thank the girl. Then with a flap of his newly fixed wings, it flies towards the green on the horizon, back to his homeland.

Whoooosshh . . . thwack.

Preeya screams in horror as the bird plummets to the ground, an arrow thrust through its body. Cold shock rushes through Arteo as his sister falls to her knees beside him with a pained moan. 'No! No!'

The little bird lies motionless, rainbow wings unmoving, black eyes not seeing the sky above. The arrow pierced its heart. If not for the cruelty of such a senseless kill, one might wonder at the skill of the archer.

Preeya reaches towards the bird with shaking hands, then gets slowly to her feet, brushing at angry tears. Arteo follows her glare to see Syrana standing nearby, a satisfied smirk on her face, bow in hand. Ristos stands next to her, clapping and cheering. 'Bullseye, sister! Nice shot!'

Preeya stomps over to them, her hands glowing, chest heaving. 'You . . . you inhuman *beast!*' she screams, throwing out her hand and sending an energy blast at Syrana. The girl is not prepared for it, and the force sends her tumbling to the ground, her head hitting the ground hard. She lies on the grass, stunned.

Shock ripples through Arteo. He's never seen Preeya retaliate to Syrana's bullying before. Even from behind, he can see she's trembling with rage. He rushes after her. He is wary of what his cousins may do.

Bolara is watching from a distance and signals to Thamios. The general heads towards the children, long strides heavy like a bull.

His amusement turning to a snarl, Ristos throws an energy blast at Preeya, knocking her down. Rage shoots through Arteo. For years, the siblings have endured their cousins' bullying. They cannot take it any more.

Ristos stands over Preeya, pointing a wooden sword at her neck like their mentor had done only weeks earlier. His handsome face is twisted into a malicious grin. With a growl, Arteo rushes forward and tackles his cousin to the ground. Preeya scrambles to her feet behind him.

'You dare tackle me.' Ristos shoves Arteo as they both get to their feet. His jaw clenches. He is not aware of Arteo's training and has never been confronted physically by his cousin. Arteo's eyes dart to the wooden sword turning in Ristos's hand.

Bolara stands up from his seat, a smirk on his face as though he's anticipating the fight. The general has stopped too, his arms folded. They're waiting to see Ristos pulverize his weakling cousin into the ground.

The boys eye each other while Syrana, recovered from Preeya's energy blast, snatches a sword from a nearby rack. She throws it over to Arteo with a smirk. 'This should be interesting,' she mutters with excited anticipation. The hilt slides easily into his palm, as if it belongs there. He turns it over in his hand, glaring at his cousin.

Enough of the bullying. Killing that bird was cruel enough, *but to threaten his sister.* In the past, he always walked away from confrontations, the desire to keep the peace forever stronger than his desire to fight. But this is the last straw; he will not walk away today.

Ristos darts towards Arteo at blinding speed, wooden swords clacking painfully together, the force knocking Arteo to the ground as Preeya gasps behind him. He springs to his feet and somersaults over Ristos, narrowly avoiding a swipe with his cousin's sword.

He throws up an energy shield to block a cosmic blast just in time and retaliates with a blast of his own. Ristos gives a surprised squeak as it hits him square in the chest, sending him sprawling.

All his life, Arteo and his sister have been considered the weaklings. Ristos and Syrana train hard under Thamios and are considerably skilled. No one had any idea he wields power like this. Everyone is surprised.

Ristos gets back up, flying at Arteo with a wild scream, spittle bursting from his mouth. He swipes at Arteo's head with the sword, crunching against the defending timber. The teenagers lock into a sword fight, wood clacking and echoing, their sisters yelling and cheering them on as the guards and staff behold with interest.

Sweat beading on their brows, with angry grunts and the smacking of wood, the boys brawl for what seems an eternity. Two adolescent demigods thrust, swing, parry, evade, moving with the speed and evasiveness of two wild jungle cats locked into battle. Arteo catches sight of his sister watching him, her eyes locked in fear and excitement.

Smack, crunch . . . a hard blow to Arteo's arm is met with a hit to Ristos's shoulder. Everything his cousin throws, Arteo returns. Their teeth are clenched, tunics damp with sweat, each of them desperate for victory.

Ristos lunges—it is arrogant, foolhardy—and Arteo leaps over his head. Ristos's sword scrapes Arteo's ankles, but he lands, softly on his feet, as Ristos sends another energy blast at his midriff.

Arteo thinks of the dead bird. He thinks of the years of bullying and sneers from his cousins. He thinks of Preeya's tear-filled eyes and her awful scream when that innocent bird fell to the ground.

He leaps, again.

He avoids the blast so narrowly he feels it singe his toes; in mid-air, he shoots a blast back at Ristos, who stands stunned, tottering. His legs wobble. He starts to fall to the ground. Arteo approaches his fallen cousin, ready to finish the battle.

Syrana stands nearby, her sneer gone, shock emblazoned across her face. 'How is this possible?' she mutters under her breath.

'Enough!' bellows Thamios, slamming his sword—real, not wood — into the grass between them. The force of his anger shudders the ground shaking the trees and knocking Arteo off his feet before he can finish the job on Ristos.

Arteo jumps back up and flings his sword to the ground, breathing hard. He approaches Preeya, who has tears on her cheeks, still mourning the baby Paraka.

She puts a warm gentle hand on his arm, looking deeply into his eyes, tears still trickling down her beautiful face. She doesn't have to say it. It is on in her face; she's somewhat surprised but immensely proud of him.

Ristos recovers, brushing dirt off his pants as he jabs a finger at them both. 'You got lucky, *cousin*.' He growls. 'If it wasn't for Thamios, I'd have pummelled you back to the heavens.'

'Hard to do that when you're sitting on your ass,' Preeya snaps over her shoulder. Her eyes are red from tears, and the glare she gives their cousin is of pure hatred.

Bolara is watching from a distance, raising one eyebrow, frowning in confusion at what he has witnessed. He turns and heads to the palace.

'Come on,' mutters Arteo, taking Preeya gently by the shoulder. No more words are needed. Everyone saw what happened. They approach their parents, Queen Assyri and Lord Ranay, who come scurrying from the palace, having caught only the last few minutes of the fight.

Their mother is radiant as always, gold hair over her slim shoulders, hands clasped in her lap. Her usual smile is gone, however; her expression is one of shock and confusion. *Where had her son learned to fight like that?*

Their father stands beside her, tall and strong, regarding his son with pride. One part of him is extremely happy that Arteo fought back, but another part knows that the boy's abilities are no longer a secret. No one has seen Arteo's true power unleashed before.

One thing is for sure. No longer would Queen Assyri's children fall victim to their cousins' bullying.

✻ ✻ ✻

Bolara's quarters are majestic. Honey-coloured stones, structural pillars, chequered floors of polished marble at their feet. There isn't a single piece of furniture that isn't made by master   craftsmen, each intricate part perfected before being allowed within a mile of the quarters. If anything gets dirty or damaged, the offender is lucky to get away with their life. As moonlight pours through the balcony windows, Bolara sits in his pristine armchair overlooking the gardens, not a speck of dust on his cloak. 'What did you make of that?' he asks the general.

An untouched glass of wine sits next to Thamios's large hand. 'The boy is blessed,' he rumbles. 'Perhaps more powerful than Ristos.'

Bolara gets up, heading to his desk of polished oak. He pulls a dagger out of a drawer, lips pursed as he mulls over the scene in the gardens. Two cousins, one his own son, one the first-born of his pathetic sister.

Clashing swords, energy blasts, seeing Ristos get defeated like that. Truly, it was a spectacle. The servants were gossiping about it all evening.

He examines the dagger in his hands. It's a beauty. The blade, polished to a shine and reflecting Bolara's forest-green irises, was moulded with rungan steel, the wooden handle holding a gleaming gemstone, glittering bright like the sun. His father.

'We need to remove the boy.' He twirls the dagger in his hand. 'I want you to deal with him. He can't get in our way. It must be done . . . carefully.'

'It will be done, sir.' Thamios nods.

The general gets to his feet, leaving his untouched drink. He bows and leaves the chambers, boots thumping on the marble. Bolara takes another sip of wine, rolling the sweet, rich liquid on his tongue as he gazes outside at the full moon hanging in the night sky like a fortune teller's crystal ball.

Ritani moves from the shadows like a ghost. The half-witch curls her pale arms around her husband's waist, whispering in his ear, warm on his neck. 'The potion is almost ready, my love.'

He shifts. 'They're more capable than I thought,' he murmurs.

'Not after their potion', she replies. 'The time is near.'

Taking another long sip of wine, Bolara keeps his gaze fixed outside, wondering if he might catch a glimpse of his father. What might Suriyar think of their plans?

As though sensing his hesitation, Ritani holds him tighter, her words tickling his neck. 'You will be king soon.'

CHAPTER 7

THE COUP

The smell of old dusty books, dried leather, and crackling fire lingers in the air. A sulphuric gust wafts in and out.

Ritani hums to herself as the potion bubbles and boils. Jars of herbs and pungent tonic bottles adorn the walls. Decapitated toads and dead bats dangle from the ceiling by pieces of string, within picking distance, for easy addition to any brew.

Fragments of chopped garlic and crushed petals settle on to the wooden table and on her skin. The tiles on the floor of this secret room in the palace are stained from years of infusions.

Dried blood and splatterings of herbal tinctures are well and truly ingrained. Ritani has never had it cleaned; she believes it gives the room character.

She continues to stir the potion. The large round, carbon-stained pot nestled above the fire. A few extra items are added: a dash of herbs, one toad eye, and a strand of bats' wing. She is stirring slowly and humming away as though preparing a nice chicken broth for a cold winter's night, not a lethal concoction capable of sapping a demigod of their powers.

✖ ✖ ✖

Hirtila's troops approach. The guards have been distracted, their eyes turned away from the gates. A peaceful era has turned them lazy and thoughtless. Some have not experienced battle in quite some time, whilst others, not at all. It appears that they will provide very little challenge tonight.

Above, a flash of fiery orange illuminates a high window. When the fire blossoms, signalling the all-clear, the combination of Zartali soldiers and Thamios's soldiers move in for the attack.

'I'm going for a night ride,' says Ristos, riding his magnificent black stallion to the guards at the gate.

'But, my prince, it's night-time,' says the nearest guard, looking up at Ristos with fear. 'Surely, tomorrow would be—'

'I wasn't asking your permission.' Ristos growls. 'How dare you show such insolence. Open the gates at once!'

The guards scramble to open the gates, and when they do, they're met with an avalanche of soldiers, bursting their way through. A sea of Zartali and Thamios's soldiers.

Taken by surprise, they're easily cut down by the rebellious group. Ristos joins in the slaying and thrusts his mighty steel blade into a guard or two and then stands back to witness the carnage with a wicked grin.

He then goes in search of more guards and innocents, who dare to be within close reach. It matters not whether they are challenging or not; it only matters if they are within reach of the evil prince's blade as he goes on a murderous rampage through the streets of Pendilor.

✣ ✣ ✣

Ritani smiles sweetly at the servant bringing the drinks to the dining table. 'I'll take that,' she says, taking the tray.

'Oh, m-my lady,' stammers the serving girl, giving a clumsy curtsey. 'I-I'm sorry. I mean, thank you—'

'Run along now, dear,' says Ritani, and the servant trips over her skirts scurrying away, somewhat surprised at the politeness shown by the half-witch. Ritani quickly takes a phial of yellow potion from her dress pocket and pours a measure into each of the cups.

She carries the tray to the grand dining room, where Queen Assyri and her children are talking quietly at the enormous wooden table. Flowers align the walls, picked that day from the garden by the staff. The scent of jasmine floats through the air.

'Thank you, Aunt Ritani,' says Arteo, his brows knitting in confusion as he accepts the drink. Preeya takes hers too, and the siblings exchange a quiet glance. Queen Assyri takes her drink with a forced smile, one that Ritani has seen on her sister-in-law's lips many times.

'What are you doing, Ritani?' asks Assyri in surprise.

'Just looking to let bygones be bygones, my queen,' comes the response.

'I am glad to hear of it.'

Once Ritani has handed out all the cups, she raises her own non-potioned cup towards the group. 'To family.' Ritani smiles, pulling up a chair to gesture as though she is to sit near them. It is uncharacteristic, but they all drink anyway, and the witch smirks into her own cup. *So quick to forgive and so easy to trust.*

It isn't long before the potion works its wonders and the children's eyelids grow heavy.

'I feel funny, Mother,' wails Preeya as she starts to stagger.

'I feel weird too,' responds Arteo as he grips the chair to stop from falling.

'Ritani, what is . . . happening?' says Queen Assyri, frowning as she glances around. The world around her is beginning to warp in front of her eyes.

'A simple concoction, but an effective one, my queen,' says Ritani, examining her fingernails as the queen and her children slump in their seats. She leans towards the queen, with her dark-green eyes fixated on the staggering body. 'It removes your demigod powers from your limbs.' She leans in even closer until her lips are almost touching Assyri's ear. 'Rather fine, is it not? I brewed it myself earlier, just for you and the children.'

'What treachery is this . . .' Queen Assyri groans, trying to lift her fingers. She slumps on to the table.

⌘ ⌘ ⌘

'Another good training session today,' says Ranay as Galdin rolls up a scroll. 'The children are learning fast. Come, we should join the others for dinner.'

There's a commotion outside, the sounds of shouting and clashing weapons. The setting sun casts a bright glow through the windows, and the men frown as they glance outside.

'By the gods,' Ranay exclaims. There are Zartali soldiers and some of Thamios's men outside in battle attire, attacking our guards. 'What's going—?'

Heavy footsteps resound outside in the hall, and the door bursts open. General Thamios stands on the threshold, clutching his sword. Ranay's stomach goes cold. The gleam of battle is in his eyes as he breathes hard like a bull.

'What madness is this, Thamios?' screams Ranay.

He's attacking.

Galdin grabs the basket of fruit on the table and throws it at the general, to distract long enough, to unsheathe his sword. He then leaps up to protect the queen's husband.

He engages with Thamios in battle. Ranay watches in horror as his trusted friend blocks an attack with a metallic clang. The general is well aware of Galdin's prowess as a skilled swordsman and treats him with respect.

A parry here, a thrust there, a cosmic blast sent from Galdin is deflected easily by Thamios. A counterblast is sent from the general, which Galdin blocks.

A soldier enters and advances towards Ranay. Ranay grabs a knife from the table and throws it at the soldier. It is a skilful throw, even for a mortal. It penetrates the soldier's right eye, blood spurting forth like a fountain. The man drops to the ground. Two more soldiers enter.

One heads for Ranay, who has grabbed a sword from the ground. The other moves towards Galdin. His demigod friend turns his attention to another steel blade swirling towards him and deflects the incoming attack and swirls around to sweep with his own sword and ferociously slice at the soldier. The head comes off and rolls on to the floor, eyes wide open.

Ranay can see his friend is distracted.

Thamios senses his moment and does not hesitate. The general takes his mighty blade and drives the steel deep into the stomach of Galdin.

'*No!*' Ranay cries, icy horror flooding his veins. Galdin's eyes widen in horror, blood bursting from his mouth. General Thamios gives a satisfied snarl, yanking the blade from Galdin. Ranay slumps in shock and is detained by more soldiers who come scurrying in.

'You have got what you deserve.' He hisses as Galdin slides to the floor, painting the carpet red, clutching his stomach.

'Thamios, why!' Ranay roars, all to no avail; General Thamios only listens to one man and does not respond. The brute rounds on him, his sword shimmering with Galdin's blood.

'On your knees, Ranay.' Thamios smirks. 'You are my prisoner.'

✂ ✂ ✂

Syrana rushes into the dining room, her black hair wild, murder in her eyes. She clutches her shiny sword, approaching the young royals and the queen.

They are exhausted, groaning, and half-asleep, powerless as she stalks towards them with a smirk on her face. She's never seen the smug queen so weak, her annoying cousins so helpless. Ritani is behind her, arms folded as she notices her daughter approach them.

'What are you doing, Syrana?' blurts Ritani.

'I look forward to sending them to the gods, with my blade,' Syrana remarks, turning the sword over in her hand. 'Maybe I'll make you watch, Aunt Assyri, while I slice your puny daughter's throat.'

'Bolara will not be happy, my daughter,' exclaims the witch but does little to intervene.

With a fierce growl, Queen Assyri gets to her feet and raises her hands. They light up like the sun—bright yellow. A blast of cosmic energy is directed at Syrana and Ritani. The princess and her witch mother fly across the room with surprised cries, crashing into the wall opposite.

'You will *not* . . . touch . . . my children.' Queen Assyri grunts, every word a huge effort. The blast seems to have sapped the last of her energy. She slumps over the chair, glaring at her sister-in-law and her niece with all the hatred of the heavens.

Surprised that the queen is capable of such a feat after consuming the lethal potion sends an icy chill down Ritani's spine. Scared for her life, she scrambles to her feet and scampers for the safety of the hallway.

'I told you they weren't to be harmed, Syrana,' screams Bolara, appearing at the doorway with General Thamios at his heels. Syrana scowls at them both, shoving past the general and following her mother outside.

The queen is powerless, and the soldiers in silver armour yank them up and start guiding them outside. The children can barely walk, and two soldiers drag Arteo and Preeya, scraping their royal limbs against walls and doors. No respect is given to their title, and they are dragged like commoners outside the palace.

'Where . . . is Ranay?' asks Queen Assyri, scowling as she has to slump against a guard. No one responds. The palace is a different world; the servants are gone, and she's surrounded by enemies. Her own family has turned against her. They step into the dusk air, where more guards are waiting for them.

'My love.' Queen Assyri breathes as she sees Ranay there, a cut on his head and his arms shackled behind his back. Ranay looks at his family with grief etched on his face, red running from temple to jaw.

'They . . . murdered Galdin,' he murmurs.

Dead guards, servants, and gardeners litter the once beautiful gardens. Detached limbs are everywhere, the grass, stained red with blood, so much blood.

She steps over a body, and the face is familiar. *Master Chirok*—he has a deep gash in his stomach, and crimson stains the ground around him. The blade of Ristos has played a part here.

The Zartali soldiers and Thamios's soldiers surround the group, taunting and teasing, poking spears at anyone within reach. It is as though they have won a battle today, a fierce battle against a mighty army, rather than taking down a peaceful kingdom and a much-loved queen. If anyone dare tries to run, they will only be speared down.

There are many of the queen's faithful still alive, a group huddled with guards around them, holding one another and sniffling, eyes widening in horror as they see their queen and her family captured and treated like common folk.

Assyri, in a dazed state, spots chefs, serving girls, cleaners, some unarmed soldiers, and civilians from the town. Many are distraught as innocent family members have been slain in the carnage.

'Why?' Queen Assyri screams at her brother. Bolara is there, his arms folded and a satisfied smirk on his face that makes her stomach churn. 'All these innocent people! What is the cause of all this evil?'

'Kill them all!' Syrana squeals. Feels like all her birthdays have come at once, delight burning in her eyes.

Assyri regrets many things at that moment, most of all her kind rule and lack of boundaries with her brother and his family. She's seen how much they love evil, how jealous they are of her and her children. And now it has led to this.

'No,' snaps Bolara at his daughter. 'Suriyar would never forgive me if we slay our kin. No matter how much we may want to.' He grins, cupping Assyri's face in his fingers. She glares up at him with all the hatred she can muster.

'They will be banished to the jungle of Kalanya to live with the wild that roam there.'

A ripple of sound emits around them—shocked gasps and whispers from the survivors, mutters from the guards, gleeful giggles from Syrana and Ristos.

'The animals can feast on them.' Bolara smiles. 'Send them away.'

Assyri's eyes burn with tears as the soldiers lead her children and herself out of the grounds. Her loyal followers trudge alongside. Ranay is holding Arteo and helping him walk down the long cobblestone path.

They leave the palace behind, the jewel that has been their home all her children's lives. It has fallen under her brother and his evil.

She ignored the warning signs, taken no notice of the obvious that many people tried to warn her about for years. She's been too forgiving, holding on to the hope that Bolara could one day be good, that his children could live alongside hers in peace.

She was so very, very wrong. Now they are paying for it.

CHAPTER 8

THE LOST SOUL

U nder their master's orders, the soldiers take the survivors past the cliffs of Heldegar towards the mighty jungle of Kalanya. The effects of the potion linger, causing them to stagger and stumble. It's exhausting for them to travel so far.

The queen and her family are still dressed in their dinner clothes, their slippers ripped and frayed after the long journey over dirt and rocks. Preeya sniffles, her feet aching, their home stretching further and further away with each mile. What does fate have in store for them?

Arteo sags against his father. Ranay's expression is dark, his arm wrapped around his son. He feels like he's failed his family. Maybe there was more he could have done to prevent this. Preeya wants to reassure her father, tell him that it isn't his fault, but the words catch in her throat.

Her mother looks ill. It's a strange sight, seeing the regal Assyri walking slumped and miserable, having lost her queenly grace, dirt on her dress, and dark circles beneath her eyes.

They pass an enormous cliff face overlooking a cavernous river. The waterfalls of Heldegar are mighty and roaring, water crashing into the rocks below, throwing up cold droplets. If their situation isn't so dire, the children would have enjoyed such an exhilarating view.

None of them notice General Thamios, deep in the trees behind them. He is nocking an arrow.

Ranay turns, his eyes wide as the arrow whistles towards Arteo. Ranay leaps in front of his son. *Thwack.* He gives a low, guttural grunt as the arrow pierces deep into his chest.

'Father!' Preeya screams in horror, the colour draining from Ranay's face as he stares in disbelief at the arrow sticking from his chest. He collapses straight into Arteo.

'*No!*' Queen Assyri screams as Arteo tumbles backwards under the weight, hangs on the edge, his arms pinwheeling. His eyes lock on Preeya's, cold fear rippling across his handsome features. Preeya reaches out, but it is too late. Arteo falls.

He slips from the cliff face and tumbles down towards certain death. Jagged rocks and ravenous water await.

Preeya is numb as Arteo screams, her brother disappearing into darkness. Ranay coughs, blood bursting at his lips as he falls to the ground. Preeya hears a thump behind her. Her mother has fainted, her eyes fluttering as she slumps into the grass.

'My queen!' says a voice; a gardener hurries to her, taking her in his arms. Several guards and followers shout and scream, looking over the cliff face towards where Arteo fell.

Others approach the queen's husband, hands clapped over their mouths. Preeya collapses beside her father, choking on tears, cradling his head in her lap and looking down at his paling face. His lips quiver, blood staining his tunic, hot and red.

'Listen to me . . . Preeya,' he whispers, each word a huge effort. 'You are stronger . . . than you think.'

'Father,' she says, tears slipping down her cheeks and on to Ranay's chest. 'I'm not.'

'Listen to me,' he urges, grabbing a fistful of her dress. His hands are trembling, his face contorted with pain. He's fighting to stay here, if only to reassure his daughter in his final moments. 'The time will come . . . where you and the queen . . . will need to use your . . . powers.' He groans, bloodstained teeth bared. They clench as he hisses. 'You have to claim back . . . what is rightfully yours.'

She takes his hand in hers as she sobs. The shouts and cries around her go muffled, like she's underwater, everything blurring except the crystal clear sight of her father's dying face before her eyes.

'You must unleash . . . your abilities . . . Promise me . . . you'll unleash your full power.'

'I'll try, Father.'

'Preeya, you must promise me. The future of . . . Pendilor . . . depends on it.'

'I promise.' She sobs.

He gives a rattling sigh, his eyes rolling to the back of his head. Preeya wails, burying her face into his neck, inhaling his musky male scent for the final time. Ranay—Queen Assyri of Pendilor's beloved husband, her rock, and her beloved father—is dead.

'Get up.' A nearby soldier growls, grabbing Preeya by the scruff of her neck and hauling her to her feet.

'We have to bury him.' She chokes through her tears.

'No time,' says another guard, and Preeya watches in horror as they drag her father's body into some nearby bushes.

'The animals will have a good meal tonight.' One chuckles, grabbing her. She does not fight against his grip. To do so would be futile.

His body isn't even cold yet, and they threw him into the bushes like a discarded piece of meat. Preeya weeps, hopelessness filling her.

✖ ✖ ✖

Arteo feels the wind rush past him as he falls, cold shock prickling through him. Spray from the water hits him first, ice-cold against his skin. He braces himself for the impact, for the pain that is surely coming.

But right before he hits the rocks and death claims him, a slim ray of light shoots from the sky. The beam consumes his body, and a protective bubble forms around Arteo.

The young prince faints as the ray of light hits him, exhaustion overcoming him. He is completely unaware that the bubble is cushioning his impact, shielding him from the rocks. The topple over the waterfall, which would have surely brought death, is now just a bumpy, cushioned ride.

He hits the base of the waterfall, drifting along the river. The night comes and goes; Arteo travels further along the river, accompanied by nothing but the sound of running water and the occasional curious fish, which swims up to investigate before darting away. All the while, Arteo is unconscious and protected. Whilst the bubble is mystery enough, how is he to deal with the new attachment that adorns his face?

❌ ❌ ❌

The morning light sparkles on the water, the river calm and filled with fish that swim to the surface, scales shimmering, before darting back into the depths. King Paraksha, the leader of the Garlamon people, is fishing in his boat, humming merrily with the sun on his face.

His teenage son, Balin, sits next to him, both with fishing rods in their hands and enjoying each other's company. The king's guards and some staff are also on the boat, a thickset wooden vessel, beautifully crafted by hand.

Balin thinks he feels a fish on his hook and wrestles with the sudden resistance. However, he soon gets distracted as he sees something approaching on top of the water from the north.

'Father, what's that?' says the teenage boy, leaning over the edge of the boat and pointing a sun-kissed finger upstream.

A well-tanned boy with chestnut-brown hair wearing a green tunic of fine material is floating towards them, face up in the river with his eyes closed. His face is hidden behind a strange, black mask.

'Father, look! There's a boy in the water!'

King Paraksha turns his dark eyes to see the boy floating towards them. He turns to his guards and gestures. They quickly row to meet him, and with an effort, the king and his son haul him on to their boat. His tunic sticks to his skin, his hair dripping. He isn't moving, but his chest rises and falls.

'Is he going to be okay?' asks Balin.

King Paraksha doesn't answer. He reaches out a hand to remove the mask, but something sparks at his fingers, like an electric shock, and he jerks back. It seems the boy's mask cannot be removed.

Curious.

'Take him downstairs,' the king orders two nearby guards, who take the boy carefully in their arms and try to carry him below deck. The boy coughs and flails in panic, swiping at the guards until they lay him back down.

The king holds his shoulder, worried. What has happened to this boy to make him so fearful? Behind the mask, he sees the teen's blue eyes are wide with fright.

'We mean you no harm, boy,' says the king in his deep voice, his dark hand holding Arteo's shoulder firmly.

Gasping, the boy wheels round, his sky-blue gaze sliding from the king to Balin, who stares back in shock. 'Where am I?' says the boy to the king finally. 'Who are you?'

'We found you in the river just now. You would have drowned if my son hadn't seen you.'

Arteo's gaze flickers back to Balin, who gives him a shy nod.

The mysterious lad appears a few years older than Balin, with defined muscles that speak of work or training. However, his skin is tanned; he's no farmer's boy, and his clothes speak of wealth. What is he doing alone in a river with that strange mask?

'Why am I here?' asks the boy.

'That's a good question,' says the king, bewilderment rippling through him. 'Unfortunately, it's one I don't have the answer to. Let's start with another. What is your name?'

The boy gives a confused expression, his eyes widening. He shakes his head. 'I . . . I'm afraid I don't know.'

His eyes roll to the back of his head, and he slumps back on to the boat deck, falling unconscious.

'Take him below,' says the king in concern, and a nearby guard takes the boy in his arms below decks. 'The healer will know what to do.'

'Let's head back,' King Paraksha says to Balin, who gives an agreeing nod. He suddenly doesn't feel like fishing any more, intrigued more at the discovery of this mysterious youth and the many questions that would need answers.

⚬ ⚬ ⚬

Queen Assyri and her crew, surrounded by the dozen or so soldiers, trundle along through the forest, dry leaves crunching underfoot and sweat beading their backs. In the distance, animals howl and insects chirp, sending goose pimples stippling across Preeya's skin.

She's cried all her tears away. Her father's blood is still all over her hands, dry and cracking. The sight of Arteo tumbling over the cliff replays over and over in her mind. Her mother walks beside her, eyes red and head bent, defeated by the evil that has taken over their family.

'Here,' says General Thamios's deep voice. The guards stop with a rustle of chain mail and leather, boots crunching twigs as they come to a halt.

Assyri reaches to take Preeya's hand, squeezing her daughter's fingers. The touch from her mother does little to comfort the girl, and she fights back more tears. What are they supposed to do here? They're in the middle of the jungle with nowhere to go, very little food, and no weapons or supplies.

A few of their followers are with them, clutching one another and looking to the royals for guidance with frightened eyes.

'This is where you rightly belong,' says General Thamios as he turns to give Assyri a nasty grin. 'Welcome to your new kingdom, *Your Grace.*'

Hatred and fear surge through Preeya. One of his soldiers murdered her father and caused Arteo to die too. 'You evil, pig of a man', she screams. Thamios sneers back at her, as though mocking the teenage girl for her childish rage.

As the sounds of soldiers crunch away in the foliage, the followers come over to their queen, gathering in a circle as they speak quietly, discussing what to do next. One of the servants, a handmaiden who dresses her mother, wraps a warm arm around Preeya's shivering shoulders, murmuring words of comfort that do little to stem the girl's rising panic.

She watches her mother and her followers talking quietly, tears sliding down Assyri's cheeks, until there is a sudden crunch of leaves and twigs behind them. Soldiers approach, but they aren't from Pendilor or Zartali. *Who are these strange men?*

Preeya's breath catches in her throat as a muscular man with dark, curly hair and a beard steps out of the bushes, flanked by soldiers.

Assyri looks up.

King Ranakin, lord of the jungle dwellers, has found them. He does not look happy!

✂ ✂ ✂

Arteo slowly floats back to consciousness. The first thing he feels are the soft sheets under his aching body. When he opens his eyes, he comes face to face with a set of bright-brown eyes, the afternoon sunlight shining in them.

A beautiful scent of rose in the air. Most likely from her beautiful glowing skin. Has he died and met an angel?

He vaguely remembers a man helping him in the water, but everything is blurry before that.

He moves and feels the silk sheets against his skin. His *bare* skin.

He isn't wearing a shirt. Arteo snatches the bed sheets and glances underneath. He isn't wearing pants, either.

'Uh . . . where are my pants?' he asks, looking up to where the girl, around his age, is smiling at him. She has dark skin and long, wavy hair the colour of midnight. She's enchanting. He fights to keep his voice level. 'And . . . who are you?'

'The healer had to check your body for injuries,' says the girl, her voice light. Her hands are clasped before her, and she's wearing a dress of pale blue that's beautiful against her dark skin. She isn't a commoner or a servant. 'I helped,' she added.

'Surely, you did not . . .?'

'Mmm, yes I did.' She gives a grin, reaching to a nearby bowl to pluck out a grape. She pops it into her mouth, smirking. 'Don't worry. I've seen one of *those* before. Maybe not as big as yours, but I have seen one.'

Heat floods Arteo's cheeks. 'Please bring me my pants,' he stutters, vulnerable without his clothes. He tightens the sheets around himself as she giggles, picking up his clothes from a nearby chair, where they've been neatly folded, and flinging them to him.

She flounces out of the room, her dress rippling behind her like water. Arteo swallows, his heart fluttering. She's the most beautiful girl he's ever

69

seen in his life. Though he's embarrassed, he's secretly wishing that she won't go.

He wriggles into his clothes, his body aching likes he's been dragged a hundred miles tied to the back of a horse. He can't remember . . . anything at all. Who is he? What happened to him?

He surveys the room. It's simple, with homely wooden walls and a faded rug at his feet. The nearby table has the bowl of grapes the girl ate as well as some plain bread. A lantern, cold and unburning, sits on the windowsill, where daylight streams through the window near the bed.

A gentle knock on the door announces another newcomer. A handsome man with dark skin and a salt-and-pepper beard opens the door and stands on the threshold, eyes creased in concern, though he smiles when he sees Arteo looking at him.

'Good afternoon,' he says, his voice pleasant. 'How are you feeling?'

'You helped me earlier today,' says Arteo dumbly. 'In the boat.'

'That's right,' says the man. 'My name is Paraksha, and I'm the king of Garlamon. The boy you saw yesterday is my son, Balin, and you've met my daughter, Karina. I believe she was here earlier. What is your name?'

'I . . . don't remember,' says Arteo, running his fingers through his hair. Everything is black. What happened? Where did he come from?

King Paraksha says nothing for a moment. 'Well, you must be hungry,' he says. 'Would you like to remove your mask so you can eat? We thought it best to leave it on while you slept.'

'Mask?' Arteo's fingers move to touch the warm, soft material on his skin. King Paraksha notices the surprise on the boy's face and brings him a looking glass.

Arteo's eyes widen. He can't feel it, but a plain mask has been welded on to his face as if by magic, hiding his features. Only his mouth and eyes, blue as a spring sky, are visible. He attempts to remove the mask, but it is futile.

The king sits on a cushioned bench nearby and asks, 'Where are you from?'

'I don't remember anything.' Arteo sighs, searching his empty memory. 'Not my name, my home . . . nothing.'

He wants to break down into tears. He feels that something bad has happened, something terrible, but it's like someone has snatched away all his memories. How did he end up in the water, and what is this strange mask over his face?

'You're in shock,' says King Paraksha kindly, leaning over to give Arteo's arm a fatherly pat. 'Your memory will likely come back in time. Meanwhile, you're our guest and will be treated as such.'

'Thank you, Your Grace.' Arteo doesn't know the rules for contact with royalty, but he takes hold of the king's hand.

Paraksha looks him in the eyes and says, 'For now, we'll call you Lartak. It means "lost soul". At least until you remember your true name. Come now. We'll get something to eat.'

Lartak (Arteo) follows the king out of the modest room and finds himself in a stone corridor. Flowerpots are hung on the walls, bursts of colour among the grey stone. Sunlight shines through the windows, casting light on the flagstones beneath their feet.

Lartak looks around in awe at enormous framed paintings, elegant sculptures, and intricate tapestries flanking the corridors. Outside, the sun is starting to set, bleeding pink into the sky.

There appears to be some kind of festival in full swing here: servants wearing simple robes rush past with trays of food and drinks; people in dresses and skirts and breeches dance and sing, moving to music played on nearby stringed instruments; notes fluttering in the light breeze. It fills Lartak with calm.

He sits at a large table next to the king, aware of the many stares he's getting from the surrounding people.

Karina, the king's daughter, is over by the tables of food, her hips swaying in her dress as she smiles and dances with everyone around her— teenagers, the elderly, children, she doesn't seem to mind whom.

She takes the hands of a nearby boy of around seven, his chin stained purple with jam. He gives a delighted grin as she dances in a circle with him, her black hair dancing on her shoulders. Lartak is consumed with her every movement.

When her grinning face meets his, his stomach does a nervous backflip.

CHAPTER 9

A NEW BEGINNING

King Ranakin and his soldiers surround Assyri and her people. The fallen queen of Pendilor holds Preeya close to her, the servants and gardeners shielding what remains of their beloved royal family as the jungle dwellers approach.

Furs are wrapped around their slender, muscular bodies, black hair in dreadlocks or waves, scowls on their dark faces as they point spears towards the group. Preeya gives a scared whimper, clinging to her mother's skirts.

'Halt,' orders the king, holding up a hand as he approaches. He frowns, looking at their dishevelled clothing and dirt matting their faces.

'Who are you?' he asks in his deep voice. 'Why are you in my abode?'

The queen steps forward without hesitation, defiance in her red-rimmed eyes. Though her blonde hair is a tangled mess and grief is etched on her face, she confronts the king bravely.

'I am Queen Assyri of Pendilor,' she says. 'This is my daughter, Preeya.' The princess mimics her mother, standing up straight and looking the jungle dweller ruler in the eyes. Straightening her spine, she acts a little braver.

'And these are what is left of my loyal followers.'

'What brings you to my jungle in such a state?' The king takes a step closer to them on his long legs. A dagger is tucked into his belt, but he doesn't reach for it.

'We have been wronged,' the queen pleads. 'My people and guards have been slaughtered. The rest of us were rounded up like cattle and brought here, left to rot in these jungles.'

King Ranakin raises a bushy eyebrow. 'Who, pray tell, would wrong their queen?'

'It was my brother, Bolara,' she says darkly. Preeya sees her mother's shoulders shaking. 'He has taken the kingdom by force and murdered many innocents. My husband . . . my son . . .' She pauses and takes a breath. Preeya wraps her arms around her mother, her heart bleeding.

Arteo tumbling from the cliff . . . her father's trembling, bloodstained lips . . .

King Ranakin's dark eyes narrow in recognition of the name.

'We are aware of your brother and his general . . . and their exploits in our jungles. He has slain many of my people in his time here. I trust you were unaware?'

'If I had been aware of such crimes, he would have suffered swift punishment,' Assyri replies, anger in her eyes. 'He has done much behind my back in recent years.'

The king hesitates, wiping his brow, then casts a glance at all the fearful eyes in the crowd. 'I believe you,' he says. He has heard of Assyri's kind rule. 'It seems your brother has dealt a terrible blow against you and your family today. Any enemy of Bolara is a friend of mine.'

At the wave of his hand, his soldiers lower their spears, though several of them scrutinize the fearful Pendilorians with hate-filled gazes.

'Forgive us. The jungles have not been safe of late. But I am aware of your kind and compassionate rule, Queen Assyri. You are welcome here, so long as you pose no threat to my people.'

'Thank you, King Ranakin.' Assyri bows her head.
'You may set up here for the night,' he says and barks some orders at his followers, who spring to action.

'Come, now,' says Assyri to her followers. 'We are not alone here. We can get through this, yes?'

Her followers give hesitant nods and rush to help as the jungle dwellers return with planks of wood, thick animal skins, weapons, bags of food, and skins of water. Preeya sniffles, and Assyri takes her daughter's cheeks in her hands.

'We *will* survive,' says the queen, looking straight into Preeya's eyes. 'We will, my darling daughter. For now, we are weak and afraid, but it won't last forever. We will rebuild, and one day, justice will be served. Bolara will be held to account for his actions.'

❧ ❧ ❧

Months pass, the cold winter coming and going, the early chirping of birds and sprouting flowers showing the first signs of spring. King Paraksha's kingdom comes alive with new flowers and fruits, its people rejoicing with the new season.

They have welcomed Lartak to their community, showing only kindness and patience. His absent memory is still a sign of frustration for the boy. However, not everyone is happy with Lartak's presence.

'Anything?' asks Karina, cocking her head. She's wearing her long hair back in a braid today, strands of black framing her face. She is radiant.

Lartak shakes his head, frowning. It's been several months since he was rescued from the river by Balin and King Paraksha, but his mind is still hopelessly blank. Like someone took all his memories from before that day and plucked them out.

They venture through the village together, a fond pastime of theirs. The pair has become inseparable since Lartak's sudden appearance all those months ago.

'Balin,' says Karina sternly, turning around to see her little brother trailing after them. Just a few years Lartak's junior, the boy is fascinated by him and enjoys following them around.

'I won't get in the way,' he protests, looking around as though not interested in the pair. Lartak chuckles as Karina leads him through a row of artistic tapestries. Since he got here, she has shown him all kinds of amazing things in the town, such as difficult-looking dance routines, wondrous paintings, and beautifully carved rock sculptures that make his heart swell.

Right now, there is an archery contest in full swing, dozens of people standing outside a sand ring, thumping their fists on the fence, and cheering as several youth's fire arrows at targets, some a few hundred feet away.

With each *thwack* of an arrow, the crowd cheers, groaning in disappointment or clapping as the arrows hit or miss their targets. 'Would you like to join in?' asks Karina. Her brown eyes sparkle as she looks up at Lartak. 'I never had much of an eye for archery, but perhaps you could show them a thing or two.'

'I doubt it. I don't remember ever using a bow.' He shrugs.

She nods in sympathy as she grabs his hand. Calloused, hard palms and fingers exhibit some sort of wielding of equipment.

Nearby is Mirtan, whom Lartak has seen around a few times. He is the best archer among the group by far; as they observe, he nocks an arrow and shoots it at a nearby target, the arrow piercing the middle.

People around them cheer and shout, and the young man, around eighteen years old, shakes back his dark hair, a confident half-smile on his face. His eyes scan the crowd and settle on Karina, where he gives a confident nod.

'A friend of yours?' asks Lartak, keeping his voice light.

'No.' She sniffs.

The boy's eyes slide to Lartak, and his smile turns into a sneer. 'Watch this, Karina!' he shouts over the heads of the onlookers. Several turn to look at the princess. She folds her arms.

Mirtan fires another arrow to a target even further away. It lands in the dead centre and is met with general applause. He turns to grin at her.

'He says he likes you, Karina,' pipes up Balin from behind them. 'He said he's going to ask Father for your hand in marriage.'

'He better not,' scoffs Karina, rolling her eyes. Lartak feels a rush of mirth at her distaste for the archer boy. Though he won't admit it aloud, he is glad she isn't interested in him.

The young man suddenly abandons his position on the sands and heads for them, his bow in hand. 'Who's mystery boy?' he asks of Karina, gesturing towards Lartak without looking at him.

He stands a few inches taller than him, and he can see the tight muscles from years of training in his arms. Several nearby girls enjoy the exchange, curling their hair in their fingers as they whisper and giggle.

'I'm Lartak.' He reaches out a hand to shake Mirtan's. 'We've met before. Maybe you don't remember.'

'I'd have remembered a foreigner,' snarls Mirtan, ignoring the proffered hand. 'How about a challenge? Think you can hit that target over there?'

Annoyance rippling through him, Lartak lets his hand swing by his side. 'No, thanks. I'm just watching.'

'Come on,' goads the boy and nudges Lartak in the shoulder. 'Show me what you've got.'

'Yeah, go on, Lartak,' says Balin.

'Fine,' says Lartak, swallowing a sigh. He knows he's about to be made a fool of, knowing full well that this Mirtan is hoping to humiliate him in front of Karina. But no one will be able to say that he didn't try.

As someone throws him a bow, he places a palm out and catches it without hesitation. The bow slots perfectly in his hand, and he enjoys the warmth in his fingertips. *It's as though he's held one a hundred times before.*

He runs his finger along the wooden shaft, familiarity flooding him, exciting him. Holding a bow is as natural as pulling on a fresh tunic.

'Come on, then,' yells Mirtan.

The arrogant youth shoots target upon target, with near-perfect precision, hearing several 'oohs' and 'aahs' from the watching crowd. Lartak's neck burns as he senses Karina's gaze on him.

He raises the bow. He doesn't need someone to tell him where to press the bow, how to position his fingers, how to sight down it to see his target properly.

Twang.

Lartak's arrow hits the dead centre of a target fifty feet away. It is natural to him, and he quickly nocks another arrow.

Karina and Balin look at each other in surprise.

The contest continues.

Gasps of shock erupt from the crowd as Lartak matches all Mirtan's shots, his arrows digging into the targets, sometimes closer to the dead centre than his rival. Mirtan's face gets redder and redder, and eventually, he lets out a frustrated snarl. 'Try this one!' he cries, nocking an arrow. 'Hit the melon one hundred feet away!'

He fires before Lartak is even ready. It is a tricky shot, one that requires huge willpower and dexterity. The arrow must bend around a tree to hit a melon wedged into another tree that lies behind. Mirtan's arrow flies around the trunk, narrowly missing the bark, and lands with a *thwack* into the melon.

Lartak fires his own arrow, and it shoots past the first tree at lightning speed, hitting the struck melon as it's falling to the ground. Mirtan watches in dumbfounded horror as the people around them cheer and yell.

'That was amazing!' Karina shouts to him with an absolute stunned look on her face. Balin drops the apple he is munching on.

Mirtan throws down his bow. Several people come to clap Lartak on the back as he gives a shy smile, wondering who he must have been in his past life to pick up the bow so easily. Where did he learn these skills?

'Wow, you're better than Mirtan,' remarks Balin.

For Mirtan, this is the final straw.

'All right, mystery kid,' he snarls, marching over to Lartak and shoving him hard in the chest, almost knocking him over. 'Sparring match, you and me, right now! I'll rip that stupid mask off your face and see what you're hiding!'

'Stop it, Mirtan!' Karina cries.

'Yeah, leave him alone, Mirtan,' snaps Balin.

'Come on!' The youth's eyes are narrowed in angry slits, his cheeks flushed red, his hair in a tangled mess from where he's run his fingers through it in frustration. He raises his fist, ready to strike.

Lartak readies himself to defend. His hands start to slightly glow. Karina notices.

'What's going on here?'

King Paraksha's deep voice overpowers the mutters and whispers around them. 'What's this, Mirtan? Are you challenging someone to a fight? And our guest, no less?'

'No, Your Grace,' mutters the young man, bowing low to his king. 'Just a misunderstanding.'

'Come on,' whispers Karina, and they leave the archer behind to be scolded as Lartak's hands return to normal. Balin doesn't follow. He is enjoying watching Mirtan squirm under the interrogation of his father. Lartak and Karina leave the archery ring behind and head to the forest, giggling as they run hand in hand.

'Lartak, what happened to your hands . . . with Mirtan?' says Karina as she peers up at him, dark eyes sparkling.

'I . . . I don't know.'

She stares intently and, with a breathy voice, whispers, 'You are full of mystery, aren't you?' He finds himself grinning, exhilarated by his victory and Karina's warmth. He stops in his tracks when she leans towards him, her soft lips brushing his cheek.

His face blazes with heat as she gives a giggle and runs off, her skirts flowing behind her. Laughing, he chases after her, thinking how blessed he is that of all the places the river could have carried him, it was to Karina's side.

✳ ✳ ✳

In the six months since they were outcast from the palace, this part of the jungle of Kalanya is transformed into a bustling village. Queen Assyri, virtually unrecognizable with her long hair tied back and wearing animal furs, approaches with a bundle of firewood. Preeya is sitting drawing shapes in the dirt, her head bent.

'Preeya, sweetheart, are you all right?'

'I'm just thinking about Father.' She sighs when Assyri kneels beside her. 'And Arteo.'

'I miss them too,' her mother murmurs, pulling her into a hug. She strokes her daughter's hair, still silk-soft and shimmering. More of their supporters are around them; together, they hunt for food, build shelters, and defend themselves from the dangers of the wilds.

They lead a simple life here, but nobody has forgotten their lost kingdom and especially not those they lost along the way.

Assyri's eyes fill with fire. It is a determined look that Preeya hasn't seen in a while. 'We will rebuild,' she says. She gestures around them. 'We are rebuilding. We'll train our warriors, and we'll be ready in case Bolara'— she spits the word as though bitter on her tongue—'decides to come back and finish us off. We will not surrender meekly.'

Preeya nods, resolve filling her at her mother's words. 'I'll help,' she offers. She'll have to shed her dislike of fighting to get their kingdom back. No longer is she an innocent princess frolicking in a garden of small animals and flowers. She must be strong and determined.

She has no choice if they want to survive.

⁂

Bolara never gets tired of sitting on the grand throne. His legs stretch out before him, his chin resting on his palm, a smile curling his lips. His wife, Ritani, is at his side, looking deliciously radiant in a gown of deep-red velvet.

After they took over the kingdom, they moved into Assyri and Ranay's superior quarters, ordering the statues and paintings of the royal couple to be taken down and burned.

They watched in delight as the servants destroyed every work of art related to Assyri and her family. It is all a great game to them both.

Servants pass them in corridors and serve their meals with their heads bent. Far fewer people come to the palace to seek an audience with the one who sits on the throne.

The laughter and banter of the royal staff are gone, overtaken by fear of reprisal or punishment for doing the wrong thing. Parts of the gardens have been transformed into larger sparring sands and targets, leaving less room for gardens and more for practice.

Guards are outside day and night, fighting to be better and stronger. What used to be the sounds of chittering birds and children's laughter is now the clashing of steel and the thump of wooden dummies taking a beating.

'Y-Your Grace?'

A leader of a nearby village has come to see Bolara, walking with a slouch, eyes wide with fear. He's dressed in rags, and Ritani scrunches her nose up in disgust at the man's approach. He smells of dogs and horses, and blood mattes his worn-out boots.

'That's close enough,' rumbles General Thamios, his hand on his sword hilt as the villager halts before the throne.

'Name?' says Bolara lazily. The villager opens his mouth, but Bolara interrupts him. 'Never mind, I don't care. What are you doing here?'

'About this month's t-taxes, Your Grace,' stutters the villager.

'Ah, yes. Your village has yet to pay. Why?'

'The f-food supplies, my king. We don't have enough to feed the village, let alone pay taxes. I come to humbly b-beg for an extension, Your Grace. Farmers are working day and night.'

Bolara gives a lazy flick of his wrist, and General Thamios swallows the distance between him and the villager in one long stride. He snatches the man's thin wrist in his gauntlet and slices his hand off at the wrist as easy as a cook cutting through a cucumber.

The villager's eyes widen as he screeches in pain, his screams echoing around the throne room as red bursts from his wrist. General Thamios steps back, sheathing his blade and returning to his spot in silence.

The villager sinks to his knees, whimpering, holding the ruined stump of his arm, wrapping it up in his dirty shawl to stem the blood pumping fresh and red on to the marble floor.

'I will keep your hand as payment,' says Bolara flatly. 'Each month you fail to pay, you'll lose another limb. Pray you're able to pay next month, peasant. General Thamios likes chopping off things.'

'Th-thank you, Your G-Grace,' the villager stutters, getting to his trembling feet. More guards come and grab him by the arms as he sobs and coughs, tears streaming down his dirt-covered face. They throw him out of the throne room, and all that's left is a trail of red.

CHAPTER 10

THE STRENGTH WITHIN

Twelve long, troubled months have passed since Bolara exiled his
sister and her family to the jungles and took over Pendilor.

In the kingdom, the beloved Queen Assyri, Ranay, and their darling
children are assumed dead, and their silent followers have long since
abandoned all hope of them returning to reclaim their rightful throne,
succumbing to Bolara's iron-fisted rule. They keep their heads down, living
the best lives they can under their ruthless new leader.

However, deep in the Kalanya jungle reside Assyri and Preeya, damaged
and heartbroken but still very much alive.

Their new home in the jungle is unrecognizable. What was a year ago
a stretch of forest like any other is now a modest village. It is small, and by
no means a city or a palace, but it is bustling with activity. Tents and fences
have been constructed in neat, orderly lines, torches keeping away most of
the wandering wildlife.

They even built small dirt paths and organized sections for the
different people living there, making it as homely as possible. Pens keep
goats, chickens, and pigs, and the beginnings of vegetable patches mean the
village is fast becoming self-sufficient, though the jungle people still visit
to help and trade items they can't produce themselves.

The king's assertions did little to reassure his people that the newcomers
meant no harm, but months of peace, trading, and careful communication
helped the people of the jungle slowly trust Assyri and her people. Now

they trade and swap information like old allies, understanding that Bolara and his children are just as much Assyri's enemies as their own.

The group, who were once servants in the palace and the most faithful of Assyri's followers, live as equals here now. There is a sense of calm among the village, routines and jobs for everyone that bring a sense of responsibility and worth. However, beneath the serenity is a deep sadness.

Two crudely made graves of mud and stone sit near Assyri and Preeya's tents, memories of the father and son they lost on the way here at the hands of Assyri's heartless brother. They are not the graves they deserve, but it's the best they could do here. Everyone in the village often leaves flowers and offerings at the grave in mourning.

Her chores complete and a restlessness gripping her, Preeya snatches up her sword and ventures into the woods by herself. Twelve months of hard living has given her toned muscles and a steel edge to her that wasn't there before.

Every day, she thinks of her father and brother, so cruelly taken from them, the home she lost, and the justice that still needs to be served to her cruel uncle and his family. Her steps are sure and brisk, leaves crunching under her boots.

The village is a bustle of activity, the warmth from the torches comforting, her mother's followers giving her kind smiles as she passes. Preeya steps into the thick wilds of the jungle, the air cool on her skin, weak sunlight shining through the leaves and casting slits of light on the leaf-strewn ground. It is quiet here, giving her space to think.

The queen, now wearing simple village rags and her long hair tied behind her, sees her daughter leaving and follows quietly from behind, snatching a sword from a nearby training ring. *The jungles aren't safe for her to wander around alone.*

'Stay here please,' she says quietly to her aide, who gives a low bow, still showing respect despite the fact Assyri hasn't sat on the throne for many months. She still possesses the eloquent grace of a royal and follows her daughter from a distance, grass tickling her ankles.

Preeya walks for over an hour, quietly mumbling to herself and kicking the dirt every now and then. Assyri watches but does not intervene. She continues to follow quietly.

In a clearing, Preeya stops and attacks a tree with her sword, a fierce growl emanating from her with each swing, letting out her rage and frustration. She battles an invisible enemy, practicing her footwork, lunging and dodging unseen blows.

She is almost unrecognizable; she is a far cry from the sweet, nature-loving girl she was before all this mess happened, maturing into a young woman with fire in her heart.

'Preeya,' Assyri calls, her voice ringing over the clanging of the blade against the bark, creating deep welts in the tree trunk. Preeya looks up, blonde hair sticking to her neck as her chest heaves, the blade trembling in her hand. Her gaze softens when their eyes lock.

'You need to use more force and intent when you thrust with a blade,' says Assyri, stepping from the tree line to join her daughter's side.

Preeya grips the blade more firmly.

'Any hesitation, and it will cost you your life.'

'How do you know all this?' Preeya asks. All through her childhood, her and Arteo's training was kept secret from their peace-loving mother. To imagine Queen Assyri with a weapon in her hand is borderline laughable.

'I was not always queen, my dear princess,' says Assyri, favouring her daughter with a warm smile. 'I was trained by Chirok from childhood, right up until my coronation. There were times I had to use my sword and my powers to defend myself, you know.'

Preeya thinks back to when her mother fired energy at Ritani and Syrana the night of the attack. Preeya thought it was a last, desperate show of power to defend her children, but it makes sense that Assyri would have been taught to use her abilities.

'What did you use your powers for?' she asked.

'I mostly used them against the unwanted attention of aggressive men. Here, let me show you.'

Preeya blinks, having never heard of her mother speak of men before she married. Assyri turns her own sword in her hand. Then she shows her some moves while Preeya gapes in shock. Is this the same elegant queen who preached peace and behaved as though she never lifted a finger or touched a weapon?

What appears before her now is a woman with fire blazing in her eyes, a woman unravelled and put back together with determination and hard work.

Bolara's invasion made them both stronger, not weaker. Though Preeya flushes at her assumption her mother never lifted a weapon, she feels a fierce pride as she watches her move with skill and grace.

'I'm a little out of practice,' the queen jokes as they spar. 'I'm afraid it's been a while since I did this. But you never quite forget.'

Assyri's modesty isn't needed. She is skilled, as good as Galdin, if not better. Steel clashes as they parry and block. The queen gets the better of her daughter time and time again, finishing with holding the sword to her neck before drawing back with an encouraging smile.

'Please show me that move again, Mother,' Preeya begs when Assyri bests her with a complicated flurry. The queen obliges, teaching her daughter some moves Chirok taught her many years ago. It's a special time for them both; not only is it time they are spending together, but finally, they feel like they're fighting back.

Preeya is taken aback by her mother's extraordinary skill. She kept this secret for so long, letting everyone think she was delicate and kind and never lifted a weapon in her life. Preeya almost doesn't recognize her, but she feels nothing in her heart but love and respect.

They practice for hours, Assyri gently coaching Preeya on how to improve, small tricks, and ways to feint and fool her enemy. A light sheen of sweat on their skin, their tunics damp, they finally wander to collapse by a tree overlooking an enormous waterfall.

They munch on apples, smiling together as they make small talk. This time with her mother is precious, and Preeya leans on her mother's shoulder, peace filling her. Assyri strokes her daughter's blonde hair.

'I'm so proud of you,' she murmurs as they look at the valley where the waterfall throws water to the river far below. They spot an eagle flying above, flapping its great wings as it hunts for its lunch.

The roaring torrent of water makes Preeya think of Arteo. She chews the apple slowly, her happiness giving way to despair. She's spent many sleepless nights going over and over that terrible day in her mind, at seeing her brother's eyes widen in shock as he fell . . . down into the roaring waters, never to be seen again.

Assyri's warm fingers gently close around her wrist as she says softly, 'I miss them too.'

Preeya forces a feeble smile, swallowing her apple. She sighs. 'I don't understand, Mother. What can make a man so cruel?' She thinks of her Uncle Bolara. How could he have betrayed his own family?

'Greed and power, my dear. It blackens the heart of many people.'

'But how could he kill so senselessly? His own family?'

'It is a question that we will never have an answer to,' says Assyri sadly. 'The gods themselves have asked this same question, over and over. Not even the wisest know.'

A fierce and righteous anger ripples through Preeya. This cannot be. Their true home was stolen from them. She throws her apple core at the waterfall. They watch it sail through the air and out of sight. 'I will not let it go, Mother. I cannot.'

Assyri's pale eyebrows raise in surprise, as though she can feel the power from Preeya rising to the surface like water in a boiling pot. Preeya's skin tingles like static, her rage fuelling her power.

'I won't let them get away with this. They murdered Father, and they killed Arteo. They took our kingdom away from us, and no one is punishing them for it.'

'Then we have work to do,' says Assyri. She shows none of her daughter's fury, but the same fire burns in her eyes. 'You will have to master your skills, then we'll train our loyal followers. More will join us. The time for us to be peaceful folk has come to an end. With some hard work, we can develop capable warriors. Are you sure you're ready?'

'I'm ready, Mother. I—'

A twig snaps a distance away.

Assyri suddenly leaps to her feet, snatching a rock from the ground in a single, fluid motion. She hurls the rock over Preeya's head, and the girl watches in shock as it hurtles fifty feet through the air.

A sudden sickening crunch is heard. A soldier's head snaps back. He drops dead at the base of a tree. Assyri's aim is true; his skull is split, his head caved in from the blow. Preeya jumps to her feet. She didn't even hear them approach.

There's the rustle of cloth and scrapes of steel as four more soldiers emerge from the tree line like cockroaches, their swords out. They are wearing Bolara's colours.

Two of them glance at the dead soldier's body, and they all look enraged. The nearest has a glint in his eye, as though he's more impressed than horrified at his comrade's sudden demise.

'The little one's mine,' he snarls, eyeing Preeya with ravenous greed. A thrill of fear runs through Preeya as she grips her sword. *How did they find us here?*

Assyri gives a howl of anger and rushes the first guard. He barely has time to widen his eyes before she slices through him without mercy, finding a chink in his armour and slicing her sword up, ruining his torso. He crumples to the ground with a shocked groan.

With the grace of a dancer, the former queen of Pendilor heads for guard 2 and engages him in battle. She blocks his feeble attempts easily and somersaults over his head, landing softly and swinging her blade deftly to slice through his neck.

The guard's head pops off and rolls forward towards Preeya. Preeya can do nothing but gawk as the listless eyes are glaring at her with each revolution.

The remaining two guards head for the queen, a little more apprehensive after what they have witnessed. She bends down gracefully and retrieves a dagger hidden, strapped to her thigh. With nothing but a wristy flick, she sends it spiralling towards one of the guards. *Thwack.*

The dagger enters at the centre of his temple. If it was a target, you would almost swear it was the dead centre.

She casually approaches the last guard and jousts with him for a few seconds before sending a small cosmic bolt to his hand. He lets out a loud yelp as his jolted fingers release grip on the sword.

Preeya can see her mother is enjoying herself. *Who is this woman?*

She beheads the last one with a brutal, wet squelch, blood spraying from his neck as he collapses to his knees, dead.

Preeya is in awe. It's one thing training with her mother, but to see her effortlessly cut down enemies like they were straw dummies, she'd hidden her skills well. She's so powerful.

She looks radiant and dangerous all at once as she turns to meet her daughter's eyes, chest heaving, face alive with adrenaline. Preeya swallows.

'More will come,' says Assyri, sheathing her sword and brushing a loose strand of hair from her forehead. A smattering of fresh blood stains her tunic and her beautiful skin as she steps over twigs and leaves to take Preeya's hand. 'Come quickly, back to camp. We must prepare to defend ourselves. The time has come to start training as I fear it is only a matter of time before we will be called upon to fight for our lives.'

For the first time in a long time, Preeya is not scared. A sense of clarity sweeps over. She knows what her purpose is. She will train an army with whomever is available.

They clasp hands and scurry towards their new jungle home.

CHAPTER 11

---◎---

THE HUNTING TRIP

Over eighteen months have passed, and Lartak's body grows taller and stronger, his boyish youth melting into strong adulthood, and his muscles more defined. Even after long talks with people in the village, meditation, and even trying herbal teas brewed by the village elders who insisted they would work, his memories never returned.

Giving up on ever remembering his old life, he is now settled in Garlamon, living among the people like he was born there. Much to the delight and gossip of the people, Lartak spends most of his free time with Karina.

She has blossomed into a stunningly beautiful young woman, with a smile like the sun on a summer's day, eyes . . . diamonds that Lartak could lose himself in.

The last of her childish looks have turned to graceful womanhood, and he can't imagine ever loving anyone else. Their friendship involves them spending as much time together as possible, whether they're working or not.

They take long walks together, pick fruit, and study, sometimes sneaking out together at night to gaze at the stars, talking about anything and everything that comes to mind.

She is his best friend, and he's been in love with her for almost as long as his whole memory since he first opened his eyes and saw her standing there with that cheeky, knowing smile.

Karina's father, King Paraksha, is of course aware of their blossoming relationship, but Lartak doesn't know if the king is aware of his true feelings. They have stolen a few adolescent kisses but aren't officially courting; Lartak is nervous about talking to him about it directly.

How do you ask a king permission for something like that? Lartak is an outsider who washed up on their shores one day with no memory; Karina is the princess, the king's only daughter.

One sunny day, Lartak is helping train Karina's younger brother, Balin. The boy is maturing close to adulthood himself, his frame wiry and eager brown eyes beneath his mop of curly black hair.

He holds a slim frame and dark skin burnt further by hours in the sun, a crease in his brow as he swings his sword with exaggerated screams that make Karina roll her eyes and giggle.

'Good. Try another,' says Lartak, throwing an apple at the younger boy. With a high-pitched cry, Balin swings his blade, slicing through the apple almost at its centre.

The boy gives a delighted grin as the fruit falls to the ground in two halves. Fondness bubbles in Lartak. Balin is almost like a brother to him, and he is aware the younger boy practices day and night to master that move. He's spent almost all his allowance on apples, much to their amusement.

'All right, boys. Quit showing off,' Karina scolds, though her brown eyes sparkle. She is ravishing in a simple tunic of beige, her black hair tied in an intricate braid. 'Time for the hunt, Lartak, and my father's calling for you.' The Garlamon people hunt Burrintot for food. They have strict rules about it, targeting only adult Burrintot and killing only what they need for meat. One fully grown Burrintot can feed most of the village.

Lartak and Balin go off to grab their gear for the hunting trip. The trips are full of laughter, the people working well together to hunt the essential, valuable meat to feed the citizens waiting for them at home.

Karina brings some of her close friends as the hunt is considered a festive occasion, and celebration is always held after a satisfactory kill.

Lartak is not overly fond of killing animals. He reminds himself he's helping the people he has grown to love. They aren't hunting for sport, only necessity.

'Let's go,' says the king, who always leads the hunt. His eyes are red-rimmed, and he sways a little on his horse; he partied and drank a lot last night, and now he's paying for it. The king catches Lartak's eye, and he grins, remembering a particularly funny moment when the king decided he wanted to dance a jig with everyone in Garlamon.

'A bit under the weather, sir?' Lartak asks, leaves rustling as they ride their horses into the forest. Lartak is riding a bay mare, a calm creature with silk-soft ears he's ridden several times. The other hunters are beside them, some on horses and others on foot.

The villagers no longer give Lartak strange stares, but he's known as the foreign boy with the missing memories. Most regard him with short nods or shy smiles, and though some grumble that he's closer to the king and his family than most of the villagers, most treat him with cautious respect.

Lartak is at home with them. He takes comfort in this as they hunt the mighty creature's whereabouts.

'Nothing I can't handle,' says the king, though he groans and massages his temple. 'How about you, Lartak? You're an adult now. When are you planning on asking me for my daughter's hand?'

Lartak's cheeks warm. 'Is it that obvious?' He gives a nervous chuckle. Karina is a little behind, her long braid draped over her shoulder as she chats with one of her friends. As she laughs, their eyes lock, and Lartak turns back to the woods, his neck burning as he listens to their delighted giggles.

'She's my only daughter, Lartak. Are you sure about what you want to ask? Though I know you're a kind and courteous soul, I'm nervous about letting my daughter entwine herself with a stranger.'

Lartak's lips purse as he grips the horse's reins. He's been living with these people for a long time now; he is hardly a stranger. He says nothing.

'A mysterious one, at that,' adds the king. 'I'm not sure it is wise to let her court you.'

Neither of them realize that Karina had caught up with them. She scoffs. '*Let* me?' she snaps. 'Father, I'm a grown woman. It's about time you treat me like one.' She slams her heels into her horse's sides, and it gives a snort, trotting off.

'She's got a fire in her belly, that one,' King Paraksha remarks. 'Are you sure you would be able to handle her, Lartak?' He's grinning, as though the whole thing is a joke to him. 'Just remember, if you ever hurt her, I have a sharp sword, and I'm not afraid to use it.'

Lartak almost falls off his horse in shock, but then he notices that the king is laughing. 'I would never hurt her,' he says, choosing his words carefully. Though what Karina's father says is tongue in cheek, there is a truth to his words.

He, and the rest of the village, would never forgive Lartak if he did something to hurt Karina. He can't imagine ever doing her harm.

After a few hours, they arrive at the waterhole, a small body of water that shimmers in the sunlight where creatures bathe and drink. A small stream runs from it, the water clear and gurgling.

There are no signs of Burrintot tracks yet, so they all dismount to take a short rest. The air is full of anticipation, and several hunters sharpen their spears or splash water on their faces, chattering quietly among themselves.

'I'll be back in a moment,' King Paraksha calls over his shoulder. 'Nature calls.'

The others stretch their legs and feed the horses, speculating where the Burrintot might be. Lartak glances over at Karina, but she's talking with her friends, her back to him. He wonders if she is genuinely annoyed by what her father said.

He decides to leave her alone, examining the dirt adjacent to where the king ventured for any telltale signs of Burrintot footprints, inhaling the clean, grassy scents of the jungle. If they can work out whether the beast ventured here recently, they can make headway in tracking it down.

He's running his fingers through the grass at his feet, noticing uneven bumps in the dirt. *Burrintot tracks.* A sudden crash nearby, where the king ventured, followed by a pained yell that makes Lartak's blood run cold.

He dashes over, scrambling over branches and leaves and bursting through several trees into a vast forest clearing.

King Paraksha is lying on the ground, a nasty gouge wound in his stomach. He's panting hard, blood pumping on to the grass. His chest rises and falls as he covers the wound with red-soaked hands, his face contorted in pain. Blood is splattered on the nearby leaves and grass.

The king is injured. Badly.

'Your Grace!' Lartak shouts, darting towards him.

'Look out.' King Paraksha winces, his voice a mere breath. 'In the . . . bushes . . . it's coming . . .'

Lartak hears, before it appears. Heavy footsteps, rustling branches, and the deep, growling breaths of an enormous Burrintot. Then it gives a loud roar, shaking the nearby trees, dark eyes glinting from the bushes. Despite his better judgement, Lartak sprints towards the king.

The Burrintot bursts from the bushes with an angry snarl, great hooves pounding on the ground as it gallops towards them, its horn glinting in the meagre sunlight. It is a terrifying sight: twice the size of a horse, with a thick, leathery hide and legs thick as tree trunks.

Without thinking, Lartak throws his arms forward, and cosmic energy shoots from his palms. *Where did this come from?*

The Burrintot runs into it, bouncing off and flinching, giving an angry snarl. It eyes Lartak with angry, black eyes.

'Lartak!' King Paraksha shouts, blood bursting from his lips. Lartak leaps to the side as the Burrintot comes for him, the ground trembling with each of its mighty steps. His heart is thundering. This is the biggest Burrintot he's ever seen. He withdraws his sword, his breath quickening.

He can't go back for help, or the king will be mauled to death. No choice but to fight the beast alone.

His sword is clasped firmly in his hand. He dives towards the trees as the beast thunders towards him again; he's close enough to smell the dirt and manure on its leathery skin. As he scrambles to his feet, a wild thought flits through his mind. *Use your speed!*

The beast is powerful, but it is slow. With every charge, it needs to turn, its size its downfall. Lartak bravely leaps forward and slashes at its rough skin with his sword. One long, red welt appears in its side, and the Burrintot turns with an angry growl.

I have to tire it out.

Taking great care not to lead the beast near the king, Lartak dodges and dives out of the way of the beast, jabbing and slicing and sending more cosmic bolts where he can. On their fourth round, the Burrintot surprises Lartak, turning at the last moment.

Its horn tears through Lartak's armour, leaving a cut on his arm. His heart pounds with excitement, thrill rushing through his veins. He barely winces at the pain.

He glances at the king, whose face is contorted in pain as he holds the terrible wound in his stomach. His lips suddenly move, and though Lartak can't hear, he can read his words: '*Watch out!*'

Lartak narrowly avoids the incoming Burrintot, leaping out of the way and delivering a stab to its rump. The beast is covered in blood, snarling and breathing hard, steam bursting from its nostrils as it rushes at him again. This time, Lartak doesn't dodge quickly enough and gives a cry as the beast buffets him in the side.

He's thrown to the floor, the hard-packed dirt beneath him, the sword almost slipping from his hand as pain explodes in his skull. He grips the blade in his fingers, narrowly avoiding his wrist getting crushed by the beast's huge foot.

Hot, putrid breath spills over Lartak's face as the monster stands over him, pressing against the protective cosmic shield protecting his midriff. The horn pushes against it, trying to penetrate and crush him into the ground.

It growls, its destructive horn inching ever so closely as it snaps and snarls. The boy struggles to escape; if he scrambles out from beneath the creature, it'll drive its horn into his back. *The shield is weakening.*

Hopelessness descends on him. In moments, the beast will crush him with its weight or gouge him with its enormous horn. He breathes hard through his teeth, struggling as the monster's forceful push slowly starts to penetrate the shield. Soon he will be crushed to the forest floor. *I'm going to die.*

Karina's face bursts into his mind.

He can't die here. He will not die at the hands of this creature. Lartak gives a scream and angles his sword upwards as the Burrintot pushes down.

A small hole opens in his shield. With all his strength, the blade drives deep into the Burrintot's rough hide, piercing the chest.

Hot blood splatters on to his face as he gives a bestial growl. The animal on top of him gives a groan, its legs falling beneath it. It rolls, crashing to the ground with a rumble so loud that several nearby birds flap into the sky, squawking in terror.

The beast is dead.

Lartak breathes hard, his ribs aching as he gets slowly to his feet. He wipes the back of his mouth, and his wrist comes back red. His arm stings, but he flexes the muscle. The wound isn't deep.

'King Paraksha!' he shouts, darting towards where the king is lying and collapses beside him. 'Your Grace, I will summon help?'

Blood bubbles on the king's lips as he stares in horror at Lartak, dark eyes moving down to his ruined abdomen. Lartak quickly rips the sleeves of his tunic, using them to stem the blood seeping from his stomach. His robes are dark red.

'Help!' Lartak bellows over his shoulder. 'Someone help us! The king is injured!'

Karina suddenly bursts on to the scene with two soldiers behind her. Balin is on their tail and blanches when he sees his father, his brown eyes widening in horror. One of the guard's curses, his eyes sliding from the king to Lartak to the dead Burrintot.

'You took it down by yourself?' the guard asks in bewilderment, looking at Lartak's red-stained sword still buried deep in the Burrintot's heart.

'Never mind that right now. Get him to the healer!' the other guard barks, dashing for the king. He and the guard gently pick him up, and he yells in pain.

Karina holds her face, her eyes glassy as the guards carry their king into the trees and back towards the waterhole. Lartak watches, swallowing. A pool of drying blood is evident where he lay only moments earlier.

If only I got here sooner.

Looking confused and dazed. 'I'm sorry,' he croaks. Karina hurries over, helping him to his feet. He didn't realize before, but he's shaking. His hands and arms are covered in blood; whether it's the Burrintot's or the king's, he can't tell.

He gives a rattling sigh, retrieving his sword from the Burrintot's chest with a squelch as the others gaze, wiping the blade on the grass. Balin is sniffling.

'He's dying,' says the boy, his eyes full of tears. 'Oh, no, no . . .' Karina's eyes shine with passion. She grabs her brother by the shoulders.

'Listen to me,' she says, her voice low. 'You're right. He's dying. There is only one way to save him.'

Balin gives another sniffle, fiercely wiping at his eyes. 'We need to find a Lawky's nest.'

Lartak approaches them as Balin swallows and gives a determined nod. 'Okay . . . okay, sister. I know where one is.'

Lartak hesitates, not wanting to intrude on this family moment. But curiosity prevails. 'What's a Lawky?' he asks.

'A mystical bird that resides in this jungle,' says Karina. 'One of their feathers can heal almost any wound when mixed with common herbs. It might be enough to help him. I . . .'—she fiddles with her tunic—'I hope so.'

'I'll get one,' says Balin again, and Karina embraces him, planting a swift, sisterly kiss on his forehead.

'I'll go too,' says Lartak, sheathing his sword. 'You'll need my help.'

Back at the waterhole, the people are gasping and muttering to see the state of their fallen king. A healer is strapping up his wounds, wrapping bandages around Paraksha's ruined stomach and another deep wound in his shoulder. But he shakes his head, his face grim.

'My supplies are limited here,' he says, looking up at Karina. 'We need to rush him back to the village.'

She nods, her face hard, but Lartak can see that her hands, curled into fists, are trembling. Pity ripples through him. Though there is no memory of his parents, the king has become somewhat like a father to him.

It's tearing him apart to see King Paraksha in so much pain, so he can't imagine how Karina and Balin must be feeling.

They strap the king to his horse. His eyes are rolling to the back of his head, bile at the corner of his mouth and his tunic covered in drying blood. The air is solemn; even his horse is sombre, standing obediently.

Half of the villagers accompany the king, forming a protective circle around him as they crunch through the brush back towards Garlamon. The guards and a few other volunteers go back to the forest clearing to retrieve the Burrintot's body. A few of them give him quizzical looks when the guard tells them Lartak took it down on his own.

'Does that hurt?' asks Karina, nodding towards Lartak's wound.

'No,' he says, in truth, but he lets her quickly dress it using one of the medic's bandages. Her eyes are filled with tears as she works, her gentle fingers wrapping the bandage around his arm. Their eyes meet, and her breath catches.

'Go to your father,' he whispers. The others are nearly out of sight, hurrying to take their king to safety. She nods, her cheeks flushed, her eyelashes sparkling with fresh tears.

'Please hurry,' she whispers, and she presses her lips against Lartak's for a brief moment before pulling away. She hugs her brother, sniffling into his shoulder. He hugs her back. 'Be safe, both of you.'

They stare as the others clop away back towards the village. No one is chatting or laughing, all concerned for King Paraksha.

Karina looks back once, sadness in her eyes before ushering on her horse. The young men stand in silence until the group is out of sight, and they're left alone with the sounds of the forest.

Balin lets out a long breath. 'Let's get going.'

They crunch through the wildlife; Balin hesitates. He turns towards Lartak. 'Did you really kill that Burrintot all by yourself? The guards said you did. It usually takes five or six of us to take down one that big. It was enormous.'

'I did what I had to,' says Lartak, too worried about the king to talk about the battle. His heart is still racing with the thrill of the skirmish, but it is almost suffocated with the awful image of King Paraksha lying in his own blood.

The fear is cold, primal; he doesn't want him to die. They have to hurry and find this Lawky bird and retrieve its feather.

'How did you kill it, Lartak?'

Lartak can sense that he has some sort of abilities and is getting stronger every day. He gives a vague half-shrug, remembering how his muscles ignited with vigour, his cosmic energy ignited at will, and how he sank his blade deep into the Burrintot's heart.

'I got lucky, I guess. Come on. Let's find that Lawky. Where should we look first?'

The youths head deep into the forest, each step leading them further away from Garlamon, from Karina. Determination drums through Lartak. They must find a Lawky's feather and get back to the village as soon as they can, or King Paraksha will not survive.

CHAPTER 12

THE MAJESTIC LAWKY

Bolara stands in the war room, an enormous map spread upon an oak table, the corners weighed down with tomes from the palace library. General Thamios is at his side, both men poring over the map. The kingdom of Pendilor is in the middle, designed and painted by a skilled artist who placed their kingdom at the centre.

'This one next,' Bolara rumbles, pointing a regal, ringed finger at the village of Sparat several dozen miles southwest. 'They have good fields of grain that will help feed the army.'

The army is an ever-expanding force. Bolara did away with the peace-loving guardsmen who worked for Assyri and employed only those thirsty for training. They train and spar constantly when they aren't invading nearby townships and forcing them under his rule.

Those still loyal to Assyri are immediately snuffed out, if found. His soldiers encourage townsfolk to snitch on one another, bribing them with food and gold.

Some people are only too happy to rat out their neighbours, whisper of them wearing Assyri's colours, talking about rebellion, or reminiscing about her rule, in exchange for a sack of potatoes to feed their families.

'Start with the small villages,' snarls Bolara, sliding his finger along the worn parchment and to nearby settlements, most of them little more than farming villages. 'Once we have garrisons stationed, we can employ the young people and expand the army. If we control the farms, we control the people and trade. Then we can move towards the kingdoms. Kyetin will be first.'

'Then Garlamon,' adds General Thamios, pointing to the southern kingdom. Bolara nods. Thamios is one of very few people who can interrupt Bolara and not lose a limb.

'I am concerned about talk of a rebellion. Assyri may have secured warriors from that jungle king pheasant. Once we secure all the other kingdoms, we will destroy what is left of the jungle and my sister's so-called rebellion. By then, we will be strong enough to deal with Suriyar, if required.'

Thamios nods.

'Ristos', Bolara barks. His son, now nineteen, appears in the doorway. He always wears a dagger at his belt, his boyish youth melted into the figure of an athletic warrior. His powers were unveiled on his eighteenth birthday, and none were surprised that he holds Shakti 5 powers. He and Bolara went through half the palace's wine reserves in celebration.

He and Syrana often lead the assaults on the small towns and villages. Any hint of rebellion is instantly quenched. Stories are already floating around the palace about his children's ruthlessness; often, they execute villagers just for looking at them wrong. Bolara doesn't much care if the rumours are true or not. What is important is that they inspire fear.

Just last week, Syrana led a small battalion to a nearby farm. They didn't damage the farm itself but set afire a mill that had several people inside after the farmer snatched up a sword to fight. The man was forced to witness his family perish before he was hanged on the noose a day later.

'Do not lose hope!' the farmer croaked to the silent crowd, seconds before he was hanged. 'Queen Assyri and her children will return! Do not lose faith, for our true ruler will come back and save us all!'

A crack to the skull was earnt, right before the executioner forced him into the noose, but words can have an impact. The thought makes Bolara's fists clench. He will snuff out any whisper of resistance.

⚔ ⚔ ⚔

Jiola is a modest village settled between two hills. The worst thing they have encountered in fifty years is a couple of kids almost drowned in the lake a few years ago. The people who live here are simple and hard-working, and their lives are peaceful . . . until the day Ristos and Syrana arrive with a battalion of soldiers.

The sound of running horses shake the ground like an incoming storm. Seeing them come from the horizon, the mayor locks himself in his house like a frightened child, cowering as the villagers flee from the swords and spears.

The horses sweep along the paths and past the farmsteads, screams erupting as arrows fire through the air.

The soldiers enjoy frightening the townsfolk; arrows litter the grass, spears hitting trees, fences, and some innocents. The rest scatter.

'Must be hiding,' says Ristos, his armour glimmering as he dismounts his stallion, Syrana right behind him. 'The mayor.'

Not long and they kick in a door housing a skinny, balding man cowering behind his bed. Ristos grabs him by the collar and drags him outside, where the soldiers are gathering the villagers together.

'Here is your brave mayor!' Ristos bellows at the trembling villagers. Most are in rags or torn tunics, terror in their eyes as the enormous figures in armour and surcoats surround them. 'Hiding in his home!'

He throws the man to the ground, where he sprawls into the mud with a whimper.

A tomato comes flying through the air, exploding on the mayor's temple. A ripple of laughter runs through the soldiers.

They press vegetables and fruit into the villagers' hands and half-force them to punish the mayor's cowardice. Soon he's covered in juice and bits of vegetables, trembling on the ground with his hands over his head.

Syrana cackles with laughter. 'Now run, little villagers!' she cries, snatching up a spear. 'How fast can you run?'

A wild bloodbath follows. All a game to them. A vicious game of hide- and-seek ensues, where villagers who don't run fast enough are cut down. Ristos sets the mayor's house on fire, black smoke curling into the sky as he laughs.

'P-please,' the mayor whimpers, crawling along the dirt, then reaching out to grab Ristos's tunic. 'P-please stop this madness, Your Highness. I'll d-do anything.'

Ristos shakes off the mayor's stained fingers in disgust. 'Is that a backbone?' he remarks and slaps the older man on the back. He leans towards him. 'Are you ready to surrender your village now?'

'Yes, Your Grace! Absolutely!'

'Fall back!' Ristos bellows, and horses return, many of the soldiers with bloodstained swords. Bodies litter the farm, the dirt stained red.

Horse hooves thunder towards them. The mayor barely turns around before he's met with a meaty *thwack*, and his head is separated from his shoulders. A shocked frozen gaze as his head soars through the air.

'Like a bird.' Syrana laughs, sheathing her sword. The gifted eighteen-year-old showed Shakti 5 abilities on her last birthday, like her brother. As they monitor the soldiers round up the surviving villagers, she slips off her mount and appears at her brother's side.

'He had just surrendered, sister,' he says with a forlorn tone, knowing that his sister is capable of simple ruthless acts, depending upon her mood.

'I didn't like the way he looked at me,' she replies with a scowl on her face.

⚔ ⚔ ⚔

The forest grows thicker, hills turning to mountains with enormous cliffs. According to Balin, the Lawky makes its nest high on cliff faces like an eagle.

Once they reach a cliff face, they tie up the horses to some nearby trees, where a small stream and a patch of lush grass await. Lartak pats his mare's neck. They have to hurry.

They have supplies from the hunt, Balin anticipating that they'll have to stay in the forest for at least one night. They make camp beneath the trees, and the sky stays mercifully free of rain. Though they take turns keeping vigil in case of Tolverines or Burrintots, the fire they built will keep them away.

Lartak snuggles into his bedroll, staring at the flickering flames. His pulse is quick with worry. Every moment they waste, King Paraksha gets sicker.

They rise as soon as the sky fades to dawn, skipping breakfast. They walk in silence, heading north to where the ground gets hilly.

A crease in Balin's forehead tells Lartak the younger boy is worried about his father too. He's about to say something, anything to help soothe him, when Balin points towards a nearby cliff rock. 'Up there.'

The edge of a cliff side is reached. Lartak peers up; *doesn't look so high, but they'll have to climb.* Not quite a vertical face, and many ledges exist to put their feet. 'Lawkys live in caves where most animals can't reach. One's up there, I'm sure.'

'I guess it'd be too much to ask for this bird to live in a tree where it could be easy to catch?' Lartak offers, in jest.

Balin grins. 'What would be the fun in that?' The smile slips off his face as concern clouds his young features. 'Come on. Let's get going.'

They tie strips of cloth around their hands for grip, examining the cliff face. 'Tell me about this bird,' says Lartak.

'Well, she's massive,' says Balin.

'Helpful,' he remarks. 'Have you ever seen one?'

'Yes, I have,' Balin snaps. 'I stumbled across one by accident when I was nine. Chased me for miles, and its sharp talon scraped me.' He lifts his shirt and shows a faint, pink scar on his chest.

Lartak always assumed sparring had caused the injury.

'When it flew off, I managed to grab a tail feather. Shines like a rainbow. I took it back to the village, and a healer mixed the tail feather with his herbs. Healed three sick people and a wounded warrior that day.' Balin appears pleased with himself.

'So to answer your question, Lartak, it's a huge bird. Extremely dangerous. Tail feathers like a rainbow and a sharp, colourful beak. And lives up there.' He points to the cliff face again. 'Oh, and another thing, the healer believes we cannot kill the bird, or the magical tail feather won't work.'

'If this creature contains amazing healing powers, why don't we capture it?' Lartak asks. If they had a whole flock of Lawky's at their disposal, they could heal the sick with ease.

'Because they're massive and dangerous,' says Balin. 'Hunters have had their faces ripped off. This is not a bird you can keep captive.'

Lartak swallows. He hopes they'll be able to take this bird by surprise. He can't let King Paraksha die after everything he's done for him.

They clamber up the cliff face, the sun peeking from the clouds and shining its glory on the dry walls. There are plenty of footholds in the rock and even several larger ledges where they can stop and rest.

'How many people did you say this Lawky killed?' Lartak asks, panting as sweat beads his forehead.

'Um . . .' Balin's face is screwed up in concentration, his fingers scrambling for the next shelf. 'About a dozen, I think. I . . . *arrgh!*'

'Balin!' Lartak yells in alarm as the young boy loses grip, fingers slipping from the rock. He dangles from one arm, hanging fifty feet above ground, his feet dangling in the air.

'Help me!' Balin screams, hanging on with one hand.

'Hold on! I'll come to you!' Lartak calls, peering along the cliff face at him. Sweat pours down Balin's ebony face as Lartak's heart thunders. He'll never forgive himself if Balin falls, never. He edges over until he is within reach.

'Take my hand!'

Balin grits his teeth, reaching up to grab Lartak's fingers. He grabs at them, but his sweat-slicked hand slides from his grip.

Balin sobs, grasping at grass sticking out of the cliff, feet scrambling for purchase on the rock. 'Help me, Lartak. I don't want to die.'

'You won't die!' Lartak growls. 'Balin, look at me. You're going to be fine. Grab my hand. There's a ledge here. I'll pull you up.'

The boy reaches for him again, and this time, Lartak grabs his wrist. He yanks him upwards to a ledge. Balin scrambles his way there and pants on the ledge, his chest heaving, wiping at the tears on his cheeks.

'I nearly . . . died . . .' He gasps, brown eyes widening in horror as they peer down to the ground far below. The fall would have likely killed him as jagged rocks lay below.

'Well, you didn't.' Lartak pants. 'Come on.'

They scramble up the cliff, not talking as fatigue pulls at their muscles, concentrating on every movement and testing every ledge before putting weight on it.

There is not much wind, fortunately, just a light breeze that tickles their hair. The treetops move farther away.

They reach the top, scrambling to the grassy bank where they lie on their backs, chests heaving as they gasp for breath. 'Wow,' Balin says, recovering first and sitting up, his eyes shining. 'That was scary.'

'Let's maybe use a rope when we go down.' Lartak wheezes, getting to his feet. The sun is shining its glory on the treetops below, green leaves shining. Snow-speckled hills stand on the horizon. It is a beautiful sight.

But there isn't time to stop and admire the view. With every passing heartbeat, King Paraksha grows weaker.

'Is this it?' Lartak asks, looking behind them. A rocky, grass-strewn plain is before them, dotted with trees. The wind is a little stronger so high up, cool and refreshing.

A loud screech rings across the plain, startling the boys. Balin's eyes widen.

'There it is! The Lawky!'

A gigantic bird is in the air, its wings fully spread. Holding an enormous, long beak, bright green with streaks of blue, orange, and purple.

Its chest is the colour of buttercups, and its talons, electric blue. Another earth-shattering screech reaches their ears, almost shaking the earth.

'That's it.' Balin breathes. He's shaking. 'Oh gods, I forgot how huge the thing is.'

The bird stops, suddenly turns, and rockets down at them like a lightning bolt, its talons razor-sharp. Death swoops down upon them. For a moment, Lartak simply gawks. This creature is as huge as a Burrintot.

'Get down!' he cries, shoving Balin to the ground. Lartak doesn't have time to, and the wing clips him with bruising impact, but better than those sharp talons.

The boys scramble to their feet and run away from the deadly cliff, Lartak unsheathing his blade, fear tumbling through his mind.

They need a tail feather, but they cannot kill the bird. The Lawky's tail streams behind it as it flies back up into the air. Each flap of its wings is like a drumbeat.

'Come on,' Lartak shouts, his tired legs burning as they avoid another deadly swoop by the bird. 'We have to tire it out . . . injure it, somehow.'

Balin takes out an arrow and shoots towards the bird's wing. A clumsy shot that misses. The Lawky gives another screech and swoops down to them.

The boys dive either side, and Lartak gives a cry, swinging his sword. An angry scream from the bird tells him his blade connected. Blood drips from its injured wing as it flaps away, landing on the ground with a rumble.

It hops on its feet, black beady eyes landing on Balin. 'It's seen me!' The boy panics, backing away.

It hops over to him, its colourful beak shining in the sunlight, deadly as a Tolverine. It jabs its beak forward, narrowly missing. Balin falls down, smashing his face on a rock.

Lartak gives a yell and rushes for the bird, tackling it. Like running into a wall. A few feathers fall to the ground as the bird staggers. The Lawky flaps its wing and jabs at Lartak. He grunts, the wind knocked out of his lungs as the beak delivers a bruising jab to his chest. He falls to the ground, wheezing.

Balin gets off the ground, screams, and dodges the beak, red pouring from his nose. He rolls over and gets to his feet. He takes out his short sword, holding it in front of him, hand trembling.

'Balin!' Lartak wheezes, throwing an energy blast at the bird as it moves in for the kill. The Lawky gives a mad squawk, flinching from the invisible shield protecting Balin.

He gets to his feet, his chest aching, muscles burning, and grabs the rope at his waist. He swings it like a lasso and throws it towards the bird.

He misses.

Balin steps back, swinging his sword wildly for survival as the Lawky advances on him with an almost humanlike chirp, akin to laughter. The tail feathers, as long as Lartak's arm, stream behind the bird like a shimmering rainbow.

Lartak throws the lasso again and grins in satisfaction; the rope lands around the bird's beak. He frantically ties the other end to a strong oak.

The Lawky goes insane. Flapping and squawking, Balin forgotten, as it hops, panicking at the rope around its beak. Lartak runs and leaps on its back, stopping it from taking to the air.

'My gods!' Balin breathes as Lartak is on its back, riding it like a horse. He yanks the rope, pulling back the bird's head by the beak, struggling to stay upright as it bucks and flaps. Lartak isn't sure whether to scream or laugh; the Lawky gives a violent hop, almost throwing him off.

'*Balin!*' Lartak bellows, struggling to keep hold of the rope as he holds on tight with his thighs. '*Grab a tail feather now!*'

Balin shakes his head and comes to his senses, scrambling to his feet. The Lawky gives an angry flap, hopping around on the grass with Balin running after, trying to catch its tail feather.

'*Aargh!*' Balin yells, jumping on its tail. The Lawky gives an ear-bleeding screech and bucks so hard that Lartak goes flying. The Lawky snaps the rope and advances on him, wings spread.

A glinting talon slashes out, and pain burns in Lartak's shoulder. Another energy blast throws the Lawky back, and Lartak swings his sword with a cry. It slashes across the Lawky's talons, chopping off two of them.

The Lawky gives a pained scream, flapping into the air, crimson spurting from its talons and on to the grass.

'No!' Lartak cries as the bird flaps into the air, still able to fly with its injured wing. It shines like a colourful rainbow as it flaps into the sky, its flight clumsy, getting further and further away with each heartbeat.

'Damn it!' Lartak cries, throwing down his sword. He clutches his injured shoulder, his palm coming back red.

'How did you do that?' asks Balin, coming to his side. His nose is bent at a strange angle, and red is pouring down his lips and chin, spilling spots on his shirt. He wipes it impatiently.

'I don't know,' responds Lartak, knowing what Balin is referring to. 'The energy just comes out when I need it.'

'You must be a wizard of sorts. I knew you were dangerous when we picked you up that day in the boat.'

'Okay, I'm dangerous . . . fine, but the creature is getting away!' Terror seizes him. 'It will take *ages* to catch it!'

'Good thing I managed to grab this, then,' says Balin, grinning as he holds up a long tail feather.

Lartak stares at him. For a moment, he wants to strangle him. Then he laughs, slapping Balin on the arm. 'Great work.'

They collapse on the grass, watching as the Lawky disappears into the clouds. Lartak can sense new bruises forming, aching from where he fell and where the beak punched his chest. His shoulder is scratched, but it doesn't appear bad. He tests it, pushing himself up. He can use almost all his strength.

'Come on,' he mutters. 'It will be dark soon, and we need to get back down that cliff.'

Balin ponders about the new abilities he witnessed from Lartak but knows it is best to not discuss them with anyone else. Lartak trusts he does not need to ask this of Balin.

❊ ❊ ❊

'Thank the gods!'

Evening arrives when they reach Garlamon, their horses tired out. They've barely slipped from the saddles when Karina runs towards them, her black hair streaming behind her. She wraps Lartak in a warm hug, kissing his masked cheek.

'I'm here too,' grumbles Balin. 'How's Father doing?'

'He's stable,' says Karina, drawing back to hug her brother. 'Oh, Balin! What happened to your nose?'

'Battle scar,' says Balin, strutting his chest. The blood has mostly gone from his face, but brown stains adorn his shirt, and his nose is bent to the left.

'Did you find it? The Lawky tail feather?'

Balin gives a lopsided smile, holding up the enormous rainbow-coloured feather. She snatches it from his fingers, and they run back the rest of the way to the village, where a healer is waiting.

He grabs it from her and rushes into a nearby hut, where people usher him inside. The scent of boiling herbs reaches their noses, and Balin screws up his face at the putrid aroma.

Karina sighs, hugging herself. 'Now we wait.'

✂ ✂ ✂

The king is delirious, his eyes closed and sweat beading his skin as his head moves left and right, eyelids flickering. He doesn't recognize any of them. Heat permeates off his form, the thin blanket over him soaked. Karina sniffles, squeezing his fingers.

The king mutters something, completely incomprehensible. Behind his daughter, the healer chops up the tail feather and adds crushed herbs to it. He quickly feeds the concoction into the king's lips, holding his head up like he's a weak child.

'Drink, Father,' Karina whispers. 'This will help you heal.'

The king manages to swallow, lying back with a sigh, bits of herb clinging to his lips. Fear clenches Lartak's heart. What if they were too late?

'Might take a while to work,' says the healer quietly, and a warm hand touches Lartak's shoulder. 'Your wounds need tending, and some dinner awaits. We'll know by morning.'

Lartak leaves the tent, Karina and Balin at his heels. Karina's eyes are weepy red, and she glances back at the tent. 'I think I should be with him.' She sighs. 'I know I can't do anything, but . . .'

Lartak understands her sentiment. It's almost like they're betraying him by leaving him alone.

They head to their home, where healers hastily clean and dress his injured shoulder. Hardly any pain as the demigod blood allows him to heal quicker than most.

From the next room, Lartak hears an audible crack, and Balin yells, '*yeeooww*'. He comes back a moment later, looking sulky, his nose straightened and a satisfied-looking healer behind him.

After washing their faces and dressing into fresh robes, a cook gives them vegetable soup. Lartak didn't realize how starving he was and spoons it rapidly into his mouth, the spicy carrot and potato spilling over his tongue. Karina doesn't eat anything, pushing her food away. Balin picks at his food.

'I'm going back,' she says. 'Stay here.'

'No way,' says Balin, getting to his feet. They all go to the king's tent. Some colour is back in his cheeks, but he still isn't awake.

'Did it work?' asks Karina anxiously.

'Some time is needed princess,' says the healer, looking exhausted. 'I'm afraid I've done everything I can. All else is up to the gods.'

'Thank you,' she says, lightly touching the thin man's arm. 'Go, rest.'

He bows to them all before leaving the tent. They take seats around the king, Karina chewing her lip as she takes his hand in hers. 'Come back to us, Father,' she whispers.

❋ ❋ ❋

Lartak wakes up with his neck bent painfully against the chair rest, his arms folded. He fell asleep in the night. Early sunlight streams through the window, where Karina's head and arms are on the bed, her back rising and falling slowly in sleep. Balin snores beside him.

As Lartak gazes towards the king, he opens his eyes. The delirious mumbling has ceased, and he blinks around in confusion. Then he sits up.

'What's for breakfast?' he asks, his voice croaky but animated. He throws off the thin blanket and gets up, stretching like it's a normal day.

Karina jumps awake, her dark eyes widening as she beholds her father.

The healer walks into the room and drops the tray he's carrying with a terrific crash. 'My king!'

'I'm starving!' says King Paraksha, grinning around at them all. He doesn't mind that he's naked, save for a cloth around his waist, blood-crusted bandages around his abdomen and shoulder. 'I feel like I haven't eaten in days.'

'I'll organize some breakfast, sire,' says the healer, signalling to one of the staff.

'Balin, wake up!' Lartak shakes the boy, who awakens with a jerk, staring up at the king.

'Father!' Karina gives a squeal, leaping over his bed to throw her arms around him, showering his face in kisses. 'Oh, Father, we thought you were gone!'

'The Lawky feather worked,' says Balin, jumping to his feet and embracing his father. 'Lartak and I got one for you.'

'You did?' asks the king, reaching over to give Lartak's uninjured shoulder a squeeze. He puts an arm around Balin and hugs him. 'Both of you are brave.' His dark eyes gaze intently. 'You saved my life, boys. Thank you.'

A smile spreads across Lartak's face. All he cares about is that the king is safe. He appears healthier than ever, his eyes bright. The Lawky feather really is magic.

Karina gives him another tearful hug, then reaches over to Lartak, giving his hand a squeeze. King Paraksha observes with a knowing gaze.

They leave the tent and gasps and cheers rise as people come to see their king. 'He's alive!' someone shouts, and the news spreads quickly. People cheer, and it isn't long before the celebratory sounds of string instruments spring up from the streets.

'We have two reasons to celebrate today!' his strong voice booms out to the villagers as they gather. 'My recovery, which wouldn't have been possible without the help of these brave young men.'

Balin and Lartak give sheepish grins as a hearty cheer rises from the people.

'The second reason is that my daughter has found an appropriate suitor!'

Karina gasps as another huge cheer erupts from the villagers. Gratitude floods Lartak as the king grabs his hand. He grabs Karina's with his other hand, and raises them into the air. Karina throws her arms around her father's waist and squeezes him, much to the delight of the spectators.

'Thank you, Father,' she whispers, her eyes glassy with emotion.

'I'll be proud to call you my son,' says the king, pulling Lartak into a hug. Lartak can't believe it. He's finally received the approval he has been craving. He is as happy as he can remember.

CHAPTER 13

***

A STRANGE ENCOUNTER

Queen Assyri frowns at the horizon, her hair blowing in the gentle breeze. Her insides are clenched tight. She always gets nervous sending spies back to Pendilor. If they are caught, they won't make it back, and if Bolara interrogates them, there is the risk they'll be tortured, and they'll all be found out.

Assyri trusts her people, but Bolara's evil has no limitations. She has no doubt that he would utilize the most excruciating of techniques to get the information he needs.

She clutches the folds of her skirt in her fingers, watching the empty hills. *They're already late. What if . . .?*

Relief floods her as horses appear on the horizon, the familiar sounds of their hooves thumping on the grass. Her spies are unhurt, traveling with a good pace.

She breathes in relief, rearranging her features to calm wisdom. She may not sit on the throne any more, but she's still their leader and must inspire their confidence.

'My queen', says Erendis, who used to be a gardener for the palace. Since growing a beard, he's become unrecognizable to Bolara's men and can slip in and out of Pendilor posing as a merchant from Trithi, next town over.

'Bolara's making plans to overthrow all the kingdoms. He's starting small, taking over villages, but his goal is complete takeover.'

'I see,' she says, her heart sinking. She should have known it wouldn't satiate him to rule over Pendilor; no, he wanted the whole planet.

Every day, more and more people trickle into the forest, whispers of the queen and her daughter's survival spreading hope throughout the land.

Survivors from destroyed villages and people from Pendilor who'd had enough of Bolara's hard rule, pack everything they can on to their backs and move to the forest.

Though difficult to find jobs and feed everyone, every new soul that makes their way to the forest to join her cause is a gift to Assyri. She greets every man, woman, and child with fond familiarity, hugging and kissing them all in welcome.

Their village is no longer a humble gathering of survivors. Fast becoming a city. Well over seven thousand now reside here.

'Preeya', says Assyri when she finds her daughter. Most new people don't recognize her at first when they come to the forest. The meek teenage girl who spent her time looking at flowers and chasing butterflies has vanished.

A layer of muscle from training sits beneath her skin, the innocence replaced with hard determination. She's cut her hair short, claiming it gets in the way, the remains of the blonde locks tied back into simple braids or tails. She dresses in practical tunics and pants instead of dresses, and there is always a sword at her side.

'Mother', she says, gracing the queen with a rare smile.

'I need you to train the newcomers,' says her mother. 'Men *and* women, and any child who is willing. Bolara may have spared our lives last time, but when he amasses a force strong enough to challenge the very gods, he'll come back. We won't get caught out next time.'

Preeya nods. 'More numbers. Good, we'll need them.' She marches away and greets the closest groups. 'Any of you know how to fight?'

Assyri bristles with pride. It is like her husband and Arteo, Gods rest their souls, have loaned their strength to her daughter. She is now a mighty warrior.

⚘ ⚘ ⚘

'Once more!' Preeya snaps, surrounded by villagers. They're a mismatched bunch: bakers, blacksmiths, barbers, milkmaids, and everyone in between. Some are wearing finer cloth of the middle class, others wearing rags with unkempt hair and dirt smeared on their faces.

Doesn't really matter. They're all equal and ready to fight for their homeland. Preeya is ready to train every last one of them. The ones who watched her grow up stare with wide eyes. Where did the innocent young girl who loved frolicking in the gardens and feeding birds go?

'Come on.' She growls at a nearby young man around her age. He swallows and gives a feeble swing of his sword.

'Aaaand you're dead,' she says, defending with ease and holding her own blade near his throat. 'You,' she barks at a woman with an infant on her hip. The woman looks around in alarm, then puts down the child and approaches.

She fights with more vigour than the boy, at least, but it is clear she's never picked up a sword in her life.

'All right, everyone.' Preeya sighs, massaging the bridge of her nose. 'In front of a dummy, now. We need everyone who can fight. If you can't, cooking, cleaning, and healing are your priorities, yes?'

To Preeya's surprise, the mother steps in front of a dummy, holding the sword in front of her with fire in her eyes. The young princess nods in approval.

Workers, maids, and soldiers stand shoulder to shoulder, hitting dummies and practicing their footwork. Some are nervous, glancing at others in confusion like they don't know which is the pointy end. Others attack the dummies with angry roars and too much power, exhausting themselves in a few clumsy attacks.

'A little higher. Watch your footing. Sidestep like I showed you. Parry!' Preeya barks as she wanders up and down the group, correcting postures and giving advice. Though she shouts, she isn't unkind. Remembering the patient guidance she grew up with and her mother's coaching, she helps her followers with firm but patient teaching.

Hours later, there is some small improvement. Preeya wipes the sweat from her forehead, smiling and slapping backs.

If they continue working hard, they might have a chance of surviving.

❈ ❈ ❈

Several clouds streak across the early morning sky, but the day dawns warm. Lartak, his belly full of breakfast, steps around a street corner to hear a familiar voice floating towards him.

'. . . An emerald so beautiful that it is said to have fallen from the moon,' says Balin. He's surrounded by a group of children, all wearing the same furs and kneeling before him, listening. 'Hidden deep in a tree in the Kalanya jungle.' He whispers the last two words, making the children giggle.

'Making stuff up again?' says Lartak loudly, folding his arms. The kids turn to look at him with bulging, brown eyes. Some of them are wary of the handsome, masked stranger; others look at him with curiosity.

'All true', says Balin, his face falling. 'My mother told me.'

Balin and Karina don't talk about their mother much. Lartak knows she died when Balin was eight and Karina was ten, of a complicated illness. Death came quickly. No time to try and save her with the Lawky's magic. She's buried at the edge of a nearby forest, beneath a mighty oak.

Karina visits the grave sometimes, but Lartak doesn't want to interfere, letting her have the private time on her own.

'You said it's real?' he asks Balin later. 'The diamond?'

'Emerald. And yes, my mother did not lie,' he munches on an apple. 'Laying deep in the forest. The tree's so huge it appears to reach for the skies, so they say.'

Lartak thinks on it as they wash up at a nearby stream. He hasn't heard of or seen a tree in this forest *that* tall. Though the mask is still on his face, he can't remove it. Still it is easy to see how his features have developed; he has handsome, chiselled cheekbones and eyes the colour of a spring sky.

From daily training, his body is muscular and strong, sunburnt from hours spent outside. Since Karina is now his promised, this gem would be the perfect gift for her.

'You want it, don't you?' Balin asks, as though reading his mind.

'Karina would love it,' Lartak admits.

Balin pretends to retch. 'A waste of a good gem.' He grins, getting up. 'Come on. Why don't we go and find it?'

They joke and tease each other as they throw away their apple cores, mount their horses, and head deep into the forest, venturing into territory outside the usual boundary. Their swords at their sides and bows at their backs.

Lartak wonders if he ever had a brother before he lost his memories. He loves Balin like a sibling; he's truly blessed to have been given this incredible family. He doesn't think much about the life he had before this one; it is all still blackness, like he didn't exist before he washed up in Garlamon.

'What would Karina even do with the gem?' Balin teases, interrupting Lartak's thoughts. 'Too chunky to put around her neck? She wouldn't even know the full value of it.'

'Says the guy who can't tell a short sword from a steak knife,' Lartak remarks. 'Don't deny it—we all saw you trying to carve your meat with a sword from the armoury yesterday.'

'And you let half of Garlamon see it before you told me,' Balin grumbles.

Lartak laughs and punches him on the arm. Balin punches him back, and soon he's chasing him on horse, through the jungle, laughing and yelling.

An owl hoots somewhere, and they stop. They dismount and walk through some dense foliage, leaves crunching underfoot. They're deep in the trees now. The leaves are thick, and the sunlight meagre, casting strips of golden sunlight before them. Lartak feels uneasy, like something is watching them. 'Be careful,' he whispers.

A sudden, strange wailing to the left. Balin clutches his friend, looking scared. It sounds like an animal in pain. 'Come on,' mutters Lartak, and they push through some trees to find a Tolverine.

Absolutely enormous. With a shaggy coat and long fangs, huddled in a forest clearing. She's clearly in pain, a deep gash in her side and another on her face, dripping red. Her body is shielding a small Tolverine, a baby trembling near her stomach, the size of an adult dog.

Circling her are two Burrintots, not as massive as the one that attacked King Paraksha but still dangerous, snorting as they close in on the mother and its pup. A third Burrintot lies dead nearby, vicious slashes in its coat.

'By the gods,' Balin whispers.

The Burrintots charge at the mother Tolverine as the baby shivers. Out of instinct, Lartak throws out a hand, and a shield forms in front of the mother. The Burrintots bounce off it with confused, snarling roars.

The mother painfully pushes herself to her feet, hackles raising as she growls. There's blood on her teeth.

The baby scampers towards the bushes with a scared whimper. The second Burrintot lowers its horn, ready to charge and skewer the poor baby. Lartak charges after it, leaping over boulders and under branches, a fierce desire to protect the pup, overwhelming his senses.

The forest rumbles as the Burrintot gallops towards the baby. A second blast bursts from Lartak's hands, slamming into the Burrintot and knocking it off balance; it slams into a tree trunk with a crunch. The baby is safe for now.

The Burrintot shakes its enormous head, dazed, and turns to face off with Lartak. Balin yells something, but Lartak doesn't hear; blood rushes through his ears, animating his limbs. He unsheathes his sword, heart pounding.

The animal charges. He throws himself out the way of the glinting horn, stabbing the Burrintot's side like he did with the one in the forest clearing. It barely makes a scratch through the rough hide.

The second Burrintot tears towards Lartak. He dodges but feels a stinging tear at his back where the horn catches him. He groans through his teeth, pain flaring along his back.

'I've got this one!' yells Balin, facing the smaller of the two. He goads the Burrintot to chase after him as he heads towards the trees, armed with his bow.

Lartak dodges and ducks, avoiding getting skewered and delivering several slashes when he can. The Burrintot suddenly catches him by surprise, and it pins him against the tree.

The rough bark flares agonizingly up his injured back, and he yells through clenched teeth, grasping the horn and pushing away. The Burrintot snarls and snaps with its blunt teeth, catching Lartak's shirt and almost tearing it.

Lartak gives a yell, and an energy bolt bursts from his palms, throwing back the Burrintot. It shakes its head, growling as a small crack appears in its horn. Lartak watches, shock flooding him. *His cosmic blasts have become more potent.* Without hesitation, he swings his sword and slices off the horn.

The creature lets out an almighty howl and stands dumbfounded. Lartak gives a yell and slams his sword point towards its face. The blade enters the eye. With a slow, low-pitched groan, the Burrintot collapses to the ground, crimson bursting from its eye, with a crash that shakes the trees. 'Balin?' Lartak calls. The boy has scrambled up a tree, the second Burrintot growling and nudging the bark with its horn. The beast is peppered with arrows, like a pincushion, bleeding from its many wounds.

Slow circular movements follow, then the Burrintot drops dead☐

'I'm fine! Get the Tolverine!' Balin shouts, nocking another arrow☐

He pushes through the bushes and branches and finds the baby cowering behind a rock, looking like a scared puppy. 'Hey, little guy,' says Lartak, his blood-drenched sword at his side.

⚜ ⚜ ⚜

Preeya sighs, running fingers through her blonde hair. It is exhausting work training the new recruits. Most of them have never handled a sword. She should at least be grateful that they're so willing to fight for her mother.

They'll learn in time; she just doesn't want to send anyone to battle before they're ready. They have a couple of brave farmers and merchants on their side. Bolara has armies of trained soldiers.

With thoughts running over and over in her mind, she loses track of how far she has ventured from camp.

She hears something ahead: shouting and the pounding of large footsteps. Her brow creasing, Preeya heads towards a clearing. She stops when she sees a young man, a strange black mask covering his face, made of muscle, and built like a warrior. He's holding a bloodstained sword, standing over a terrified looking baby Tolverine.

'Hey!' she yells, launching a blast of energy at him. How dare he bully the animals of the forest? Frustrated from training, Preeya wants to let out her pent-up energy. 'What do you think you're doing?'

The boy staggers but stands his ground. She has her sword at her side, but she snatches up a nearby branch. She doesn't kill people unless they attack her first, but she wants to teach this stranger a lesson.

The Tolverine backs away as she gives a roar, swinging the branch at the stranger. To her surprise, he neatly dodges the first two blows. She feints and hits him in the ribs hard.

'Stop!' he shouts, not hitting back but defending himself, blocking her blows with his sword. 'What are you doing?'

'It's my business if people are hunting innocent animals here!' Preeya shouts in a rage and keeps on swinging.

He somersaults, parries, sends out defensive blasts, and finally swings his sword through the branch, decimating it.

⌘ ⌘ ⌘

Lartak backs away in alarm as the pale-skinned, blonde-haired girl gives an animalistic cry of fury, swinging the huge branch at him. He blocks it with his sword.

She snarls and sends a blast of energy his way; he blocks it with one of his own. Her eyes widen in surprise for a moment, but then her face twists into fury, and she raises the branch.

He avoids the incoming assault and smashes through the branch. 'Stop it!' he shouts again. 'Are you insane? I was *helping* it!'

He's never met anyone else who isn't from Garlamon before. He would have been excited to meet her were she not trying to kill him with a stick.

Footsteps suddenly sound behind them, and the girl leaps back, the shattered branch falling from her fingers. The mother Tolverine limps towards them, the surrounding branches bending easily as she pushes through. Balin is behind her, the bow at his back. 'The Burrintot's dead. I . . . Lartak?'

His mouth drops open as he spots the beautiful girl. Her eyes widen as she spots the Tolverine. She backs away. 'Wait!' says Balin.

Lartak swivels around. The Tolverine pup scampers past Lartak towards its mother. She touches noses with the baby, her eyes slowly closing for a moment.

She glares at Lartak with huge, brown eyes. He swallows, not moving. The Tolverine's back almost reaches the treetops. His fingers grip the sword. He prays he does not need to draw it.

Then the enormous creature does something that makes both boys gape; the creature lowers her head in a slow bow. Lartak's heart fills with warmth, and he lets out a breath. He nervously nods back.

The jungle goes silent; the birds don't sing, and twigs don't crack; it's like the whole planet has stopped to witness the understanding between man and nature. The puppy quivers as its mother bows to Lartak in thanks for saving her child.

'Where did that beautiful girl go?' asks Balin in surprise. Lartak whirls around, but the blonde-haired warrior girl has disappeared.

✂ ✂ ✂

Embarrassment flutters through Preeya as she pushes through the trees back towards the village. So that strange young man in the mask wasn't attacking the Tolverine; he was helping it. She's never seen a Tolverine bow to a person before. *He must have saved her baby.*

He was highly skilled and used energy blasts, something only people with high Shakti powers can do.

Who is he?

✂ ✂ ✂

Lartak is quiet as they clean weapons and dress their wounds. Balin assures him the scratch on his back from the Burrintot isn't deep. They carve one of the Burrintot's while the Tolverine and her baby sit nearby and feast on the other. They will save the meat and take it back to the village.

Balin again raises the possibility of Lartak being some sort of wizard or warlock after his display today.

Lartak is only half listening. He can't stop thinking about the feisty young woman who cared about the animals of the forest and attacked him with such fierce intensity. He has never witnessed such an awesome female warrior before. *She has the same abilities as me.*

Who is she?

CHAPTER 14

●

THE FIRE OF THE DRAGON

A breezy day abounds in Garlamon, puffs of white clouds floating in the vast sky, blowing hair, and refreshing skin. The height of spring, and everyone appears to be in a cheerful mood.

Lartak and Karina walk along the fields near the tree line, hand in hand, talking about everything from cooking to the different animals of their world to their hopes and dreams for the future. Balin tags along, and although they pretend that he's a pain, they don't really mind his company much.

'Are you two going to have lots of babies when you're married?' Balin asks, half-jogging to keep up with their long strides. Karina blushes, her ebony cheeks darkening as she shoots him an angry glare.

'Shut up, little brother,' she snarls and swipes at him, but he ducks out of her way, laughing.

'Isn't it about time *you* found someone, Balin?' asks Lartak. 'Claim yourself a nice companion instead of following us around all the time?' He grins to show that he's joking, but Balin appears panicked at the very thought of courting, although he does occasionally dwell on the mysterious girl in the jungle.

He appears to fall into deep thought, lagging behind as they make their way back towards the village. A quiet peace exists this afternoon, smoke from campfires curling into the sky in lazy, grey wisps.

The familiar, comforting scent of crackling firewood and grilled vegetables floats through the air, making their mouths water.

'Oh, gods. I forgot to collect the herbs.' Karina sighs as they arrive at the gates. 'I knew I'd forgotten something. We need them for dinner tonight. I'll go get them.'

'I'll come with you if you like,' says Lartak.

'Lartak! Balin! Will you come and play with us?' shouts a little girl, running down the street towards them. One of her shoes is missing, and her brown eyes are shining with excitement.

A smaller boy, her brother, runs behind her, wearing nothing but cloth around his waist. He giggles as he swings a wooden sword. 'Show us how to shoot a bow. Will you? Pretty please?'

'It's all right. Go and play with them.' Karina smiles, reaching to cup Lartak's masked face. 'I'll be back soon.'

After watching her run back to the fields, Balin and Lartak play around with the children, practicing shooting with a training bow and the straightest, bluntest twigs they can find.

'Draw it back like this,' says Lartak, showing the little boy, correcting his footing, and showing him how to pull back the string of a bow. The boy pulls at the string, then stares at the bow. He drops it to the floor with a clatter and runs off.

'Are you saying I gathered all those twigs for nothing, little man?' says Balin, his face falling comically. 'Come here!' He runs towards the chubby child, snatching him up and tickling him until he squeals.

'Let me try,' says the little girl. Her black hair is tied in thick braids. Where she and the other children once looked upon Lartak with fear and distrust, now they show only admiration and respect. Adults are good at hiding their true emotions, but children never hesitate to let their true feelings be known.

Aside from King Paraksha's blessing to marry his daughter, the friendship and friendliness of the children of Garlamon have been the best thing about gaining the people's trust here. Ever since saving the king, Lartak has been well-loved by the people, and sometimes he is asked to help train their children.

Lartak snatches up the bow and starts coaching the little girl. She's more enthusiastic than her brother, a little crease between her brows as she frowns in concentration, shooting twigs towards makeshift targets.

He's giving her tips on how to improve when footsteps, quick and uneven, pound through the square, accompanied by fast, panicked breaths. They cut through the quiet peace like a blade. Everyone glares up.

A soldier is running through the streets, terror like Lartak has never seen before on his dark features. Something is horribly wrong. Icy dread clings to Lartak, a sensation that is both unfamiliar and frightening.

'He's here!' screams the soldier as he tears through the streets, glancing behind him, pushing past people, and knocking them flying. 'The dragon . . . Gazzadeil! He's back! Run for your lives!'

For a moment, a shocked silence. Then screams erupt around them. People jostle and shout, running around, snatching up weapons, and banging on doors. The town bell rings somewhere in the distance.

'Mama!' The little girl dashes past Lartak and into the arms of her mother, who scoops her up, holding her close. Balin dashes over, the small boy still in his arms, and she takes him with a gasping 'Thank you, my prince,' before joining the panicking throng.

The atmosphere has turned from jovial and peaceful to horrified bedlam in a split second. Numb shock stirs through Lartak as people rush past him, jostling him, shouting for loved ones. 'Did he say dragon?' he spurts.

The air has changed. Drier, warmer, and the breeze has vanished.

Something like battle drums, slow and steady, sound in the air, coming from the very sky itself. Several people scream and cry as an enormous shadow envelops the town, casting them into darkness.

An enormous, scaled creature, a snake with wings and scales like plate armour, swoops over the town. Three times bigger than the Lawky bird, bigger than a Burrintot, or even a Tolverine. Lartak's heart pounds in his chest, and for a second, he and the dragon are the only things that are real.

'Get down!' Balin yells, tackling Lartak to the ground. Sound crashes into his ears: the shouting, the jostling, the whisper of steel as swords are drawn, the crying of children as their parents rush them to safety. All the young men can do is watch as the dragon gives an earth-shattering roar, shaking the ground beneath their feet.

Fire bursts from its mouth, bathing them in heat; people scream and duck as a nearby paddock catches fire. Fierce flames crackle in the field, belching smoke into the sky. The air is dry and hot, almost choking.

The dragon swoops down to another field, grabbing several bleating sheep in its vicious claws. When it climbs back into the sky, great wings beating like drums, it has three more in its mouth, dripping blood and bones as smoke bursts from its nostrils.

Slits of yellow for eyes. Scales shimmering in the firelight. Powerful and awful, majestic and terrifying.

'Lartak, come on!' Balin yells, yanking Lartak by the arm. 'We need to find cover.'

'Balin!' Lartak grabs his shoulders. His senses come out, and when he drags his gaze from the dragon, his thoughts straighten out. 'What about Karina? She's still in the fields!'

Balin's dark cheeks pale to a tan as he swallows. 'I . . .' His lip trembles as his dark eyes peer over Lartak's head to where the dragon is still swooping through the air, burning everything in its path.

'I'll get her,' says Lartak, looking worried. 'Go make sure those children and their parents are safe. Then find refuge yourself?'

Before his future brother-in-law can argue, Lartak darts towards the stables, shoving past people and ducking with the others as the dragon swoops overhead. Terror is thick in the air, people screaming for loved ones, carrying sacks and weapons.

Three horses are in the stables, panicking and snorting at the commotion outside. Lartak grabs the reins of the nearest mare, soothing her with a gentle voice and petting her nose. She snorts, calming at his touch.

'There you go. Good girl,' he murmurs, fighting to keep his voice level as terror for Karina swims in his guts like oil. 'Everything's okay. Let's go find Karina.'

The mare doesn't have a saddle, no time for one. He jumps on the horse and bursts out of the stables. People leap out of the way, forming a path for him as he canters towards the herb garden, the mare's mane tight in his fingers, his heart punching frantically at his ribs as though trying to burst from his chest.

More fire has erupted around the town. A barn burns nearby, dry heat hitting him, filling his throat, and hot on his skin. The sky is blood red, thick smoke rising to the sky, obscuring the dragon. Why is such a monster here?

Fear squeezes Lartak's heart as he slams his heels into the horse's flanks, hooves pounding on the dirt ground, people shouting and screaming nearby. Is Karina all right? Did she hide? Or is he too late?

Please be all right, Lartak prays, his burning eyes scanning the ground. He reaches the herb gardens; half of them are on fire, plants shrivelled and black or still burning. Terror grips him as he peers around, searching frantically for his love. Nothing here except torched fields.

The bodies of sheep and chickens, gashes in their bodies and their black eyes sightless and wide open, lie scattered and lifeless all around. But no people. No Karina.

'Karina!' he croaks, his throat dried out from the smoky air. '*Karina!*'

He hears a sound in a nearby cow paddock and sprints over, praying he isn't too late. He'll never forgive himself if something happened to her, never.

'Karina!' he yells when he sees her. She's behind a fence, soot on her face, and the edge of her dress is singed. To his horror, she's bleeding from her head, but she stirs when he yells her name again.

She's forty feet away. He rides the mare hard, the mare snorting as they gallop towards her. Thirty feet.

A terrific crash rocks the fields like an earthquake as the dragon lands in front of Karina, smoke bursting from its nostrils, claws digging into the blackened grass.

An enormous, ugly thing, with black scales littered with scars, beady yellow eyes, and countless fangs dripping saliva and gore. It approaches Karina, looking at her with greed.

'*No!* ' Lartak bellows, urging the mare to gallop faster, his heart screaming.

The dragon inhales. Smoke dances at its nostrils, its chest glowing as it prepares its fire.

It's going to kill her!

He'll never reach her in time. The mare gallops, hooves pounding; Lartak reaches out.

Karina turns to the dragon and opens her eyes, sad acceptance on her face. The dragon opens its mouth, ready to fry her.

With a desperate scream, Lartak jumps off the horse, smothering her. He throws out a protective shield, and it surrounds them. The flames, red hot and deadly, glow orange and burst from the dragon's mouth, engulfing the shield, trying hard to penetrate and consume the inhabitants.

Lartak and Karina are protected for now. Still, the heat is intense. They are surrounded by the flames, but unharmed.

Sweat pours down Lartak's face as he holds the shield in place, not knowing how he's doing it but knowing in this moment that if he lets go, or if his energy levels deteriorate for a second, it will be all over.

The shield is weakening. He cannot maintain it much longer. It is about to give way. There is no way out. Soon they will be consumed by the flames. Lartak peers down at Karina with love in his heart, knowing that he cannot protect her from the dragon's venom for much longer.

The shield slowly starts to dissipate, then a bright burst thunders from the sky. It showers Lartak and Karina, causing the dragon to cease his fiery burst and take a step backwards. The protective wall fully dissipates. The earth is scorched, the nearby fence black and burning, leaving a circle of unharmed grass around him and Karina.

The dragon snarls, stepping back, glaring up at the sky warily. He does not attack again, just stands silently still, breathing deeply, and stares hard at Lartak.

Lartak's horse races towards them on pounding hooves. He picks Karina up, taking care not to jostle her injured head, and throws her over the back of the horse before jumping on himself and riding off, glancing back at where the dragon watches him.

Staring with intent, something like mad intelligence in its eyes. *Why did the dragon stop?* Lartak doesn't know if shock or hatred adorns its scaly features.

As they scamper off towards the tree line, he glances back once more. The dragon appears to smile at him before spreading its enormous wings and heading back into the sky.

⚹ ⚹ ⚹

The waterfalls flow mighty and strong with constant, comforting roars, throwing icy droplets on to the nearby rocks. It is a quiet place, a treasure in the forest, the kind of haven where people go to think or meditate.

The dragon's fire hasn't touched this place, and sunlight shines through the leaves above, casting slits of gold on to the leaves and branches at their feet. Karina sits on a rock, Lartak looking at the cut on her head.

'Is everyone at the village okay?' she asks, wincing in pain as he dabs at the cut with a damp strip of cloth from his tunic.

'Everyone will be fine,' he says, voice gentle. 'We lost some livestock and fields, but that's it. How are you feeling?' he adds. Her head has stopped bleeding, and although she appears tired, she's alert.

'I'm fine,' she says, her voice quiet. 'Lartak, you're hurt too.'

'It's nothing,' he says, glancing at the burn on his shoulder. He can't remember how it got there. The flesh is dark red and sensitive.

Karina has a bag of herbs with her she was picking up, so she wraps some in some fabric from her dress. 'This might help,' she says, pressing it on to his shoulder.

Their faces are close. Lartak can see the crease of worry in her forehead, and her brown eyes shine as she gazes up at him. The spray from the waterfall has settled in her black hair like tiny diamonds.

He was so afraid of losing her. 'When that dragon landed in front of you, I . . .' His breath is caught in his throat. 'I've never been so scared in my life.'

She moves closer. He can feel her warm breath on his lips, see the dark freckles on her nose. Her soft lips meet his, and heat rushes through him. They've kissed before, but never with so much desperation and passion. He pulls her close. Her body trembles against his.

'I love you,' she murmurs into his lips. He kisses her cheek and her forehead, caressing her back with gentle fingers.

He kisses her cheek and her forehead, caressing her back with gentle fingers. Her hands move beneath his shirt, leaving burning trails in their wake. She kisses him again with a fierceness, a possessive want that makes him groan. Slowly, they shed their clothes, fire on their skin, and love in their hearts. Nothing but the waterfall and the birds to witness their passion.

✂ ✂ ✂

The sun is lowering when they return to the town, hand in hand, the horse clopping alongside them. Wheat fields and paddocks are blackened and burned, the people of Garlamon picking their way through remains and examining animal corpses. Greyish smoke still trails the sky, but the worst is over.

'Thank the gods! Where have you been?' King Paraksha shouts as soon as they arrive through the gates, pulling Karina into a tight hug.

'I told you she was fine, Father,' says Balin behind him. 'Lartak, the wizard, would never let anything happen to her.' His grin falters when the king turns to glare at him.

Lartak also gives him a stern gaze, which makes him casually turn away. 'I'm sorry, Papa,' says Karina, hugging him back, and the king's face softens. He holds her at arm's length, looking her up and down.

'Never mind, so long as you're both all right,' he says, pulling Lartak into a hug as well, almost crushing him with fierceness. The king isn't hurt, but Balin's clothes are singed, his curly hair an unruly mess. The scent of fire is still strong in the air.

A lot of the livestock has been slaughtered, and many of the wheat fields have been reduced to ash, says the king. 'There are a few people with the healer, tending to burns. Hopefully, they'll be okay.'

They head home, a servant lighting lanterns and fetching them all herbal tea as they settle on to armchairs and pouffes. Karina keeps catching Lartak's eye, and they share a shy discreet smile as she pours the tea for them all. Balin catches the glances and says, 'What's up with you two?'

They just smile.

'The last time we saw that dragon was a few years ago,' says King Paraksha darkly. 'Not long before you joined us, Lartak. We lost two people back then.'

His jaw tightens as he rubs his chin. 'There were no casualties this time, thank the gods.'

He continues. 'We are a little unsure sure why he left so quickly this time.' 'He destroyed a lot of our crops last time too,' says Balin. 'Seemed like he was searching for someone and just torched any in his way.' He pauses. 'I thought, for sure, he would destroy some more folk this time as well.'

'I will hunt down this dragon and put an end to this,' says Lartak abruptly, and everyone turns to stare at him.

He stares back. 'Someone has to deal with it, and I was able to create a strong enough force field to protect us from the flames,' he says, looking towards Karina. 'I have some sort of powers.'

'I knew it. You are a wizard,' shouts Balin.

Karina is concerned. The thought of Lartak going after the dragon does not sit well with her, but she knows it must be done. 'I don't know what Lartak did, but he threw a shield around us, and it protected us. The flames could not penetrate it.'

'I also witnessed this when the Burrintot almost killed me. I wasn't sure if I was delirious,' says Paraksha, looking at Lartak with gentle eyes. 'You have been gifted with abilities, from the gods.'

'Perhaps,' Lartak responds.

'This isn't a task to be taken lightly though. Are you sure?'

'Yes, I'm sure,' vows Lartak, nodding. 'This Gazzadeil. I'll track it down and destroy it. It will never harm Garlamon again.'

CHAPTER 15

―◎―

THE MIGHTY GAZZADEIL

Lartak enters a part of the forest where few ventured. Tired feet crunch on the uneven stony ground as he approaches the cavern holding the dragon's lair. He brushes away the assortment of virescent vines, which adorn the entry.

With each step, his heartbeat increases. Pounding like a steady drum, increasing in intensity and speed, straining to escape through his chest and flee from the impending challenge.

Stories of just how many others have died before, leading to a cold shiver running directly down his spine. He keeps going, though. He will not turn back.

The cave mouth lies dark ahead of him, like a glimpse into the heart of midnight or a jagged cut through the world into some deeper blackness beyond. It's like the kind of space which could swallow a man whole.

Takes all he can muster to force himself to step over the threshold.

The filthy scent of stale water blended with rotting corpses fill his nostrils as he enters, somewhat surprised by how much of the interior of the cave he can see once he is inside. It helps that it opens out into the sky above, no doubt giving the dragon another way out.

Strange light of a kind also comes from pillars set around the walls, glowing faintly as if to illuminate the efforts of human hands to reclaim a space not meant for them.

Cave is the wrong word for this place. More like a cavern, larger than any Lartak has seen in his life, thick mist flowing across the floor, looking to sweep all in its path.

He moves forward, looking around carefully to find some sort of advantage in this place, some spot which might let him survive where others have not.

Silence surrounds him, the mist seeming to smother all else. The silence builds, like a pressure against Lartak's skin. A spring-loaded tension with the certainty something is coming. He would have preferred the mighty roar of a lion to the eerie silence.

Another step forward, and he stumbles as the floor gives way beneath him, a step down to the true level of the cavern's floor hidden by the mist.

Lartak manages to catch himself in time, the scrape of stone against his palms. He lowers himself down. Now the mist is everywhere around him, shadows shifting in the darkness.

Some of these shadows are stalagmites, pointed like spears, or perhaps like waiting teeth, lurking to pierce the bodies of any who fall. Lartak can see bones scattered around the base of one, a bloody smear darkened almost to blackness on another.

More bones lay on the floor of the cavern, telling of how many have tried this before and failed. Tales of the unwary. Tales of many a warrior who have come before to try and beat the mighty Gazzadeil.

Lartak can feel some of them crunch underfoot, hearing the crack as his weight shatters them. Would his bones be joining them soon? No, he will not think like that. He cannot fail.

As if the thought of the dragon had summoned it, a whoosh of air buffets through the cavern, pushing aside strands of mist, taking away Lartak's place to hide. The rush of it strong enough to knock him against the stone of one of the stalagmites.

He is kept from being swept away by clinging to it with all the strength he can summon. As he is knocked from his feet, he senses the air in the cavern change, becoming hotter and more humid, the air itself seeming to boil with the promise of what is to follow.

Gazzadeil swoops into the cavern as Lartak regains his balance. The creature—it is everything legend describes, and more. It is huge in a way no animal has a right to be, certainly nothing that can hang hovering on leathery wings.

Iridescent scales take the light that is there and twist it in a hundred directions. It shines with blinding radiance. Claws the length of swords flexed, and the stench of stale death to follow, hang in the air.

A reptilian gaze sweeps down over Lartak, hard and cold, intelligent and unyielding. Maybe a hint of confusion evident, perhaps at the way the boy does not betray the terror of all Gazzadeil's other victims. Lartak holds his ground, refusing to retreat, knowing to do so now is to die. The mighty beast admires such courage.

The dragon pumps his wings in strokes, which build the ferocity of a storm behind them. The wind whips at Lartak's strong body and buffets him to knock him from his footing.

He braces himself against the stone, hanging on, refusing to fall in the face of the onslaught. His balance and abilities allow him to find gaps in the rush of wind, secure grip for his feet, unlike others who have fallen.

'I have been expecting you, prince,' the dragon bellows; his words carry through the cavern in a deep, ominous tone, filling it. The voice itself is a weapon, the ferocity grinding at Lartak's heart, his bones.

'Prince?' Lartak responds, staring up at Gazzadeil. 'Why do you call me prince?'

'You are here to claim your destiny,' the dragon replies. Another wingbeat buffets Lartak, but he is ready for it.

'I'm here to stop you,' Lartak shoots back. 'You shall leave Garlamon be! There will be none taken. No more killed.'

'Why do you think you can kill me when so many have failed?' Gazzadeil demands. The sound following might have been a laugh, only it is amplified until it booms like thunder. 'I will crush your bones and feast well today, young prince.'

As the dragon speaks the words, its mouth strongly parts, revealing an orange glow, rapidly building into a gout of fire. He pours down towards Lartak. No time to dodge, but then he had never planned to dodge.

Calling on the powers which lie within, he pushes energy out into a shield meeting the flames while they are still the length of a man away from him. He can feel the deadly heat as they strain against his protections.

The force of the fiery blast impels his feet to gradually slide backwards as the power is intense. With one hand, he is drawing his bow. The shield holds firm, while strong fingers set arrows and let them fly.

He sends them sizzling towards the dragon's eyes, its mouth, its heart. Three arrows fly in less than a heartbeat, only to find themselves consumed by the heat of Gazzadeil's breath.

Lartak flicks his bow aside and moves to another stone, letting his cosmic shield drop so the flames hit the floor where he once stood. He needs to conserve his energy for this battle.

Gazzadeil drops to the ground of the cavern with a thud of flesh resembling an earth tremor. He slams a clawed foreleg down in the spot where Lartak stands, but Lartak is instantly dodging, weaving, drawing his sword, and swinging one-handed at the dragon's flank.

The blade deflects from the hard plates of Gazzadeil's side. Lartak swerves to duck as the dragon strikes out again, this blow bringing the crash of falling stones and boulders as it slams into the walls of the lair.

From his crouch, Lartak leaps, feet finding purchase on the tallest of the nearby stalagmites. He crouches atop it, sword poised, breath pumping harder now as he tries to calculate the next angle to attack from.

The dragon also pauses, pulling back and watching him like a snake, determining the best position for next strike.

'You are stronger than most,' Gazzadeil says. 'But that is not enough. You will still die if you do not embrace your destiny, young prince.'

'What destiny?' Lartak demands. 'I am no prince!'

'Believe and you will take your rightful place. Fail, and—'

With no more warning than that, Gazzadeil leaps forward, bellowing forth another burst of fire, slamming into the stone of the stalagmite beneath Lartak's feet. It crumbles beneath the force of the onslaught, and

Lartak throws himself clear to avoid being caught up in the flames which now wreathe the ground beneath.

He hits the ground hard, rolling and coming to rest on his back for a moment, staring up at the points of stalactites clinging to the roof of the cavern. Flames reach out to him, inviting him to join the others who had made the mistake of venturing in.

Gazzadeil sweeps his tail round, striking the cavern wall. The force in the impact rings through Lartak's ears. He hears the crack as stalactites above separate from the ceiling; sharp-edged stone starts to fall like rain. All directed at him.

'You are not worthy,' Gazzadeil roars, sending a burst of flame to follow. Lartak throws up another shield, feeling impact after impact against it.

He scrambles clear and launches an almighty leap, moving from stalagmite to pillar, somersaulting gracefully, until he finally finds a perch above the dragon.

Gazzadeil is unaware that Lartak has narrowly avoided his ferocious attack. The air is filled with rock dust as much as mist now. Visibility is poor.

'You're not as strong as you think,' Lartak says. He takes a breath, summons his powers, and sends blast after blast of cosmic energy towards Gazzadeil. They strike the dragon, one after another, and despite the dragon's great size, they are enough to send him slamming into the cavern's wall.

Sensing his chance, Lartak leaps towards the fallen shape of his foe, sword in hand. The dragon is quicker than he thinks though, leaping clear and taking to the air once again.

Between the mist and the rock dust, Lartak can barely see, and he strains all his senses, trying to work out where the beast has retreated to.

He holds his sword ready in hand, turning slowly, watching out for any sign of Gazzadeil. When the dragon's voice comes again, it is both a shock and a relief, the sound of it cutting through the still air.

'Embrace your powers, young prince. Take your place by the side of your sister, Princess Preeya of Pendilor.'

The words cut through Lartak sharper than even the dragon's claws. The tearing reality of them open something within him, and in that moment he . . . *sees.*

Memories flood him, one after another. He remembers childhood antics that had nothing to do with dragons—bullying from his evil cousins, Ristos and Syrana, training sessions with Galdin and his father. He remembers rummaging through the forest with sweet, innocent Preeya.

Playing game after game against a magical backdrop of green pastures and running water. The smell of Yackenhaus filling the air, his favourite of all the dishes served in their household.
Those years were blissful, wondrous.

He remembers his mother, Queen Assyri, tending the bruises from his falls. Her face is above him, angelic and perfect. The voice is calming, soothing, seeming to take away all the pain, inside him.

'Be careful, my beautiful prince. You do not know your own strength,' she would say.

Other memories flood in, and these *hurt*. He remembers the moment his Uncle Bolara overthrows the kingdom. Memories now run red with a sea of blood.

Death after death fill his thoughts. They had been pushed out, forced to run, forced to leave everything behind. Innocent, loyal folk were slaughtered for no reason.

Then the moment when an arrow was launched at him. His father, Lord Ranay, flinging himself in front of it to save him.

Lartak can still see the look of horror in Preeya's eyes as she reaches out to him but cannot save him. He tumbles over the waterfall and deep into the river.

In that moment, the entire cavern shakes with anger, and the sun blasts its way through! Light and energy consume him in an instant, bursting so bright that Gazzadeil reels back.

Lartak is frozen, the energy piercing every fibre of his being, every cell of his body seeming to burn with it at once. His body lifts into the air and lightly twirls about as the light envelops him. It slowly drops him to his knees.

He transforms into who he has to become. No, into who he always was.

Lartak feels his features changing, the protective mask melting away into a pool of wax at his feet. His entire being energized, as though touched by Suriyar himself. His full plethora of powers are unleashed. He knows who he is in that moment.

'Arteo. I'm Arteo.'

Arteo, heir to the throne of Pendilor, son of the queen who has been betrayed.

He remembers all.

'Now you recall', screams Gazzadeil, viciously swooping for the prince as he becomes his true self, wings outstretched enormously, claws ready to rend and kill.

Lartak—*Arteo*—readies his sword. Leaps as the dragon comes at him, somersaulting over the incoming assault and landing on the dragon's back. He plunges his sword down, striking into Gazzadeil's flesh, and *this* time, it bites. It bites hard, deep into the flesh beneath the scales.

Gazzadeil shrieks in response and plunges down towards the ground, stalagmites snapping as his bulk slams into them. Arteo leaps clear, landing softly, dodging as the dragon turns and flings bursts of orange flame at him.

There is a desperation to Gazzadeil's attacks now, blow after blow coming with ferocious intent, claws and flames seeming to blend together in a hurricane of death.

Arteo dodges each attack as they come, ducking, weaving, jumping. Agility unseen before.

He casually goes down on one knee, throws his arms back, and musters all the inner strength he can draw. He pushes forward with all his might, throwing his illuminated hands towards the dragon.

A thick yellow-and-orange stream of pure energy shoots out at such a ferocity the beast is stunned and slams against the cavern wall.

He strikes again and again, jumping around the beast with such deftness. The dragon's flames now holding less intensity, under the onslaught.

'This is not possible,' Gazzadeil roars. 'No demigod wields such powers!'

Arteo holds out his hand, and his bow leaps into it, and the arrows he nocks are now energized with pure cosmic force. They spear out, piercing the dragon's wings and pinning him to the wall of the cave.

He fires again and again, energy bolts bursting on the weak underside of the dragon.   Arteo skips aside from another blast of flame, somersaults again, and lands on Gazzadeil's shoulders, his sword poised before one great yellow eye.

'Yield or die,' he says

The dragon struggles to free itself with all its might, the motion like a roiling cascade of flesh beneath Arteo's feet, but the boy keeps his balance, and the cosmic arrows are holding his opponent firm. He draws back his sword.

'Yield!' he screams as he raises his sword, ready to provide the final blow.

'I . . . yield,' Gazzadeil says at last, slumping his shoulders and going still. 'You are worthy of your destiny.'

'I came here to protect the people of Garlamon. You are to leave them be, Arteo says.

'As you wish,' Gazzadeil replies with his head bowed down.

Arteo removes the arrows from the beast's wings, the energy dissipating smoothly.

'Then go.'

The dragon moves to the centre of the cavern, beneath the light pointing to the way out above. He flaps his powerful wings to hover above the boy. 'One last thing, Prince Arteo. You have vanquished me and spared my life. When you call upon me in battle, I will be there.'

He gives Arteo no time to respond. With another strong sweep of those wings, the dragon soars above. With a few more, he is up and out, into the beautiful sunlight.

Flying gracefully towards the crown of rocky grey mountains with snow-topped peaks. In just seconds, Gazzadeil is gone, and Arteo is left to ponder what just happened.

He sits his weary, aching bones down for a moment, squinting towards the sun, peering towards his grandfather. Thinking, maybe Suriyar is looking back in approval at what transpired.

One thing is certain in his mind. He is no longer Lartak. He is no longer a lost soul. He is Prince Arteo, the heir to the kingdom of Pendilor.

CHAPTER 16

───────◉───────

THE PRINCE RETURNS

Horse hooves pound on the grassy hill, shaking the ground as a massive force from Pendilor moves towards Kyetin. The city is prepared, archers lining the walls and a group of soldiers waiting to meet them on the battlefield. Though they are brave, they are no match for Bolara's mighty incoming army.

Enemy arrows rain down upon them, most blocked by Syrana's and Ristos's cosmic barriers, snapping uselessly against the invisible shields. The soldiers ride to the gates, their horses armoured, swords in their hands, and the thirst for blood in their hearts. They bombard the heavy wooden door with attacks of their own: fire and mighty clubs.

It doesn't take long for the wood to splinter and break. Bolara's troops pour into the street of screaming civilians and stunned guardsmen.

'At least they put up a good fight.' Ristos laughs, decapitating a nearby merchant with a clean swing of his sword. The head rolls along the cobblestones at the feet of a woman, who screams, clutching her face.

Two guards come to meet them, but Ristos throws out his free hand and hurls them from their mounts with a cosmic burst of energy. A quick death follows as Bolara's soldiers finish the job.

'Get the queen!' Bolara bellows to General Thamios. 'Bring her to me!'

General Thamios slips off his steed and heads for the castle gates, swinging an enormous claymore and shooting cosmic blasts left and right. He is so terrifying and enormous that the few guards who dare face him are cut down in seconds, and a trail of corpses is left behind. He slips into the castle.

The kingdom of Kyetin puts up a brave fight, but they're no match for the demigods. By the time General Thamios appears, dragging Queen Shyana by the elbow, her wrists tied behind her, they're surrounded by hundreds of bodies.

The rest of the civilians have scattered, seeking refuge in their homes or taverns, fleeing the chaos of Bolara's army. Syrana crushes the head of an oncoming guard with a lazy flick of her wrist, giggling as he collapses to the ground, twitching.

'Stop this! Please, I beg of you!' the queen screams in horror, her head turning from side to side looking upon all her dead citizens, a smattering of guards' bodies around them. She's an older woman with grey streaking her brown hair, light-brown eyes darting around her dead people. 'Stop this madness! We yield! We yield!'

'We yield, I say!' Syrana mocks in a high-pitched voice. Ristos snorts a laugh.

'Good work, everyone,' says Bolara. He's wearing a handsome surcoat over his armour, and several guards surround him. 'Recoup and restock. Seize any weapons you can find. We'll take Garlamon by month's end.'

'What about her?' asks General Thamios, giving the queen a shake. She grunts, anger flitting across her motherly face as she struggles against her bonds.

'Throw her in the dungeons,' says Bolara. 'Her *own* dungeons,' he adds with a nasty grin as Ristos and Syrana exchange delighted smirks. 'If her people do not support our cause, we will extinguish her.'

Thamios nods.

Bolara continues, 'Next is the kingdom of Garlamon. They have five thousand troops, according to scout reports. We will take all their men.'

He roars the last few words, and his soldiers and his children whoop and cry, raising their weapons. Each one of them is hungry for more blood.

General Thamios, accompanied by a dozen of Bolara's soldiers, heads back into Queen Shyana's castle and forcibly takes her down into the castle dungeons.

'You'll stay here until the king of Pendilor has need of you,' said General Thamios, not taking care to be gentle as he shoves the woman into the nearest cell. Straw and hay lie scattered at her feet. A bowl of water sits in the corner, and a bed that is made of rock is situated under a single, barred window.

'King . . . there is no king of Pendilor!' Queen Shyana snarls, grabbing the bars and glaring at General Thamios with all the hatred in the world in her light-brown eyes. 'There is only *one* ruler of Pendilor, and that is Queen Assyri!'

'Assyri is long dead,' General Thamios sneers. 'Your only option is to give up your weapons and your resources. King Bolara's men will be stationed here, and you will join the Pendilor Empire.'

'You can take our kingdom, and you can force my loyal soldiers to fight,' she says, her eyes glassy. Tears slide down her cheeks, and she fiercely brushes them away.

'Take our land and our food. But there's one thing you'll never take from us, and that's our hearts. The true rulers of Pendilor will return one day. You and your army, and that disgusting monster who calls himself king, will be hung for murdering innocent people!'

She spits in his face.

General Thamios takes out a handkerchief from inside his gauntlet, slowly wiping at the glob of spit that has landed on his cheek. When he speaks, his voice is like thunder.

'You will obey instructions or be slayed,' he says. 'I won't kill you . . . yet. Bolara is your king, dear queen, and will soon rule the world. You would be best advised to take him as your ruler and bow to him.'

He stomps out of the dungeons and through Queen Shyana's castle as Bolara's troops slit the throats of the maids and guardsmen who resist. His metal boots thump and clink as he goes, deep anger stirring in him.

❦ ❦ ❦

Arteo's heart races as he rides with all his might back to Garlamon, almost buckling under the memories washing over him. Classes in the gardens. The quiet halls of the palace decked in tapestries and paintings. His Uncle Bolara's attack on his family.

Family . . . for years, Arteo didn't know who his family was. How could he have forgotten everyone? His darling mother, his slaughtered father, the sister he grew up with?

The cool wind blows on his face. Without his mask, he feels naked and vulnerable, but at the same time, it's like he's emerged from water and is seeing and breathing properly for the first time. Everything is clear to him now. He's no longer the lost boy with no memories. He's a warrior, grandson of the mighty sun god, and with great Shakti powers.

He's a prince.

He rides into Garlamon, and people turn to stare at him. Confusion clouds their faces. A group of women nearby giggle among themselves, wondering about the handsome stranger, but Arteo only seeks Karina.

She's playing with some children, looking radiant, locks of her curly black hair falling over her shoulder. At the whispers and stares, she follows the others' gazes to Arteo, sitting on his horse and looking at her.

She recognizes him at once, his figure, his clothing, his hair. Her expression melts into one of love. He dismounts from his horse and runs to her, sweeping her up in his arms. She cups his face in her warm hand, and he closes his eyes; he can feel her fingers on his naked face, her touch like silk.

She embraces him, her sweet-smelling hair on his cheek, her arms strong and warm. She doesn't say anything. She doesn't have to.

Realizing who he is, the villagers run to them, calling and shouting. 'Did you slay the dragon, Lartak?'

'Tell us how you killed it!'

'Did it hurt you? Did you catch fire?'

'Of course, he didn't catch fire, stupid! He's right there!'

Arteo isn't interested in retelling the tale of the dragon. That's the job for writers and bards, not him. Karina's hand firmly in his, he searches for King Paraksha. Balin gapes when he spots the maskless Arteo, watching in stunned silence as they enter the king's tent.

'Lartak, you're back! I—' King Paraksha's dark eyes widen, and he laughs aloud and pulls Arteo into a fatherly embrace. 'Your mask, it's gone! Have you . . .?' He raises an eyebrow knowingly. 'Perhaps something happened to you, hmm?'

'Yes, Your Grace,' says Arteo and quickly explains to all of them everything he remembers. The memories almost choke him into tears, remembering growing up with his sister in the palace and how their cousins bullied them, the secret training sessions out of their mother's sight, and that terrible day when Bolara and his children attacked and stole the throne. 'They killed my father,' he says, now sitting on a stool with Karina at his side, rubbing his back. 'Shot him with an arrow. He collapsed on to me, and I fell . . .' He closes his eyes, a shuddering sigh shaking his whole body. 'After that, I lost my memories. The mask . . .' He touches the soft skin of his face. 'I don't know how it got there, maybe the gods, but it hid my identity, I suppose.'

'And now?' says the king softly.

'I have to see if my mother and sister are all right,' he says, gaining his feet. The king nods.

'Absolutely, you should,' he agrees. 'Lartak—'

'Arteo,' says the younger man, smiling. 'My name . . . is Arteo.'

Saying it aloud makes it feel real. He is not Lartak; he never was. With his name and his memories, he is whole again.

'Arteo,' King Paraksha says it as though he's tasting it on his tongue. 'Yes, it suits you.'

Karina stands, hugging herself, her eyes glassy. 'You're leaving,' she says. It isn't a question but a statement.

Arteo nods at her, his heart cracking in two at the pain on her face. 'I will return,' he promises. 'But I have to go. I need to know if they're all right.'

The word quickly spreads that Karina's promised is leaving. His mask removed and his memories returned. Some people mutter that the battle with the dragon addled his brain while others celebrate the news. Others are sad to see him go. The little girl and boy they played with before Gazzadeil attacked give him sad waves as he passes them.

'I knew you were some type of special wizard, but even more than that, you're a demigod,' exclaims Balin. 'Can I come with you?'

Arteo snatches up his bow. He stares at it. He remembers all his lessons. No wonder he left Mirtan in the mud that day.

No wonder he could fight and slay the Burrintot. He was trained to be a warrior. He opens his mouth to respond, but King Paraksha rumbles, 'Balin, this is a journey Arteo must take on his own. Surely you know that.'

Arteo's and Karina's eyes meet. Perhaps it is because he is leaving, but she has never looked more beautiful. Paraksha drags Balin away, and Arteo approaches his future wife, cupping her face in his hands.

'I promise I'll come back,' he whispers as she sniffles.

'You better,' she says, a single tear running down her ebony cheek. 'You better come back to me, Arteo.'

He kisses her, savouring the taste of her lips before drawing back. If he lingers any more, he won't go.

She waves to him, a mixture of anger and acceptance on her face. He rides off, villagers waving, his heart split between grief for Karina and excitement for his family.

✖ ✖ ✖

Arteo's uncle, Bolara, said he was sending them all to the Kalanya jungle. That was over two and a half years ago. If his family are anywhere, it has to be there. The thought that he was living mere miles away from them this whole time is both infuriating and welcoming. The jungle is vast though, and the chances of running into them would have been minuscule.

His horse, freshly fed and watered, rides with power and grace, slowing only to clop between trees as they get thicker. Each passing moment leaves Arteo wondering if he's doing the right thing, abandoning his new family for his old one. More than once, he doubts that they're still alive. But he must know the truth. Steeling himself, he presses on.

The sun is high in the sky, and the heat extra radiant. Upon reaching the edge of the jungle, he pauses for rest, not knowing which direction to head as he gazes at the massive sea of green.

The virescent hues are the foreground, the background, and as high up as you can see. The heat and humidity press in on his skin, making sweat pointless. The sounds of the insects, the birds, and the larger animals create a symphony of nature. The air tastes both sweet and fresh, like flowers blooming on your tongue.

A Paraka bird chirps loudly whilst nestled on a tree branch. Arteo smiles at the little creature, remembering the little one that Preeya had saved, many years ago. It looks like the spitting image of it.

He chooses to head east. As he slowly canters off, the bird chirps loudly and swoops near his head. He stops for a second, slightly bemused, and continues on. The bird squeals and swoops near his head again and quickly nestles back on a tree branch of a massive oak, facing west.

'What's going on, little fella?' he says.

Contemplating for a second, he scratches his chin, then turns his horse around and heads in the direction of the bird. The little creature lets out a friendly chirp and continues to head west through the jungle. *Strange . . .*

Arteo canters after him and weaves his way through the densely packed brush and vegetation. His little friend pausing and chirping to ensure the prince is not lost.

It isn't much longer before he hears the sounds of chopping wood and voices. He rides towards it, where two guards are waiting. The bird lets out one final friendly chirp as if to say goodbye and then shoots off towards the sun. It disappears from sight. Arteo rubs his eyes and peers again, but the bird is nowhere to be seen.

'Hold it!' barks one guard as Arteo slides off his horse, his hands in the air. Arteo and the guard gasp at the same time as they recognize each other. He didn't use to be a guard; he was a gardener back in Pendilor.

'M-my prince!' the guard stutters, staring from Arteo back to the other guard, who stands there looking bewildered. 'It is you! Everyone thought you were dead!'

'A long story, my friend,' says Arteo, smiling as the guard falls clumsily to his knees. 'No, no need for that. Stand. Please, are my mother and sister all right?'

'They are, Your Majesty,' says the guard as Arteo clambers back on to his horse to follow them. The sounds and smells of a town are getting nearer, the voices of a hundred bustling people, the scents of cooking and chimney smoke. 'Your sight will lift the spirits of all who see you, my prince.'

The main village is new but impressive. Houses have been constructed from tree trunks and stone, with fences and signs painted with dye from flowers. Sweet scents of fruits and herbs waft through the air. The village is one with the forest, the jungle trees high, providing shade, smoke curling around their leaves.

Arteo's heart nearly bursts. Around him are people from Pendilor, his hometown, people he hasn't seen for a long time, some pale but many nicely tanned like him. Most ignore him, not realizing who he is. He goes through them slowly on his horse, memorizing each face, looking for signs of his mother or sister.

'This way, my prince.'

The sounds of a woman grunting and the clatter of weapons grab his attention. Fifty or so people have gathered in a training square with targets and dummies. In the centre is a girl with a lean frame and built of muscle, her blonde hair tied back and a ferocious snarl on her face as she hits a dummy with a sword. She's skilled, she's intense, she's . . .

The young woman he saw in the forest after saving the baby Tolverine.

Panting, sweat on her brow, she turns to the crowd as he dismounts his horse.

Preeya. *My sister.*

Love spills in his heart like a broken dam in a mighty river. He leans on his mare for support as tears burn his eyes. She is stronger, different, more mature, but it is her. The same little girl with whom he played with. The same beautiful girl that helped take care of all living creatures.

He waits, crossing his arms and blending with the crowd, just another observer. Preeya points to a series of targets. In the middle is a stump, an apple on top of it, a hundred feet away.

She snatches up a nearby bow and nocks an arrow, aiming. She breathes slow, taking it in her sights and . . .

Gasps and exclamations of shock ripple through the crowd as a second arrow comes flying through the air with a whistle. It pierces the apple, shooting it off the stump to where it rolls in the grass. Preeya whirls around, shock on her face, and her eyes land on Arteo.

He grins at her, lowering his bow.

Shock is on her face, which melts into one of disbelief. For a moment, she shakes her head, suspicion flashing across her pale features. Then she's laughing, and as he steps towards her, she comes running, her blonde hair flowing behind her like a river of gold, her steps hard and fists closed.

She stops a foot in front of him and punches him hard on the shoulder.

'Ouch!' he cries, rubbing it. 'What was that for?'

'For not coming back sooner,' she snarls, then she breaks into a grin. 'Arteo, I can't believe it! It's been well over two years. We thought you were dead!'

She throws herself at him, her arms wrapping him tightly around the neck as she sobs, kissing his cheek, growling about how much she missed him and how much she hates and loves him. 'That was you . . . with the Tolverine, wasn't it?'

'Yes, it was,' he replies. 'What's going on here?'

Arteo breaks away from Preeya, wiping away tears of his own. An enchanting woman with Preeya's blonde hair appears, wearing a simple tunic, the sleeves rolled up. She's got fit, her body muscular, the gentle beauty replaced by hard strength. Her elegant eyebrows shoot up.

'Mother,' he says, his heart melting. The gaping crowd part for their queen as she runs to him with a cry. She hugs them both tightly to her, and Arteo wraps his free arm around his mother, unable to stop the emotion choking his throat and burning his eyes.

They rock together with their arms around each other, crying and laughing. He holds them tightly, the mother and sister he forgot and remembered, crying for his lost father as others clap and cheer around them at their beloved prince's return.

⌘ ⌘ ⌘

Bolara sips at a goblet of wine, troubled thoughts settling on his mind like mud after a landslide.

'More and more people all across Zeldigar are joining Assyri's little village in the forest,' says General Thamios. He jabs a finger at the map between them. 'Before long, they'll have a rebel force, and we'll have a battle on our hands.'

Bolara doesn't like that one bit. His sister and niece were supposed to die in that forest, eaten alive by Tolverines, not survive all this time and build a rebellion.

'And if Garlamon joins Assyri?' he asks, swirling his wine. The risk of the powerful kingdom joining her is a very real possibility that needs to be crushed before it becomes reality.

'The forest where we abandoned them is near their village.' General Thamios shrugs. 'And their kingdom *is* known for being fair and righteous.'

It makes Bolara sick. He has a sudden, violent urge to throw his goblet across the room but thinks better of it. His general mustn't see him lose control. 'Thamios, take Syrana with you to go and meet Garlamon's king. A frontal attack would . . . sour their opinion of us. Their five thousand troops would fare better in our hands, but if they refuse to join us, we must destroy them.'

Bolara enjoys Syrana's bloodlust, but she has come to recklessly kill anyone in her way lately. She will listen to the general. Perhaps this meeting will teach her that sometimes, it is important to be diplomatic.

'Yes, Your Grace,' says General Thamios, getting to his feet. 'Anything else?'

'I want Ristos and Hirtila to finish with the rest of the small villages,' says Bolara, staring at the empty fireplace, its fire diminished last night, leaving glowing embers. 'Then we will assess our total numbers.'

General Thamios leaves with heavy, clinking footsteps as Bolara takes another long sip of wine, sighing as it suffuses in his belly. Though he'll never admit it aloud, Bolara has been afraid to kill Assyri outright because of fear—of their sun god father.

But it turns out that his sister, hiding in the forest with her little rebels, is becoming more and more of a thorn in his side with each passing day.

CHAPTER 1 7

◎

GARLAMON UNDER SIEGE

Two days have passed since Arteo was reunited with his mother and sister. He is impressed with the village they've built for themselves in the Kalanya jungle.

Not only have they survived, but they're building and training, waiting for the day when they will defend themselves against Bolara's men.

Assyri gives him a tour of the massive training grounds with people hitting or shooting arrows at countless wooden dummies and targets. Huts with rooms and rooms of kitchens with enormous pots to feed the people, and farms growing rows of cabbages, carrots, and potatoes. Two small smithies, where soot-covered workers give his mother respectful nods and Arteo friendly grins.

Meanwhile, he explains to her all about his memory loss, about how everything was blank when he was washed up on the shores of Garlamon, where King Paraksha took him in, and he fell in love with the princess, Karina.

He tells her of helping them hunt Burrintots, which his mother frowns at until he explains it was only for food. He recounts the day that the king was gored by the rhinoceros-like creature and how he nearly died of his wounds.

'Balin, that's the prince, and I went into the jungle to find the Lawky bird, this enormous creature with tail feathers that heal when they're boiled with herbs. King Paraksha was so pleased we saved him

148

that he finally accepted me and let me court Karina,' he says, his heart warming as her smiling face appears in his mind. 'I wish she was here to meet you, Mother,' he says with a sigh.

'We will meet when the time is right, Arteo. It is just such a shock. I can't believe you've been alive all this time,' says Assyri, her eyes glassy as she stops to cup his face in her hands.

He almost forgot what a mother's touch feels like. Whatever, or whoever, wiped his memory must be immensely powerful. No one can explain the mask on his face that slipped away after he fought the dragon.

The cool touch of her fingers is heavenly against his cheeks, conjuring memories of his childhood and bringing a peaceful warmth over him like a blanket. He hugs her, holding her close and inhaling her clean, flowery scent. 'I don't know what protected me, Mother,' he says.

Assyri glares at the sun as though looking for a sign and responds, 'Only the gods know, Arteo . . . only the gods.'

'I'm sorry I wasn't here to mourn for Father,' Arteo says with tears welling in his eyes.

'That is not your fault, child,' Assyri says. 'You are here now, and that is all that matters.'

They head back to the training area, where the enormous crowd of people are standing in front of dummies or in pairs, faces hard as they spar, practicing parries, dodges, or mighty blows. Preeya walks between them, offering advice or demonstrating fighting stances.

Arteo recognizes servants, gardeners, and cooks from the castle, transformed into strong warriors with muscles and determined frowns. They respond to their leader with shouts and admiration.

Even teenagers younger than Preeya are evident, some little more than children, training as hard as the adults as sweat beads on their foreheads.

'She's whipping them into shape,' says Arteo, impressed.

'She must,' says Assyri, her eyes distant as she watches her daughter. 'They look to her now.'

'What of Bolara and my cousins?' asks Arteo. The name is like poison on his tongue, and he pushes down the anger that flares in his chest at the thought of their murdered father and lost kingdom.

149

'There are rumours,' she says. 'He's been taking over villages and towns for the past year or so. He's establishing influence everywhere, posting soldiers, building barracks, and fortifying. It won't be long before he conquers more. My spies say he wants to take over the whole planet.'

The unpleasant thought sinks in as Preeya approaches, sweat shining on her pale forehead, strands of blonde locks sticking to her neck. She snatches the goblet from Arteo's hand with a grin and drains the cup. 'It is so great to have you back, Arteo,' she says warmly.

He barely hears her. 'I need to speak to King Paraksha,' he says. 'I have to warn him, check that they're safe. They might need me if Bolara goes to Garlamon next.'

Preeya opens her mouth to respond, but she's cut off by the sound of thundering hooves approaching. The trio look up to a bearded man approaching on horseback.

'My queen,' he says, breathless. 'My prince, my princess.'

'Speak, Erendis,' says Assyri, not unkindly.

'News of Bolara,' he says, slipping from the horse. He's wearing a simple tunic, and countless sacks are attached to the horse's saddle. 'He's sending a regiment to Garlamon. To secure their allegiance.'

'He's going there right now?' Arteo shouts in alarm. 'I have to go back and make sure everyone's safe!'

Bolara is bloodthirsty. What if he reaches Garlamon before Arteo does? He can't let that happen. Worry for his new family battles longing for his mother and sister.

'You can't go. You just got here,' says Preeya, her eyebrow cocking as she folds her arms. 'You need to help our army prepare.'

'They've taken care of me ever since Father died, Preeya,' says Arteo, looking at her. Her coldness is surprising, but only a little. They thought he was dead until two days ago. 'I understand you don't want to see me leave again, but . . . I cannot turn my back on them.'

'But you can easily turn your back on us!' she fires back. 'We need you!'

'That's enough,' says Assyri. 'Go, Arteo. With my blessing.'

He nods in relief, but he can't leave with his sister mad at him. 'Preeya,' pleads Arteo as Preeya's lip trembles. '*Please* understand. Karina's going to be my wife one day. She is my true love. The king and his people protected me and cared for me. I need to do this.'

She gives a stiff nod, then flings her arms around him. 'Make sure you come back, big brother,' she mumbles in his ear, sniffling as she pulls back. Arteo wraps his mother in a fierce hug, then runs for his horse, praying he's not too late.

✄ ✄ ✄

Garlamon isn't so difficult to find once you know the way. General Thamios's spies have kept eyes on the forest village for months now, and they've cut a path through the jungle towards the village with ease. Syrana sits on her horse, shifting in her seat as she itches for bloodshed.

Chimney smoke rises into the air between tree branches, where several colourful birds flap, riding the breeze above the leaves. Here, deep in the forest, there is little but the sounds of chirping crickets and murmuring creatures. Syrana can't wait to paint the leaves red.

'There will be no unnecessary killing today,' rumbles General Thamios as though he can sense the thirst for blood drumming through Syrana's veins. 'We're here to have a discussion with their king, and nothing else. Your father wants his forces, so we'll take every soldier we can get.'

'Can we kill a few hundred?' she retorts, slinging her hair back. 'No, we cannot. We need all the numbers we can muster.'

'And if this king of theirs resists?' she asks.

Thamios pauses. 'Then we will show the appropriate amount of aggression. We will persuade him to join us.'

'Ugh. You take away all the fun,' she snaps. Sometimes, she can't bear the sight of the surly general. At least Ristos has a sense of humour.

She is determined to kill at least one person in Garlamon, no matter what General Thamios says. She entertains herself with daydreams of murder and battle as she follows General Thamios through the thicket.

A thousand armed men at their backs, they ride for the gates of Garlamon. The trees thin out, taking them closer to the village. The fields around them are damaged as though there has been a large forest fire here.

For a moment, Syrana wonders if someone, somehow, beat them to Garlamon and attacked, but behind the gates are the sounds of people walking and talking, the bustle of a thriving village.

There aren't many guards at the gates, but as the soldiers make their way across the field, the atmosphere in the village changes. People call for the king, scrambling to fetch him while children glare through the fence, their eyes wide.

They have reached the gates, sitting back straight on their mounts, when the man who must be their king meets them, his dark face grave. He has a neatly trimmed beard, and he wears simple robes, not the expensive silk with gold embroidery King Bolara wears.

'I am King Paraksha of Garlamon. How can I be of assistance?' He bows politely. Behind him is a young woman with long black hair and bright-brown eyes—his daughter, perhaps.

She's so delicate and innocent looking that it sets Syrana's teeth on edge. She eyes the princess with a sneer, fantasizing breaking her pretty little neck.

They dismount, approaching the king and his daughter. Silence descends on the village, and General Thamios's voice is deep and clear. 'Greetings, King Paraksha. King Bolara of Pendilor sends me to you for . . .'

General Thamios's words fade to the background of Syrana's mind as the girl peers at her with a cool gaze. It isn't full of fear or wariness as with most people who lay eyes on her. Just silent judgement. Red hot anger flares through her.

'It's been a long ride,' she remarks, approaching the princess of Garlamon. 'You, girl. Get me a drink of water.'

The girl's dark eyes narrow. 'The well is over there,' she says waspishly, gesturing to a stone well several feet away. 'Help yourself to some.'

Syrana smirks. If Garlamon resists, she'll be the first to die. And she will enjoy a slow kill with this feisty creature.

They glance to where the men are speaking, where King Paraksha is shaking his shaggy head. 'No, I don't agree,' he says. 'You can't just conquer and kill everything you touch! What about Queen Assyri's rule of peace?'

'Queen Assyri is no more,' snarls General Thamios as several of the soldiers behind them gesture to their men. Hooves thunder on grass as the soldiers rush to surround the gates. 'I'll ask you one more time. Support our cause and hand over your soldiers, or watch your village burn to the ground.'

'This town can withstand dragon fire!' says a teenage boy around Syrana's age, appearing behind the princess. His black hair is a mess, and he has food stains on his shirt. 'You can't hurt us—aargh!'

A guard has grabbed him by his curly, black hair. The princess tries to rush to his aid, but Syrana grabs her by the wrist, locking on to her hand. When she tries to yank away from her grip, she slaps her hard. The princess falls to the ground with a wail. Syrana slowly pulls out her dagger.

'Karina!' cries the king.

'No!' General Thamios roars, looking towards Syrana. 'We'll give the king one more chance! Comply, or we'll burn your daughter at the stake as an example. You will see what happens to those who refuse Bolara's hospitality.'

'You won't hurt my children!' the king roars, raising his hand. He strikes out at General Thamios, who avoids the blow, and punches him in the stomach. Paraksha buckles over before he's restrained by guards.

Syrana snickers. *Now* it's getting interesting.

The princess is defiant, her eyes shining as she says, loud enough for everyone to hear, 'Then you must burn me.' Her voice trembles. 'For we will never yield to this evil!'

'How righteous and brave,' Syrana remarks, slapping Karina down to the ground again when she tries to rise. A lump starts to form on her right cheek. 'I'm sure your people will remember your sacrifice when they're lying dead in the mud.' She cackles.

Thamios nods, and several guards grab the princess as the king tries to fight his way through the many guards now surrounding him. Glee beats feverish in Syrana's heart. Some action, at last!

They tie Karina to a nearby wooden pole as her little brother sobs, a pitiful, weak sound, like an injured goat. Syrana longs to smack him in the head and shut him up.

More of the Garlamon people are coming, staring in shock as they tie their princess's hands with rope behind the wooden pole as they restrain her brother and father. Most of them are holding children close or whispering among themselves. Syrana hopes they'll rush in and fight so she can get her sword bloody.

'Gather wood and kindling,' she snaps at the nearest soldiers, who bow and hurry to collect firewood. 'You're going to burn today, precious thing. Your screams will be heard for miles around.'

Syrana grabs a fistful of Karina's hair, yanking her head back. The girl winces through her teeth, eyes glassy with hate-filled tears.

'My, my, your hair will burn up, and you'll be nothing more than charcoal.' Syrana giggles. 'Maybe I'll burn your family as well, one by one. Or stick their heads on spikes and attach them to the gates, then throw their bodies out for the vultures. Then everyone can see their darling king and prince every time they visit.'

The boy's wails grow louder. Karina's lip trembles as she stares defiantly at Syrana. Her chest heaves up and down; this girl is scared to death. *Utterly delicious*, Syrana thinks.

'You're braver than most, at least,' Syrana remarks. 'Such a shame that won't save you from the gods.'

'My princess,' says a man's voice near her. Heat washes over her as he holds out a flaming torch. The man's eyes in his visor, a bright green, flicker between the torch and the Garlamon princess. Syrana ignores his hesitation and snatches the torch from his fingers. The time is ripe to see this little princess burn.

CHAPTER 18

THE MIGHT OF THE GENERAL

'How many soldiers does Bolara have?' asks Assyri. The training is put on hold as the queen, Preeya, and their best spies collect in a tent to discuss next moves. They have to prepare for the coming war. Time is running out.

'Thirty thousand strong, Your Grace,' says Erendis. Though he used to be a simple gardener, his skills as a spy have exceeded beyond anything Assyri expected. Over the years, he has collected invaluable information for their survival, from Bolara's battle tactics to his spies' locations. She trusts him with her life.

'Even if Garlamon joins us'—Assyri sighs—'we'll only have twelve thousand soldiers of our own. It isn't nearly enough to face him.'

'What about King Ranakin?' offers Preeya. 'He's been helping us, and they have just as much a reason as we do to fight against Bolara.'

Assyri gives a nod. She's heard the stories from the jungle dwellers of her brother and his children hunting their people for sport. When she first heard of it, she was mortified she didn't know about it. It was a huge risk for King Ranakin and his people to trust her, and she swore to avenge every single jungle dweller who died by her brother's hands.

'You're right. I must go to him and seek their aid.'

Preeya opens her mouth, but Assyri takes her by the shoulder. 'Stay here, please,' she says. 'I must see him on my own. Train the soldiers and take care of our people. Let them know a battle is coming, and all those able to fight must prepare. I'll be back with more men and women to fight for our cause.'

Jaw tight, Preeya closes her mouth, nodding.

'With me,' says Assyri to her aide, a lithe woman from a fishing village with remarkable skill with a spear. They both head out into the daylight, where a bird caws above them. Anxiety bites at Assyri as she packs food and a change of clothing into a sack. Will Ranakin join their cause? Did Arteo reach Garlamon in time?

There's no time to lose.

� ✳ ✳

'Any last words, my lovely?' says Syrana, savouring the terror on the young princess's face. The flickering flame of the torch bathes her skin in heat, just shy of painful. Karina struggles in her bonds; tears meander down her bruised cheek. There's no way out.

The soldiers have piled hay and wood around the girl. A crowd of Garlamon people have gathered a safe distance away, many of them sobbing, holding their children close, and hiding their gazes from their princess.

None of them dare to approach as Bolara's armed soldiers are a formidable force.

Cowards all, Syrana thinks. *Are none of them brave enough to face us and try to save her?*

A few men rush forward. They are cut to shreds by Bolara's soldiers. A pool of limbs and crimson litter the path to the princess of Garlamon. The rest of the crowd do not move. They sob tears and wait for the inevitable.

Karina says nothing, staring straight ahead with a determined look on her face. She's ready to die for her people. So honourable it makes Syrana's spine itch. She hates how pure she is, everything Syrana is not.

Syrana holds the torch close to the wood, ready for it to catch fire.

Gruummble. The ground violently erupts. A few of the soldiers exclaim in shock, hands around their sword hilts.

Syrana glances at General Thamios, whose eyebrows are knitted in confusion. The ground trembles again. Then several shocked gasps erupt as something soars through the air. A horse gallops towards them, but it holds no rider. It stops with a snort before the soldiers.

Syrana looks around as something plummets from the sky. A man. He lands on the ground with a terrific crash, sword slamming into the grass, shaking the whole village like a mighty earthquake.

The impact throws several people down; the torch flies from Syrana's fingers as she hurls through the air with a gasp. Pain bursts in the back of her head as she hits a nearby tree. She coughs, sharp pain in her back as stars burst in her eyes, and red pours from her head.

Her vision growing black, she slumps to the ground, unconscious.

✂ ✂ ✂

Arteo's body is illuminated, his eyes glowing white as his muscular body slowly rises.

'What in the heavens is this?' General Thamios snarls. He's a little older than Arteo remembers but still hard as stone, those evil eyes never changing. Many of the soldiers stare at Arteo in awe, mouths agape.

The torch is on the ground, burning harmlessly in the dirt. Karina is safe for now.

'It must be the power of the gods,' a soldier mutters, backing away.

'Got to be,' agrees another, who appears as though he can't decide whether to step back or throw himself to the ground in worship.

'Enough of that nonsense,' General Thamios snaps, stepping forward. As the energy surrounding Arteo's body dissipates, the general's cold eyes narrow in recognition.

'Take your soldiers and leave, Thamios,' says Arteo, gripping his sword as he steps forward. The cosmic energy snuffs out, but the nearest soldiers still back away at his appearance.

Arteo is made of muscle now, the last of his boyish innocence swept away. A large crater carved in the ground where he landed. Thamios, however, doesn't flinch. A small smirk tugs at his mouth.

'You should be dead, boy,' says the general, unsheathing his sword. It glimmers in the sunlight. 'It is time for me to rectify that. Stay back, everyone; this kill is mine to enjoy.'

Many of the younger soldiers are all too happy to stay out of the fight; others stand with hands on sword hilts, their faces hard as they await orders.

Arteo twirls his sword in his hand, feeling the power ripple up his arm, animating his limbs. The training he forgot about for years comes back to him as clear as day. The hours of practice, the years of instruction, set him into a fighting stance, holding the sword with the knowing grip of someone who knows how to wield it.

This will be the hardest battle he's ever fought. It is for the lives of people he loves. People who took him in as one of their own. Karina, Balin, King Paraksha. The town of Garlamon.

As the young prince and the general circle each other, all eyes are on them. Syrana is still knocked out, slumped against the tree.

Sensing his opportunity, Balin sprints to Karina, cutting frantically at the ropes around her body and wrists. The guards' gazes are fixed on Arteo and General Thamios, not noticing the teen cutting his sister free. They both join King Paraksha, who slowly backs away. *Getting more forces, perhaps?*

A surge of adrenaline runs through Arteo. One he hasn't felt before. A primal thirst for battle.

Arteo gives a roar, throwing a blast of energy at General Thamios. He deflects it with energy of his own, giving a mocking chuckle that makes Arteo's blood run hot. Their swords meet with a mighty clash. Sparks fly, and trees shake. Block, swing, block, parry.

Arteo narrowly dodges a stab and sends another strong wave of energy at General Thamios, who deflects it with ease with an almost lazy flick of his wrist. Then the bigger man throws out a hand and sends a blast of his own. Arteo defends himself, casting out a shield to deflect it.

'Little Arteo is all grown up,' says Thamios, coming at him with a swing of his blade that Arteo blocks. The weight is heavy on his arms, making him want to wince. 'But you're still weak. Just like your father.'

'Don't talk about my father!' Arteo growls, attacking with his sword. The steel clashes, sparks flying, and Arteo ducks a wild swing from the general, the steel whistling past his ear. His blood is drumming in his head. Death hurtles past him.

'Or what? You'll kill me?' General Thamios parries Arteo's incoming blow, shoving him forward with an armour-clad arm. One of the Garlamon citizens screams.

Arteo dodges the deadly blade and swings his sword with a cry. General Thamios gazes in shock at his arm, where a small gash drips blood.

The sneer disappears, replaced by fury. General Thamios was playing with him before; now he is ready to fight for real.

Guards and citizens hurry to scramble out of the way, wincing and snatching up children as the pair battle. Their weapons clash as they fight, block, and swap blasts of energy.

A nick here, a cut there. Arteo winces as his wrist drips crimson. He must find a weakness in the general, but an obvious one does not exist. This is a machine designed for warfare. Thamios does not lose in battle.

Wind howls above, the staring citizens little more than a blur. For a moment, it is just the general and Arteo, one fighting for conquest, the other for his family. Sweat soaks their foreheads, fury blazing in their eyes like an inferno, their breathing hard as they exchange blows and energy blasts. General Thamios is more experienced, but Arteo is agile and has speed on his side.

The people of Garlamon gaze helplessly, some sobbing quietly, others with tension, silently cheering Arteo on. The soldiers watch too.

The fight goes for what appears an eternity, neither warrior yielding an inch. Arteo sends another blast at the general. It is deflected easily, and the larger man moves forward. The cosmic power from Arteo is weakening through fatigue. Thamios can sense the upper hand.

Arteo lashes out with his blade. It is deflected, and the general thrusts forward. Arteo gasps in shock as the cold steel of General Thamios's blade pierces his stomach.

A cosmic blast of energy bursts from General Thamios's fingertips, throwing Arteo to the ground and crashing the air from his lungs as agony rips through his abdomen.

He groans, the sky swimming above, as General Thamios moves to stand above him. Arteo feels like his ribs have caved in and his stomach ripped from his body. He wheezes, trying to take in gasping breaths.

Blood bursts from his stomach, hot and fast. Somewhere far away, a woman is screaming. *Karina's voice.* Dark fuzzes appear at the edges of his vision.

'You are weak,' says General Thamios again, standing over him, blocking the sunlight. He pins him to the ground, a gauntleted hand around Arteo's neck, choking him. He holds his sword, the tip ready to thrust into Arteo's heart. The boy wheezes for air, pain tearing through his stomach, black spots bursting across his vision.

I'm dying.

'Would you like to know a secret, boy?' General Thamios hisses, so close Arteo can feel the spittle land on his cheek, his cold eyes boring into his. 'The arrow that killed your father was one I meant for you.'

Fury rips through the pain. Arteo's vision sharpens. A mighty roar from deep within his soul bursts from his lips. His entire body lights up. Anger and hate and righteous fury send a blast of energy, from every fibre of his being, outward.

General Thamios's eyes widen in shock as he's thrown backwards to the ground. Arteo is still bleeding, but he breathes. He gets to his feet, groaning through his teeth, taking no heed of the blood on his clothes or the gash in his stomach.

All that matters is he wants to hurt the general as much as he can. To inflict pain and stop this evil man.

Body alight with pure power, Arteo swings his sword. General Thamios blocks it, but Arteo's sword cuts clean through the blade, the useless halves falling to the ground.

Shock turns to horror as Thamios backs away, stumbling on some uneven ground. 'This is not possible,' the general shouts.

Arteo bellows at the top of his injured lungs like a wild animal. He swings with the dull side of the blade, and there is a sickening crack as he crushes his enemy's arm.

General Thamios screams in agony, falling to his knees, gaping at his ruined arm. It swings uselessly at his side.

General Thamios uses his good arm to send another blast of energy, but it's clumsy, panicked; Arteo deflects it with ease and surges forward with his last remains of energy, swinging his sword with all his might, screaming a mighty war cry.

The blade slices through General Thamios's neck with a meaty *thwunk*.

Silence descends on the battlefield as General Thamios blinks dumbly before his head topples off. His body collapses to the ground, the head rolling before coming to a stop, eyes staring sightless at the sky above.

The power fades from Arteo's body as he collapses to the ground, his free hand clutching at his bleeding stomach. His limbs are cold. Nothing is left.

Light footsteps rush across the field; Karina is rushing towards him, her wrists reddened from the rope, her eyes watering. She collapses beside him and holds his head as he coughs. 'Arteo . . . my darling Arteo.' Icy numbness spreads through her body. The prince is dying.

✄ ✄ ✄

Syrana groans as her eyes open, blinking in confusion. She lifts a hand to touch her forehead, and her fingertips come back red. The scent of soil is on her clothes; she's lying against a tree.

She winces as she sits up and stares straight ahead at a field where the people are gathered. The girl is no longer tied to the wooden pole. Her fists curl in fury.

A gasp rises among the people as someone is beheaded. Syrana swallows, her throat is dry as she recognizes the armour, the shape of the man.

General Thamios is dead.

She recognizes Arteo but is unaware he is fatally wounded. *He should be dead.* For the first time in a long time, fear clenches around Syrana's heart. She's never seen anyone beat General Thamios in a battle before.

She gets to her feet, pain slicing through her skull where she hit her head. It's crusty with drying blood.

She whistles for her horse and clambers on to the saddle. Nearby, soldiers follow her through the forest. No one says anything, but they are all thinking the same thing: *Arteo must be a god to have killed their general.*

Syrana's fingers clench on the reins as fury pounds through her. She must get to Bolara and tell him. Arteo is alive and dangerous. She rides away in a fluster.

✖ ✖ ✖

Cold fear clings to Karina as she holds Arteo close, whispering his name. His stomach is a red mess, blood bubbling at his lips and shadows around his eyes as he peers up at her.

Her father is behind her some distance away, having gathered his own soldiers. Garlamon's troops come riding over, spears and bows in hands.

'Drop your weapons!' bellows King Paraksha as the people form a protective circle around Arteo and Karina. 'Drop them right now, or we'll kill you all!'

There is a clatter of steel and wood as the guards drop their swords and bows to the ground. Karina struggles to register what is going on. Her eyes burn with tears as she cradles Arteo's head in her lap.

She presses her hands on his stomach wound to stem the bleeding, not caring that crimson runs over her hands and on to her dress.

'Help him!' she screams at some stunned nearby villagers. 'Fetch the healer, now!'

'Karina . . .' Arteo says. His voice is a whisper, a pitiful, weak sound that sends terror through her. His lips are trembling, his eyes half open and looking around as though searching for her.

'I'm here, Arteo,' she says, hot tears sliding down her cheeks. 'I'm here.'

'Take your people . . . to the Kalanya jungle,' Arteo whispers. 'Find the . . . village. Find . . . my mother. They'll be safe . . . there . . .'

His eyes close, and his head slumps. 'Arteo? Arteo!' she cries, shaking him. A healer finally runs over, crouching beside them. 'Tell me! Tell me he's not . . .'

The healer, his face down caste, presses two fingers against the pale flesh of Arteo's neck. 'There is a pulse,' he says. 'But very faint. He does not have much time, my princess.'

'They won't be bothering us again,' says the king's voice.

He stops before them. 'Good gods! Arteo! You! Fetch bandages at once!

The healer scurries off as Karina sniffles. In that moment, she hates everyone around her. Most of all the headless corpse several feet away. If Arteo dies, she's not sure she will survive.

She loved him that moment he was dragged from the boat into the healer's room. He is her one true love.

'We have to help him,' says Balin as her brother's warm hand lands on her shoulder. 'We'll find another Lawky feather. We will, Karina. We will.'

The king responds, 'By the heavens, we will. He saved us all. Balin and I will go right now. He will survive, Karina. The gods' blood is in him, which will help.'

His last words are filled with desperation that winds tight around Karina's heart. She watches as they wrap the wound on Arteo's stomach with bandages that rapidly turn crimson.

She tells them what Arteo said before he fell unconscious, her own words barely more than a stutter. She repeats herself twice before they understand her.

'Daughter, you will lead our people to the jungle,' says King Paraksha, reaching over to tenderly wipe away a tear on her cheek.

'I'm staying with Arteo,' she says, her voice stiff.

'With Balin and I gone, you are their leader,' says her father. 'Bolara will come back with more troops. They'll come straight here and slaughter all our people. Balin and I will get the tail feather. You must take our people to safety.'

They both gasp as Arteo is taken away on a stretcher, his head lolling and his eyes closed. Karina's heart thunders beneath her ribcage.

Swallowing, she nods. She can't help Arteo right now, but she can help their people. She runs to the stretcher, carefully moving some hair from Arteo's forehead. It's stuck together with drying blood. His skin is still warm, and she can hear the faintest of breaths from his lips.

'Come back to me, my beautiful Arteo,' she whispers and kisses him gently on the lips. Her heart breaks as they put the stretcher on to a wagon while others attach horses to it. Her father gives her an encouraging nod, and he and Balin clamber on to their mounts and ride off into the forest. This time, they'll take Arteo with them so they can heal him right away. *What if I never see him again?*

Karina wants nothing more than to curl into a ball and sob, but when she turns around, everyone is looking at her. Merchants, blacksmiths, soldiers, and housewives.

All of them are watching her, helpless, with haunted eyes. Children sit on their mothers' hips or cling to their dresses, waiting. Her heart turns to steel. She can't fall apart now. It is up to her to help these people.

'Gather only what is necessary,' she says to them. 'Clothes, blankets, food, and medicine. Then we'll go and search for Arteo's family. They will take care of us.'

She forces a smile as her eyes meet with a little girl, the one Balin and Arteo were playing with when the dragon attacked. 'The bad men are coming back, and we have to escape them. Go!' she urges, and people start scrambling. 'Gather only what is necessary and be back here as quickly as you can!'

As people call out to one another, packing sacks of grain and wheat on to wagons and bundling blankets into sacks, Karina glances towards the forest. Arteo said his family were somewhere in the jungle, right under their very noses this whole time. She just hopes they can find them.

She senses darkness without her brother, her father, and Arteo. Like part of her is missing. But she must be strong for her people.

'Ready?' she asks as citizens gather on the outskirts of Garlamon. Some people have brought horses laden with goods; others are carrying enormous sacks on their backs. One woman guides a whole brood of children, each with sack hoods over their heads and wraps around their feet.

They begin their trek into the Kalanya jungle. Karina doesn't know what awaits them, but she trusts Arteo with all her heart. She takes one last look at the dead general, his head several feet away. No one is burying him. No one cares about him. The memory of him stabbing Arteo in the stomach makes her hands tremble.

Her final thought when looking back at their abandoned village is of the girl who almost burned her to the stake. A young woman with raven-black hair and a killer's eyes. Fear prickles her heart.

CHAPTER 19

The Impending War

Assyri now has seven thousand brave supporters on her side. If Garlamon joins their cause, that will boost their numbers up to twelve thousand. But it still isn't enough; according to the spies' reports, Bolara troops comprise thirty thousand highly skilled soldiers.

'We'll secure another ten thousand if King Ranakin joins us,' Assyri says to Preeya. 'He's the best chance we've got.'

'Be careful, Mother,' Preeya whispers, hugging Assyri before the queen gets on to her horse. She gives her daughter a small smile and mulls over their situation as her horse's hooves thump with familiarity on the grass, her aide at her side.

It is a steep task to defeat Bolara's army, so every bit of help is required.

⁂

Several miles away, over treetops and through hills, more horse hooves pound on the grass, crunching dead leaves and snapping twigs as Balin and King Paraksha ride through the forest as quickly as they can manage.

Arteo is strapped on to a horse as firmly as they could secure him. The young man occasionally mutters to himself, his eyelids flickering. He's delirious.

'I pray to all the gods that we aren't too late,' Balin mutters as they're forced to slow down, the trees growing thicker and the path giving way to overgrown grass and plants. They ride as swiftly as allowed to reach the cliffs of the Lawky bird, but with every passing moment, Arteo is slipping away. 'The wound is deep. He might not make it.'

'Don't say that,' says King Paraksha, a light sheen of sweat on his forehead, fatherly concern in his features. 'Don't even think it, son. Arteo will not die. He cannot die.'

The tone of desperation in his father's voice is more frightening than the prospect of losing Arteo. Balin steels himself. They caught the Lawky bird once; they can do it again.

Their horses slow to a stop as they reach the bottom of the cliff. The grey stone looms above them, smaller birds squawking from nests in the rock. At least the weather is clear; they won't contend with strong winds or wet stone.

'How is he?' asks King Paraksha as Balin slips off his mount.

'He's breathing,' he says, and they both gently remove Arteo from his horse. A strong frown appears on his young face, his breathing ragged and uneven. The bandages are crusty with dried blood.

'Let's stabilize him in that small cave over there,' says the king, and together they carry the young man and tuck him into a cliff face. They quickly build a fire to ward off any animals. 'No hope of carrying him up the rock face. This will have to do.'

Arteo lies in the uncomfortable cave, his eyes squeezed shut as his lip trembles. There isn't much time. Balin and King Paraksha toy with the idea of having one of them stay to monitor him. It does not make any sense as both of them are required, if they are to contain the Lawky bird.

Father and son start to climb the cliffs in silence, the worry hanging between them like a storm cloud.

⚜ ⚜ ⚜

Fury still beats fast in Syrana's chest as she snaps at a stable boy to put away her horse before racing into the palace, taking the stone steps two at a time.

'Welcome back, my princess. Would you like some tea after your long journey?' asks a maid, scurrying up to her.

'Out of my way,' Syrana snarls, shoving the maid to the side. The maid bows and disappears in a flurry of skirts.

Syrana catches Ristos in the corner of her eye, and he runs after her, the unspoken question palpable on his face. She says nothing to him, searching for her father.

The half-witch Ritani and King Bolara are sitting at the large oak table in the dining hall, Bolara holding a golden goblet of wine in his fingers. He straightens ever so slightly at Syrana's appearance.

'Father,' she says in the doorway, her chest heaving. Blood still mattes her dark hair, crusty and dry, and she's still wearing the leathers she left in. Her head aches, and excursion burns in her muscles, but there's no time to relax. 'General Thamios is dead!'

She hears the sharp intake of breath from her brother behind her. Silence descends on the dining hall like a shadow. The candles appear dimmer for a moment. Bolara gets to his feet, fire in his eyes. 'What did you say?'

'General Thamios,' blurts Syrana, 'has been killed.'

'*No!*' Bolara roars, and he hurtles the goblet across the room, purplish liquid streaming out on to the flagstones. The goblet bounces off the stone wall with a metallic clang and rolls into a corner. The king breathes hard, clenched fists on the table. His half-eaten meals sits forgotten. 'When? How?'

'It was Arteo,' she snarls, the name like bile on her tongue.

'Arteo? The boy is dead,' shouts Bolara.

'He isn't,' Syrana snaps. 'He's back, somehow. And he's stronger. He beat the general in a battle. Slashed his head right off his shoulders.'

She doesn't want to tell her family that Arteo's mere appearance slammed her so hard in a tree she had been knocked out and missed most of the fight.

'It matters not,' says a calmer voice, though it still holds a steel edge to it. Syrana and Ristos's mother, Ritani, is wearing a fine gown of red velvet, dark hair piled in an intricate style on her head, pale hands clasped in her lap. 'We secure double their number of soldiers, perhaps more. We will meet them on the battlefield and crush them.'

Bolara sinks on to his chair, his fists still clenched. 'Yes . . . mmm . . . Yes, you're right.'

'Father, there was something different about him.' Syrana steps forward. 'He's stronger. He glowed, like a blue flame. I've not seen it before.'

Bolara is ready to throw something again but thinks better of it. A maid scurries in to clean up the mess as another fusses over Syrana's cut on her head. She sighs but lets the maid fuss over her like a mother hen.

Ristos comes up beside her, staring at her with tight lips.

'What?' she snaps, daring him to ask her why she didn't try and save General Thamios, why she didn't challenge Arteo to a duel herself.

He smirks at her and turns to their father. 'We can't stop our plans now,' he says.

'Meet her on the battlefield,' says Ritani. Everyone knows who she's referring to. 'Send a messenger to the forest. So many refugees there now that they'll be easy to track down. Tell them to meet our armies by the cliffs of Heldegar in three days' time. She cannot escape.'

Bolara stays sullen, stroking his chin and glaring out the window. Syrana can't blame him for his bad mood. General Thamios has been in their lives since she was a baby, training her and Ristos and helping them reach their true Shakti 5 potential. The general was always revered for his leadership and war craft. The two of them now need to take more responsibility.

'I'll crush them all,' Bolara snarls, thumping the table. A maid brings a fresh goblet of wine, and he snatches it off the table, taking a noisy, angry slurp. 'I'll cut off Arteo's head myself as his mother screams. Then I'll take Assyri's, then Preeya's, and they'll all adorn the castle walls to remind everyone who is the true king!'

✂ ✂ ✂

The jungle dwellers flank Assyri, guiding her to their king, Ranakin. Years of mutual support, trade, and help have built a foundation of trust between Assyri's people and Ranakin's, but the brave jungle dwellers are still cautious of outsiders.

It is rare that a foreigner is allowed to approach their king in his palace, queen or not. After Bolara's cruel antics, the palace has been heavily fortified, and Assyri feels a rush of respect for the people who live here and fight to survive.

The palace is dug into the cliff. Spikes of wood have been erected around the stone structure. Ivy grows on the walls, slits in the walls for its guards to fire arrows at approaching enemies.

Solemn-looking guards move aside to let Assyri through, the six guards around her clutching spears, silent and suspicious as they guide her to their ruler. She is checked twice for weapons, and she swallows. Even after all this time, she still isn't trusted.

One more thing for which her brother and his family must pay the price. 'My king, thank you for seeing me,' says Assyri, bending a knee to King Ranakin. He is slouched on his stone throne and doesn't look happy to see her. His brown eyes narrow and scrutinize her with suspicious caution as she gets to her feet. 'Thank you for everything you have done to help my people so far. We are forever grateful. Without you and the kindness of your people, we may not have survived these past few years in exile.'

King Ranakin nods and then grunts, as though he's waiting for her to get to the point.

'I come here begging your aid once again. We need your soldiers to come and join us in the fight against Bolara's tyranny. He is tearing across this land, burning and conquering every town and village he lays his eyes on. It won't be long before he attacks the kingdom of Garlamon. His army grows stronger by the day, and his troops vastly outnumber ours. Please, we need your help to challenge him and stop his brutal rule.'

The words have not left her lips before King Ranakin is already shaking his shaggy head. 'I'm not interested in foreign battles,' he says, sounding almost bored.

'Your Majesty, this is a fight for survival,' says Assyri. For a moment, a flicker of bitterness flashes through her. She was once the queen of Pendilor; now, to everyone around her, she is little more than a peasant begging for the king's attention. 'If we don't fight Bolara now, he will come here! And not only with his children but with tens of thousands of troops who will slaughter you. This is just as much your fight as ours.'

'It is not my battle,' he snaps at her, finally meeting her gaze. 'I will not surrender my people to war.'

Frustrated tears burn Assyri's eyelids, but she refuses to weep. 'Please, good king, I swear to you that every soldier who fights today is fighting for their lives. To do nothing will lead only to death.'

'Thank you for your audience, Queen Assyri, but it is time for you to leave,' says the king, giving a fake smile that appears more like a grimace. 'I have been lenient enough with your people, letting you hide in my land, sending you food and aid.'

'Please', says Assyri again, taking a step forward. The guards around her point their weapons at her, the sharp steel of a spear blade inches from her neck.

'Do not test my patience,' says the king. 'My people have been slaughtered by your kind in the past. You cannot expect us to fall at your feet and give up our strength for you now.'

'I am *not* my brother,' says Assyri, an edge to her voice.

The aide steps forward, then stops at a warning glance from Assyri. The jungle dwellers turn their weapons on her, something like distrust, possibly hatred, in their dark eyes. It makes Assyri's heart crack in two. Their people have been allies for so long, yet they distrust so easily.

She turns and marches towards the door, only catching the king's last words to her. 'I pray the gods are with you.'

She stops, her fists clenching. 'I pray they are with all of us, Your Majesty,' she says as her body stiffens. 'If we are to survive this.'

Her aide at her back, they go back to their waiting horses. Assyri's fingers are trembling with frustration as she climbs on to her mount. They were their only hope. What will they do now?

⁂

Preeya throws herself into training the others, trying not to think of her brother leaving so soon after coming back and her mother on her diplomatic mission to beg for King Ranakin's help. It is Preeya's first time being away from her whole family at once, but she steels herself. Arteo endured for years without his family; she can survive a day.

Their army is small in numbers but formidable. They've trained hard and are strong and skilled, and every single one of them fights because they love Assyri and recognize her as the true queen.

Surely that's more than Bolara can say for *his* forces—if he's anything like she remembers and the foul rumours that the refugees bring with them, he has gathered a contingent of his army through force and fear, not love and loyalty.

That's got to count for something.

Preeya spars with a young woman, and though she says she has practiced a little with her brothers, it is clear the girl isn't a fighter. 'You're waving your sword about too much,' says Preeya, torn between exasperation and the bizarre desire to laugh. 'And you make it obvious where you're about to hit next. It's all over your face.'

She reminds herself not to be too harsh on the girl. They are both worried about everything that's happening, and the refugees who joined their camp have not had a lifetime of training like Preeya.

'Keep practicing,' she says, encouraging the young woman and sending her off to spar with a nearby man.

She is eating a bowl of warm stew when Assyri steps into the tent, her blonde hair tousled by travel, her face drawn with worry. Preeya quickly dabs at her lips with a napkin and rises to embrace her.

'You're back,' she says, knowing right away that the news is bad by the terrible look on her mother's face.

Assyri rubs Preeya's arms, a warm, affectionate gesture she hasn't done for years. 'Any news of Arteo or Garlamon?'

Preeya swallows the questions on her tongue and shakes her head, her lips tight. 'No, we've heard nothing yet.'

Guards and messengers have been watching the village outskirts ever since Assyri left, eyes peeled for news.

Then almost on cue, a messenger wearing a brown tunic with a satchel at his hip comes into the tent, almost colliding with the mother and daughter. 'Forgive me, Your Majesty,' he says, breathless, sweeping off his feathered hat and bowing.

'What news do you bring?' says Assyri.

'It's . . .' The messenger's dark eyes are aghast with fear. His goatee trembles like it has a life of his own. Preeya wants to shake the man and yell at him to spit it out, but she resists. Her temper is short lately.

They step into the sunshine instead, where the messenger finally gathers his wits. 'It's Bolara,' he says as surrounding people come to listen.

'He has commanded that we meet him on the battlefield at Heldegar in three days' time.'

'We're not ready,' says Preeya, cold fear spilling down her back like ice water as she meets her mother's startled gaze. 'We don't have enough soldiers. They'll crush us.'

'Perhaps that's the idea,' says Assyri, sighing as she stares into the sky. 'Mother, we have to meet them,' says Preeya, pushing away the despair threatening to overcome her. 'If he wants a battle, then let him have a battle.

I'd rather die in a fight than have him pick us off while we're sleeping.'

Assyri peers up, seeing the fire blazing in Preeya's eyes. Pride shines on her face like sunlight, and she gives Preeya a fierce hug.

'I'm so proud of you,' she whispers in her ear. 'You're right. We will meet them at Heldegar.'

When she draws back, she says, 'Start making plans for battle. Rally everyone you can. We—'

'Your Majesty', says another guard, running over in a rustle of chain mail.

Oh, what now? Preeya thinks with a groan. *More bad news?* How much more can they take?

The guard whispers in Assyri's ear, and her eyes widen as she gazes at him. He gives a solemn nod. She races for the gates, Preeya at her heels, and they all gasp as they see the people before them.

Thousands of refugees have arrived. Some with Garlamon insignias. A dark-haired girl with ebony skin and a torn dress is leading them, staggering from exhaustion. She glances up at them all, her eyes half-closed.

'Please help us,' she whispers before collapsing forward into the grass.

CHAPTER 20

THE BATTLE FOR PENDILOR

'Welcome,' says Assyri as the Garlamon folk come through the gates.

A nearby man picks up the unconscious girl, carrying her with gentle care. People in the camp hurry to fetch bowls of food and skins of water, shouting for spare tents and bedrolls.

Assyri is proud of how quickly they rally to help their fellow people.

The girl with the torn dress awakens soon after, and after drinking water and sitting down, she introduces herself as Karina. 'They came . . . many of them,' she says, her hands trembling. 'They ordered my father to join them, but he refused. They attacked, but Arteo, he—'

'Here, settle down,' says Assyri kindly. 'Take your time.' A healer appears with a hot cup of herbal tea and presses it into Karina's shaking fingers.

'Thank you, Your Majesty,' she says, taking a sip. She doesn't appear hurt, but shadows exist under her eyes, and a nasty bruise bulges from her cheek. Her face is tight with worry.

She quickly tells them all that happened back in Garlamon—the arrival of the Bolara soldiers, how Syrana almost burned her alive, and how Arteo flew in, glowing like a fiery god.

Her voice cracked as she told them of the duel with the general and the horrific injury Arteo sustained.

'He chopped his head off.' Karina shudders. 'I've never seen anything like it.'

Assyri and Preeya exchange shocked looks. 'General Thamios is dead?' Fierce pride rushes through Assyri. But also grave concern for Arteo's welfare.

General Thamios was one of the most brutal and heartless people she ever knew. She is glad he's dead. Though neither of them says it aloud, she senses Preeya is thinking the same thing.

'Then what happened?' asks Preeya. 'Where's Arteo now?' Karina lowers her head.

'Karina?' asks Assyri, her voice sharper than she intends.

'My brother and my father are healing him,' she says in a small voice. 'He's wounded, but the Lawky tail feather will save him.'

'By the gods,' screams Preeya, causing Karina to shuffle, a little uneasy. She gives a small gasp as Assyri wraps her up in her arms, pulling her close. The girl shivers in her arms.

'You have done well,' she says. 'You brought your people here even without your family.' When she pulls back, she asks, 'War is coming. Are your people ready to fight?'

'Karina brushes away the tears on her cheeks. 'We're ready,' she says. She picks up a nearby sword, testing it in her grip. 'We will help in any way we can.'

Assyri and Preeya peer at each other. They're thinking the same thing: she's not only a beauty but a fiery one. They can see why Arteo likes her.

The next morning, Pilkan, the head of their guardsman, pours over a map on an oak table. Assyri and Preeya stand either side of him, talking strategies. Karina stands before them, acting as head of Garlamon, her dark eyebrows knit with worry.

She doesn't know anything about war techniques. The kingdom of Garlamon has been at peace since she was born.

'Bolara enjoys the advantage in numbers,' says Pilkan. He endures a jagged scar on his cheek, but his blue eyes sparkle with friendliness. Right now, they're narrowed in seriousness. 'That much is obvious. We have to be clever. Make their numbers count for nothing.'

'We need to set a trap,' says Preeya, her blonde hair starting to grow back and spilling over her shoulder as she leans over the map.

'Bolara and his troops will come from the east. If we can catch them off guard . . .'

Discussions continue for hours, Karina clutching the fresh tunic Preeya gave her in her fingers, praying that Arteo is all right and on his way. She'll feel better when her brother and father are back too.

What is taking them so long?

⌘ ⌘ ⌘

Bolara sits on his stallion, gauntleted hands clutching the reins. His new armour is finely polished and fitted for his impressive and powerful form.

At his sides are Syrana, her black hair tied in a braid and wearing new chain mail, and Ristos, his eyes glinting, a sword at his hip and a helmet under his arm. Before them stand Bolara's army, thirty thousand strong.

Spread through the line are those faithful to him from the kingdom of Pendilor, wearing surcoats over steel armour, tall spears and shields in their hands, standing at formation. There are outer battalions of soldiers from conquered villages and towns, smatterings of different colours. Wisely, they come over to Bolara's side.

Scattered groups of soldiers from different places, either bought, threatened, or seduced by promises of glory and gold. Some are little more than peasants with clubs and cheap swords. It doesn't matter. Thirty thousand is more than enough to finally crush his sister and their little rebellion in the jungle.

Bolara held knowledge of Assyri's whereabouts for years, but concern for what their father, Suriyar the sun god, would do if he killed her held him back. No more.

His dream of conquering the lands across the seas and beyond will never be fulfilled so long as his sister and her children still breathe.

Suriyar hasn't contacted them for years. There is no reason he would intervene now.

'This time, no one is to be spared,' says Bolara to his children. He can almost sense the joy spilling from them, the thirst for blood he so enjoys palpable on them both. 'Slaughter every man, woman, and child who gets in your way. Surrender is not an option.'

'Yes, Father.' They both nod.

'Let's prepare the final arrangements. Then we march for Heldegar.'

✖ ✖ ✖

Assyri, Preeya, and Karina stand together in new splint mail. The blacksmiths have been working into the nights and the mornings to create as much new gear as possible for everyone. The stench of smoke and forgeries are spread miles around.

Now the three women stand with twelve thousand nervous folks at their backs who are willing to fight with them. Most of them are not soldiers. Their army consists of refugees who have learned to fight under Preeya's teaching—farmers, merchants, bakers, apothecary workers, builders.

They all have one thing in common, however, and that is a fierce desire to end Bolara's reign.

Many of them have seen their hometowns burn before their eyes, their families and friends slaughtered all in the name of feeding Bolara's hunger for power. Now they are armed, and they are ready.

'Where is Arteo? He still hasn't arrived,' says Preeya, anxiety deepening the lines in her pale forehead. He would be here, if able. Is he even still alive?

'The Lawky tail feather brought my father back from near death,' says Karina, her voice meek and uncertain. 'They'll do everything to heal him.'

'Do not fret. He will come, my sweet princess,' says Assyri, another nickname she hasn't called Preeya since she was a child. It untightens the fist around the girl's heart a fraction.

She and Karina exchange a glance. The young princess of Garlamon stays silent, her face solemn. Shouldn't her father and brother have found the Lawky bird and healed Arteo by now? They need him.

As though sensing the rising anxiety, Assyri turns to her soldiers. They all stand in mismatched armour, holding every kind of weapon from swords and shields to clubs and spears. They're silent, standing among trees and bushes, some sitting on boulders, but they all stand to attention as Assyri steps on to a large rock to address them.

'This is the day we face our enemy,' she calls, hoping her words reach them and replace their fear with hope. 'This is the day we break free from the restraints of terror. Too long have we hidden! Too long have we cowered in the shadows while my evil brother and his army invade and destroy our beautiful lands! We won't stand for it any longer. Not while there is still breath in our lungs and blood in our veins. This is the day we stand and fight!'

A cheer rises from the army.

'Today, we fight for justice. We fight for freedom. We fight for those who whisper rebellion, who refuse to live under Bolara's iron-fisted rule any longer. We may not win today, but we will send an important message. We are the beacons of light in this dark era. We are hope for the people. If nothing else, we inspire people to fight for what is right. It is a message that says it is better to die on our feet than to live on our knees!'

The cheers get stronger, a roar rising, the stomping of steel-clad feet, the clashing of swords as they bang them against shields.

The atmosphere changes to one of hope, of determination. Each one of the brave twelve thousand before her longs for freedom, and each one of them will fight until their dying breath for it.

Preeya's eyes are shining with inspiration as she marches alongside her mother, the battle drums piercing the forest air as thousands of brave people clatter through the forest towards the cliffs of Heldegar.

※ ※ ※

Grey clouds consume the sky above Heldegar, a vast open plain surrounded by rocky cliffs. Both armies meet with a clatter of horse hooves, eyeing each other from a distance.

'Look at them,' sneers Bolara from his stallion, Ristos and Syrana either side of him, as they eye the army on the other side of the plain. 'Their pathetic army actually thinks they can win.'

'We'll annihilate them, Father,' says Ristos, ushering his horse forward. The young man is responsible for the troops after the demise of Thamios.

Bolara's jaw tightens as he beholds a woman on a horse leading the enemy. She is far away, but her slender form and blonde hair, tied in a thick braid and lying on her shoulder, are recognizable right away.

For too long, Bolara let his sister live. That ends today!

'Go!' Ristos bellows, ordering the first platoon ahead. Horse hooves thunder on the grass as one thousand soldiers on horseback gallop forward towards the small army.

'Look.' Ritani laughs, the witch on her own horse behind them. 'They're already terrified.'

Indeed. Already, Assyri's troops are turning tail and fleeing at the first sign of danger. Bolara gives a smug smile. 'I would have thought they had a little more fight in them than that.'

'More! More!' Ristos yells, sending more troops. 'Chase them down! Destroy them!'

'Wait! We need to assess—' It is too late. Bolara's voice is drowned out as more troops run ahead, steel armour rustling, the ground shaking with the thundering steps of thousands of galloping, snorting horses.

Bolara watches, wondering if he will be required to do any fighting today. This is far too easy. This is . . .

A movement in the cliffs above catches his eye. Something in the rocks towering above them. At first, it almost appears like the stone itself is rippling. Then he spots shapes move among the rocks. Realization grabs hold of his guts, and he grunts in anger; *a trap is set.*

'Wait! Stop, you fools!' he shouts, but no one can hear the false king over the racket of running horses and unsheathing blades. It's too late.

The battlefield shakes like an earthquake, and before them, the ground suddenly gives way. Thousands of men and horses scream in terror as the earth disappears beneath them, caving into an enormous pit. They fall into it, the grass and dirt collapsing like it's made of parchment.

Bolara screams in fury and casts an unsavoury eye towards Ristos as several platoons disappear into the enormous pit with a terrific crash. The remaining troops stare in shocked silence as Bolara twists his stallion's reins in fury. They've been tricked. Assyri's soldiers had dug the deep trenches the night before.

Ristos can feel the heat of his father's eyes burning on his back and does not dare to turn and face him.

Arrows rain down from the cliffs on to his soldiers trapped in the pit. Hundreds of horrified screams, the whistle of arrows, and slowly, those caught in the ambush fall silent.

✕ ✕ ✕

'It worked!' Preeya breathes as her uncle's troops, thousands of them and more than they expected, fall into the pit before them. The ground trembles and caves in, the terrified whinnies of horses and the wide-eyed shock of the troops making her flinch only a little as they fall to their deaths. Arrows rain from their archers' hiding places in the cliffs.

Despite the death before her, a grin splits Preeya's face. *We have struck the first blow.*

✕ ✕ ✕

'*Go!*' Bolara bellows, urging another platoon forward. He has taken control of the troops. The horses avoid the pit, splitting off left and right to gallop around the enormous hole. His children are behind him, their silence full of meaning. They're all aggravated by the ambush. No matter: their fury will sing in their blades.

They only lost a small fraction of their army. They will still slaughter them all.

This time, they clash with Assyri's waiting troops. Unlike Bolara's, with all the same superior armour and weapons, the enemy forces are all wearing different armour, carrying whatever weapons they could find. An inferior battalion.

Bolara and Ritani hang back, watching the carnage below.

✕ ✕ ✕

Preeya and Assyri fight back to back, the years of training and preparing singing through their bodies as they block, parry, and stab enemy soldiers.

Some run towards them with wild screams, desperate to be the ones to overpower Bolara's enemies, attacking with clumsy strikes that are easy to block. Others are seasoned soldiers, fighting with skill, drawing blood.

'Are you all right?' Assyri shouts to Preeya, a deep gash on her shoulder where a sword fell on her.

'I'm fine!' Preeya yells back, blocking an incoming short sword with a terrific clash. A cosmic burst of energy bursts from her fingertips, throwing the soldier back. 'Don't worry about me! Keep going!'

The ambush bought them time, but that's all. Slowly, the enemy soldiers are overwhelming Assyri's troops. For every one of the armour-clad warrior's dead on the ground, there are a half dozen of the brave troops who followed Assyri into battle.

Nearby, a soldier cuts the head off Erendis.

'No!' Assyri screams. The spy's headless body collapses to the ground. His killer roars in triumph, appearing for a moment more beast than man as he holds up the head for them to see. Tears burn Assyri's eyes. She picks up a nearby bow and sends an arrow skittling through the air. It pierces the Bolara soldier's neck. He drops dead, crimson spilling forth.

The Bolara troops keep advancing.

'It isn't over until we're dead!' she cries, and the nearby soldiers, wilting under the pressure, stand straight. 'Give them all you've got! Make them remember us! Make them *fear* us!'

Nearby, Karina swings a sword, backing away as a soldier approaches her, a wicked grin on his lips. He raises his sword and . . .

Another burst of energy from Preeya throws him back so far he flies through the air, hitting a dead horse far away and falling slack with a dull grunt. The princesses' eyes meet, Preeya giving a nod and a half-smile. 'Come here to us,' she calls, and the trio stand back to back, defending themselves. 'I'll protect you.'

More of Bolara's troops are on their way now, including Ristos and Syrana. Familiar fear from the years of bullying, the lifetime of helplessness, settles in Preeya's chest, but she shoves it away.

She isn't a powerless little girl any longer. She hopes they'll meet on the battlefield. She has a score to settle with them both.

'The numbers are telling,' Assyri mutters, her eyes scanning the battlefield. There is no denying it; they're outnumbered three to one. The end is coming.

Ahead, about a half-mile away, Syrana and Ristos have joined the fray. Ristos jumps off his horse and engages two people; Syrana rides through the field on horseback, swinging her sword at troops, hitting several screaming soldiers. It's a bloodbath, and they enjoy every moment.

It is only a matter of time before they're all slaughtered.

Karina lunges forward with her sword and stabs an advancing soldier, straight through the heart. Preeya gives her a nod.

'I'm proud of you, Preeya,' says Assyri, only wishing that Arteo were here so she could say goodbye to him. 'I've always been proud of you.'

'Mother,' says Preeya, and she can hear the tears in her voice. 'Mother, I love you.'

'Fight until your dying breath, my darling,' says Assyri, her eyes narrowing as she holds the sword in her hand. It's stained with blood, red on her hands and her armour. 'They may have won, but we will never live in fear again.'

The Bolara army closes in.

CHAPTER 21

An Unusual Ally

The end is coming.

Bodies litter the battlefield, coppery blood and steel permeating the air like a foul perfume. The sky is red too, as though the gods themselves are mourning the terrible loss of life this day.

The grass is sticky and crimson, unrecognizable as the peaceful valley it was only hours earlier. A scattering of brave soldiers is still standing, sporting bloody wounds, hastily bandaged limbs, and eyes of fire. It is only a matter of time before they're all slaughtered, and they know it.

Every fallen soldier here died with vengeance and loyalty in their hearts until their dying breaths. Everyone is a son, a brother, a sister. Their sacrifice will not be forgotten.

The survivors all retreat into a circle, back to back, surrounded by a hundred enemy soldiers or more. Some of them have blood on their armour, their swords stained with the life of the brave warriors who joined them today to fight for freedom.

Frustrated tears burn Assyri's eyes, but there is no time to weep. If they are to die, they'll do it on their feet, fighting until their very last breaths. The world will know they fought bravely.

'Here we go,' mutters Preeya beside her, the sword firm in her grip. Her blonde hair is a mess, loose strands down her face. Drying, brown blood is spattered on her armour. 'This is our last battle?'

'We'll see your father again soon,' says Assyri, Ranay's handsome face bursting in her mind, calming her and warming her heart. 'We'll all be together in the next life.'

Karina nervously smiles. Preeya feels pity for the girl. She gives her an encouraging smile. She wishes she could rouse some words of comfort for the young princess.

A roar rises from the enemy soldiers, and they rush forward. Assyri lets out her own scream, her sword in hand and raised towards the sky, ready for the end and to take as many soldiers down with her as she possibly can.

Whoosh . . . whoosh . . . whoosh . . . The whistles of arrows streak through the air, so many that they nearly blot out the sky. Several of the enemy soldiers fall to the ground with pained gurgles, feathered arrows blossoming from their throats or their chests.

Assyri and the others whirl around in confusion. More of the enemies fall, struck by the arrows before they realize what's happening.

Karina lets out a shocked gasp as a large group of jungle dwellers burst from the forest, whooping and yelling, shaking spears and firing arrows at their enemies.

'They came.' Preeya breathes. 'Ranakin's people! They came!'

King Ranakin appears behind his soldiers, armour cladding his chest, clutching a bow in one hand, a sword in the other. He gives Assyri a stern nod before joining the fray, and gratitude bursts in her chest, animating her limbs.

The hundred or so of Bolara's surrounding soldiers are quickly overpowered; those that haven't been killed by arrows stare in shock as the jungle dwellers overwhelm them, fighting with all the fierceness of an oppressed people who finally have a chance to strike back.

Four of the soldiers run towards Assyri. One with an arrow in his thigh, limping, rage on his red face. The others are uninjured, fury in their eyes as they strike at her with flailing weapons. Assyri dodges their clumsy, desperate blows, spinning and striking back.

Her sword pierces one in the stomach, and she kicks him off her blade with a growl. A strangled cry gurgles behind her; Preeya stabs another, and he sinks to the ground with a shocked groan, blood bubbling at his lips.

Back to back, mother and daughter fight the other two. The nearest one swings, and his blade narrowly misses Assyri's ear; she slices his throat, grimacing at the waste. He is young, a boy barely Preeya's age, and in another life, he may have led a peaceful life as a farmer or merchant under her rule.

Bolara will pay for this.

'Mother!' Preeya screams.

Another soldier is swinging at her. Assyri lurches back, the blade whistling above her shocked face. So close she can almost taste the steel. She attacks back, letting out all her hatred for her evil brother burst from her.

She finishes him off with a hard burst of energy from her fingers, and the soldier flies far into the air, landing with a spine-crunching thud near the tree line, where he collapses with a groan.

Now that the jungle dwellers are here, a somewhat level playing field exists. Assyri's heart races, galloping in excitement. *They came. She didn't think they would, but they did.*

Her and Preeya's eyes meet, her daughter's face full of the same shocked adrenaline. Preeya bursts out laughing, and she understands why; the insane, relieved chortle of someone who caught a whiff of death's scent, only to be yanked back to life with renewed vigour.

✳ ✳ ✳

Bolara lets out an animalistic growl of frustration as his platoon is taken down by the jungle dwellers, pierced by arrows or spears. He didn't expect those pathetic forest people to join his sister's rebellion at the last moment.

'Archers!' he bellows. 'Fire at them! Kill them all!'

The team of archers in front nock their arrows, aiming high. Syrana is beside him, her own bow in her hands. He glances at her.

'Shall I aim for Preeya's stomach or her throat?' she asks, aiming.

'Just kill them,' Bolara snarls, not in the mood for his daughter's sadistic games. '*Fire!*'

The arrows twang into the air, blowing soldiers' hair and horses' mane as they whoosh past, flying into the sky. As the deadly projectiles shoot up, silence descends on the battlefield, unnatural and eerie. The air darkens, somehow. Ristos glances at them, confused.

Then a burst of flame, accompanied by a loud roar that shakes the sky. The arrows are smothered in fire and eventually consumed.

Bolara's troops reel back in shock, bathed in heat, covering their eyes from the sudden bright fire. The flames have reduced the arrows to useless ash that flitter to the ground like black snow.

One of the guards lets out a curdled scream, pointing a gauntleted finger to the east. An enormous black shape is flying at them, wings flapping and pounding like battle drums, all scales and teeth, the size of a cathedral.

Gazzadeil swoops to the battlefield. Riding on his back, his face twisted in fury and dressed in shiny armour, clutching to the dragon's neck with gloved fists, is Arteo.

✖ ✖ ✖

Though a lot of the soldiers were killed by the arrows, and the jungle dwellers have equalized the battlefield, the fight is far from over.

Bolara sends more platoons ahead. Soldiers dash towards Karina in a rustle of chain mail, murder in their eyes as she freezes, clutching her sword in a shaking hand.

Preeya sends a soldier hurtling away with a blast of energy, running over to protect her brother's love. Their swords meet with a terrific clash as Karina gives a small scream, backing away. Preeya counts ten of the enemy soldiers coming for them.

'No!' Preeya growls, sending another burst of energy at a soldier about to slice off Karina's head. He flies through the air with a scream, landing heavily and rolling to a stop. Karina slashes with a sword, which meets the legs of a soldier, crippling him. Preeya spins and stabs another, then moves towards Karina.

There are still seven of them surrounding them, swords and shields in hands, some looking apprehensive, others angry. Assyri is far away, fighting her own battles. Preeya blocks the path to Karina. *They will have to get through me first.*

'Ready to die, little girl?' sneers the nearest soldier. He raises his sword; Preeya gets ready to defend with all her might.

Crash.

An enormous Tolverine, one of the biggest Preeya has ever seen, comes thundering across the field. It slams into several of the soldiers, crushing them into the dirt or sending them flying.

The creature lands on one, snatching him up in its enormous jaws, and he screams as its fangs tear him apart. Karina buries her face into Preeya's shoulder as Preeya beholds in awe. She's only seen a Tolverine this size once before. 'I don't believe it. She's fighting *for* us! And who's that on her back?'

Karina peers up with glassy eyes and gives an excited scream. 'Father! Balin!'

The mother Tolverine bends down, and the Garlamon men leap off. She turns quickly and tears more soldiers apart; they're no match for her formidable claws and teeth. Father and son run to gather Karina in a hug, half sobbing and thankful she's all right.

'No time for that,' says Preeya, looking around for more approaching soldiers. More of their enemies are coming for them, additional platoons sent by Bolara.

As if in response to the incoming soldiers, a stampede of Tolverines, dozens of them, a hundred or more, burst from the tree line, teeth bared and claws glinting, their fur-covered paws thumping on the ground.

The soldiers at the front stop their march, looking terrified, their confidence faltered. They're shoved forward by their allies behind them, forced to meet the fearsome creatures in battle.

King Paraksha holds his daughter in a hug, Balin joining in. When he pulls away, his eyes fall on Assyri, who is approaching them, the slain body of a soldier behind her.

The king of Garlamon is a handsome man, with a neatly trimmed dark beard that suits him and warm brown eyes. They widen a little as they meet her blue ones, and he stutters for a moment before saying, 'Oh. My lady. It is an honour.'

Preeya and Karina allow a quick smirk in the middle of the battle.

Assyri recognizes that look. It was how Ranay looked at her when they first met. She feels heat crawling up to her cheeks.

Then she throws her sword at King Paraksha's head. It whistles past his ear, and he appears shocked, ducking out of the way. A wet squelch is heard as the blade pierces an approaching soldier behind him. The man collapses, his sword falling to the dirt with a dull clatter.

'I didn't see him coming. Many thanks.' He grins at her. Assyri retrieves her sword, wiping the blade clean on the nearby grass.

The scales may have tipped somewhat, but the fight isn't over yet.

✻ ✻ ✻

Bolara glares in horror, a cold murmur in his stomach as his troops are destroyed by the Tolverines, Arteo, the jungle dwellers, and the enormous dragon that entered the fray.

He wasn't expecting this at all. Fear is not an emotion he often realizes, but the tension of it is grasping him by the spine, twisting his guts.

Without General Thamios, he already felt vulnerable. Now Assyri has allies coming from every which way, a godforsaken *dragon*, and an army of Tolverines. This was not the easy victory he was expecting.

Arteo jumps off the dragon with a huge leap and joins the Garlamon princess's side. The false king grows in fury as the young man battles beside his sister and mother, Bolara's troops no match for Assyri's new forces and allies.

It makes him want to slice the head off his nearest soldier, but that won't help anything. He can feel the morale sinking in his troops, their confidence lowering as they mutter to one another.

Ristos curses beside him. 'Father, I've just received word from the back of the platoon.'

'What is it?' Bolara snaps, not taking his eyes off the battlefield.

'They're deserting.'

'What?' Bolara's head whirls round. His armoured soldiers, his most faithful, are still mounted, ready to enter the fray. But where there were thousands more behind him before, now stand only hundreds.

'They're deserting?' Syrana spits. 'Running away?'

Ristos gives a grim nod. 'Mostly the Kyetin and village soldiers. Leaving the battle.'

Ritani curses under her breath.

'They'll all pay.' Bolara growls, fighting to keep the panic out of his voice. *Traitors!* When this battle is won, he'll see to it that every soldier who deserted today is burned alive along with their families.

'Last platoon, forward!' Bolara commands, sending the final few thousand of his armoured troops towards the battlefield. 'Slay them all!'

'What shall we do?' asks Ritani, the witch bringing her horse up close to her husband's.

'We're leaving,' shouts Bolara. 'We need to recoup, recover, gather more soldiers. Come on!' He growls at his family. 'Leave the horses. We will seek refuge in the cliffs!'

✳ ✳ ✳

Arteo takes down the soldier in front of him, glancing towards where the enemy soldiers came from. More are coming, but only a small platoon, and many of them appear hesitant to join them.

Seeing them coming, Gazzadeil's mighty wings pound in the air. He lands in front of Arteo with a terrific crash, shuddering the ground so hard the young man nearly loses his footing.

Gazzadeil roars, his enormous jaws expand open, fangs bared, spittle bursting from his mouth as the roar shudders the battlefield.

His outcry sends birds fleeing from the trees in terror, several rocks from the surrounding bluffs tumbling down the cliff side. Horses reel in terror as the soldiers wrestle for control of the reins; others turn tail and flee before the beast. Smoke pours from Gazzadeil's nose as he inhales.

'No!' Arteo shouts, running around to the dragon's side. 'Let them run. This is all Bolara's doing.'

The dragon's great, scaled head lowers in submission. 'As you wish, young prince.'

Bolara himself disappears; Syrana, Ritani, and Ristos head towards the cliffs on the opposite side of the ambush pit. Fury bubbles through Arteo as he detects the three fleeing shapes, leaving their army behind.

Cowards, all of them!

The mother Tolverine has Karina well-guarded, standing before her with a growl as though Karina is one of her own. 'Mother, Preeya,' Arteo says, pointing. 'They have headed to the cliffs. Let's end this.'

'Gladly'. Preeya snatches up a shield from a dead soldier, testing it on her arm. They run towards the cliffs together. If Bolara and his family get away, this will all be for naught. They could go into hiding, gather their armies again. This must end today.

'Take care of her!' Arteo bellows over his shoulder at the enormous mother Tolverine, who lowers her furry head as though she understands. King Paraksha and Balin are there too, as well as Gazzadeil, who's enjoying a meal of enemy Bolara soldiers.

Karina is in the safest spot in the world right now, and that knowledge loosens the tension around Arteo's heart a fraction. The princess of Garlamon opens her mouth to argue, but her brother and father hold her back. Though it pains Arteo to leave his love behind, this is something he and his demigod family must do together, without her.

'Children, you take care of Ristos and Syrana,' says Assyri, her eyes narrowing. 'I'll attend to Ritani.'

'Mother?' says Preeya, her voice small.

'Go!'

The ice in her voice sends a small shiver through Arteo, and he nods.

'Come on,' he mutters to Preeya as Assyri chases after Ritani's retreating form. No time to wonder whether she'll be okay. They have their own challenges ahead.

They scramble up a cliff road towards where they saw Ristos and Syrana running. They struggle up a hill of falling pebbles and dust before they come to a flatter area, leaving the stench of the battlefield behind them.

A rocky plain filled with boulders and dead trees, the dust at their feet so thin, almost like sand. There's no wildlife anywhere; not even a lizard skitters through the rocks, and the only sound is the faint, far-off symphony of battle and their own laboured breathing.

The scent of smoke is faint in the air. Behind them is the battlefield, where they can still see Gazzadeil and the dark shapes of soldiers and Tolverines.

'Where did they go?' Preeya pants, looking around. 'They were right . . .' An arrow suddenly whistles through the air towards Arteo; Preeya forms a cosmic shield, protecting her brother. Ristos and Syrana appear from behind some nearby rocks, Syrana wearing her usual sneer.

Both have grown into young adults, their muscles refined, armour well made and gleaming. Arteo senses Preeya steel herself beside him.

'Time to surrender?' says Arteo to Syrana, and she scowls at him, clutching her bow so tight in her fingers her knuckles turn white.

'Where've you been all this time?' Ristos says. 'Hiding in the woods while we took over your precious kingdom? Letting your mother and sister do all the fighting while you frolicked in the woods with the Garlamon folk?'

'It matters not. I am here now,' says Arteo.

Syrana gives a loud scoff.

'Frolicking enough where he slayed your precious general,' says Preeya.

She's done cowering and being polite. Whereas her cousins bullied her when they were all children, they now look upon each other with some form of respect. Ristos lets out a growl at her words, and she enjoys a rush of satisfaction that a nerve has been touched.

'You got lucky when you fought General Thamios,' Syrana sneers. 'You caught him off guard.'

'Just like your mortal father,' says Ristos, his eyes flashing. 'The choking sound Ranay made when General Thamios's arrow hit him was like the sweetest music, so I hear.'

Syrana lets out a cackling laugh as Preeya and Arteo bristle.

'Enough talking,' thunders Arteo. 'Let's end this right now!'

Syrana lurches forward, yanking her sword from its scabbard. Preeya is ready for her, holding up her shield to block the hasty attack. Ristos attacks Arteo, and their blades clash through the valley like a deadly symphony.

⚸ ⚸ ⚸

Assyri scrambles up the cliff, panting. Every now and then, she catches a flash of Ritani's armour, or her raven-black hair as she disappears behind a rock. She must catch up with her.

The witch sat on *her* throne for years, allowing her husband to wreak havoc on her kingdom. Fury drums through the fallen queen as she follows her, determined to make amends.

Assyri is made to leap back when she's confronted by a snake. It appears from thin air, its scales brown and glistening, jaws open and showing sharp fangs. It hisses at her.

Assyri's eyes slide up the cliff. There is no wildlife up here in these barren cliffs. Ritani left this for her using her dark magic. Assyri raises her sword, waiting. The snake gives another spine-chilling hiss, eyes glinting as it gets ready to strike.

It darts for her, long fangs gleaming, and Assyri throws herself out of the way, collapsing heavily into the rocks. Pain slices up her arm as a sharp rock scratches her skin. The snake's tongue darts out, smelling her blood.

It strikes again, quick as a bolt of lightning, and Assyri gives a yell, twisting out of the way, her blade slicing through the air.

Her sword strikes the snake, cutting its head off. The open-jawed head sails through the air and down the cliff out of sight. The body flops uselessly to the ground, red spurting from the stump.

'You'll have to . . . do better . . . than that.' Assyri pants, getting to her feet.

More creatures come to attack her—wolves, hyenas, bigger snakes. Assyri dispatches them with ease. Perhaps because they're magical, but the animals are predictable and clumsy, attacking without grace or any real viciousness. Her demigod abilities are guiding her steady hand.

'Face me yourself, witch!' Assyri roars, sweat beading her forehead as she stabs a wolf in its mouth, the blade coming out through the top of its head; the fur-covered beast collapses with a high-pitched whine and rolls down the hill.

Ritani is just ahead, her raven-black hair swaying as she scrambles further up the cliff. She glares down at her and gives a wicked grin. She summons ten daggers, deadly sharp, and sends them spinning towards Assyri.

The queen, her energy draining, raises a cosmic shield. With each dagger that rams against it, clattering uselessly to the ground, the shield grows weaker.

Assyri lets out a cry when the last knife slices through her shield, cutting her arm. The wound burns, and she breathes hard through her teeth. The witch, using a final burst of magic, moves an enormous boulder to roll on to Assyri's robe, trapping her there.

'You've always been weak,' says Ritani, looking down at her with glinting eyes. 'Always. My husband is a better ruler than you ever were.'

'You're all cowards.' Assyri seethes. 'Every last one of you.'

Ritani is holding a sword in her hand, smirking down at Assyri. The queen tries to move, but her robes are stuck beneath the massive boulder. Lightning sparks in Ritani's blade, and the sky darkens, powering her weapon with hostile magic.

Bestial hunger in her eyes, the witch raises her weapon, poised to strike Assyri down.

CHAPTER 22

BATTLE OF THE DEMIGODS

Syrana hurls a cosmic blast at Preeya, a pure ripple of energy. Preeya deflects, anticipating, and the girls trade blasts. Each of them is dealt with, sending surges of energy from the clifftops like mighty shock waves. Syrana's sneer turns to shock as Preeya blocks her manic sword attack, the clashing steel sending sparks erupting from the blades. Preeya grips her sword, teeth gritted, their noses inches from each other's.

Preeya throws her cousin back with another blast of energy. Syrana snarls, her feet sliding on the ground but maintaining her balance, and surges forward again.

The years of training drilled into them, the hours and hours of practice now ring true in their hearts as they block, parry, swing, and stab for their lives.

'You have improved, cousin,' blurts Syrana, her eyes wild, strands of black hair sticking to her pale skin, 'But you will meet the gods today.' With a roar, she attacks again. Preeya evades and swings a well-timed elbow into the face, drawing blood from the evil one's nose.

'Did you enjoy that?' Preeya snaps, then resets into fighting stance, ready for another assault.

Syrana wipes at her nose. The back of her hand fills with crimson. She glares at her cousin and lets out an evil cackle, then begins a flurried attack with sword on Preeya.

The agility on display from Arteo's sister is something to behold. Sidestepping, somersaulting, blonde hair flaring, wan sunlight gleaming on her blade. She is a warrior.

Ristos and Arteo circle each other, sizing each other up. Rage thunders in Arteo's heart. The tormented childhood, the years of confusion and forgotten memories, the era of Bolara on his mother's throne. It will all end today.

Ristos makes an acrobatic leap, flipping through the air, his sword heading straight for Arteo's head. Arteo responds with a blast of energy, throwing off Ristos's aim. The boy lands with a scowl, on his feet like a cat, and their swords meet.

Weapons clash, more energy blasts roaring to and fro, deflected or dodged. One hits Arteo in the chest, making him wheeze; he manages to raise his sword to fight off his cousin's fierce attack. With a twirl, Arteo stabs with his sword, slicing a cut across Ristos's forearm.

This is no longer sparring with wooden swords. This is a fight for survival.

Syrana sweeps a leg under Preeya's feet, throwing her to the ground. Her ribs crunch on impact. Preeya gasps in shock, the rock-strewn ground hard beneath her back, and Syrana's sword comes flying towards her for the kill.

No! I won't die on my back!

Preeya rolls to the left, the sword clanging on the stone behind her. She scrambles to her feet, her armour covered in dust, panting as Syrana surges at her. Preeya defends, and the two demigod girls weave and thrust, leap and dodge, with the speed and agility of jungle cats.

Arteo and Ristos are at their best. Neither of the gifted young men look to be weakening. Both are full of fury, one thirsting for power; the other vengeance. Neither is buckling under the pressure.

Ristos's arm still bleeds; Arteo is sporting a nasty cut on his cheek, the beginnings of bruises throbbing on his right calf. Ristos's lip is bleeding; when Arteo thrust his sword pommel at his face, the red stark against his tanned skin.

Arteo swings his sword, overpowering Ristos's block weakened by his injured arm. The blade sails past his head, and the young man's eyes widen in something Arteo's never seen on his cousin's face before: *fear.*

The son of the false king backs up, his wounded arm shaking as he holds up his sword to block another furious attack from Arteo. He fires another cosmic blast, but Arteo anticipates and flicks it away.

The battle takes them through the fallen boulders; the sultry smoke gets stronger. Behind Ristos is an enormous crevice, a gaping hole in the ground with black smoke floating from below. Ristos glances back. The bottom is not visible. A fall will lead to certain death.

Myths in Pendilor say the land underneath the living world is inhabited by the great demon Drogard. The sun god, Suriyar—Arteo and Ristos's own grandfather—banished the once demigod for inhuman acts hundreds of years ago.

He resides in the depths of hell, waiting to swallow up those who dare fall into his domain. Surrounded by demons and spirits waiting to devour the soul of any who venture below.

Ristos is getting desperate. He shoots another blast at a nearby rock, sending the boulder hurtling towards Arteo. Arteo smashes it with his sword like it's made of parchment, sending blasts of fragments everywhere. Several fly towards Ristos, and one jagged piece enters his eye.

Ristos howls in pain, dropping his sword with a clatter as he claps his hands over his eye. Blood seeps through his fingertips. His foot stumbles on the rock beneath him.

Arteo glares, no emotion felt towards his cousin as Ristos slips into the crevice. He screams, grabbing the sparse grass and rock with fumbling fingers. Blood covers his palms, slick and red, blood pouring down his cheek from his ruined eye.

Preeya pants hard, pain running through her back, a cut across her ear, bleeding down her neck. Syrana is no longer smirking, nothing but hate in her gaze as they circle each other, waiting for any sign of weakness.

They surge towards each other once more, and Preeya lands a blow on Syrana's knee, slicing across the skin just under her thigh. Syrana screams, the wounded leg crumpling beneath her.

She raises her trembling left hand, ready to throw a desperate blast of energy, but Preeya dodges and swings her sword through the air. It finds its mark, almost in slow motion, and slices right through Syrana's wrist, cutting off her hand.

The dark-haired evil princess gives a curdled scream, clutching the stump as the useless limb lands on the ground, still clutching her sword.

The crevice is close behind her.

'This is for years of being such a bitch.' Preeya launches forward with a cosmic blast, slamming her cousin in the chest. She falls back with a grunt, rolling over and falling into the hole. She slams into Ristos, and his hands slip from the stone.

Brother and sister scream as they fall . . . down into the depths of hell below. Preeya and Arteo stand above the surface, their lips tight and sucking in fatigued breaths through their noses as Syrana and Ristos fall to their deaths. Their screams echo.

Soon, nothing but silence.

Preeya breathes through injured ribs, clutching her brother's wrist. He wraps a bleeding arm around her. It is over. Their evil cousins are no more.

'I can't,' Preeya whispers, clutching at him. 'I can't fight any more.' Arteo is gentle as he picks her up. They head down the cliff.

⌘ ⌘ ⌘

'More! Give them more!'

The dragon's roars rock the battlefield, and he snaps up any soldier brave or stupid enough to try to engage him in combat. He shakes his enormous head, chewing up screaming armoured soldiers. The Tolverines flatten what Gazzadeil doesn't get to first.

Assyri's remaining troops, inspired by their allies' arrival and the disappearance of their enemies' leader, fight with renewed vigour, pulverizing the last of Bolara's soldiers. A mix of refugee fighters and jungle dwellers, fighting together like brothers.

Gazzadeil's mighty fire illuminates King Ranakin and King Hirtila's battle, crackling across dry grass and showing their black silhouettes. King Hirtila, Bolara's staunch ally and a lover of violence, is wielding an enormous battleaxe, his eyes wild as he swings at the jungle king's head. Ranakin ducks and dodges the heavy blow.

'This is for my people!' Ranakin bellows, burying his sword into King Hirtila's stomach. The evil ruler's eyes widen, the battleaxe clattering to the ground as blood bursts from his lips. 'Never again will you hurt my jungle folk!'

A cheer rises from Assyri's remaining troops as Bolara's forces scatter, running from the battle they can no longer win. King Hirtila sinks to the ground with a pained gurgle, his eyes closing. King Ranakin pants hard, his tunic sticking to him like a second skin.

Paraksha withdraws his sword from the chest of an enemy. A loud squelch follows. He glances towards his children. They're fighting, whilst under the protection of the mother Tolverine. Balin is finishing off any enemies the Tolverines leave in their wake.

'Look!' Balin shouts, pointing to where a young man runs towards them from the cliffs, carrying a woman. It's Arteo and Preeya, bleeding and injured, but very much alive.

Karina squeals and runs to Arteo, where she hugs him, careful of his hold on Preeya. She inhales the excursion and the blood on his body, never been happier to hold him.

'Take Preeya to safety,' blurts Arteo to Balin. Preeya's eyes are half-closed, like she's about to collapse. Balin puts an arm around her and lifts her from Arteo's arms.

Preeya protests weakly but leans towards the boy, clutching her ribs. The boy has a firm grip of her.

'Where are you going?' pleads Karina in alarm as Arteo turns back towards the cliffs. 'Is it not over?'

'I must find the true queen of Pendilor,' he responds and plants a quick kiss on her cheek. 'Take care of my sister!' he yells behind as he darts back towards where his mother disappeared earlier.

Karina assists Balin in helping Preeya to safety, near the tree line and behind the mother Tolverine. 'Why is he so stubborn?'

'That's my . . . brother.' Preeya pants. 'Either of you got any water?' Balin rifles through his satchel and pulls out a water skin. Preeya takes several grateful gulps, sighing as Karina checks her wounds.

The boy is mesmerized by her beauty and glares deep in her eyes as he continues supporting her. 'By the gods, you are an angel,' says Balin.

'How old are you, boy?' Preeya snaps back. 'You look like you're fourteen.'

Balin straightens his back. 'Well, I'm eighteen years, and—' Before he can finish, the beautiful girl passes out. He carries her with tenderness to the healers.

'He's coming back, isn't he?' squeaks the princess to Balin, anxiety in her dark eyes.

'He always does, sister. He always does.'

✄ ✄ ✄

Assyri grunts in pain, holding her injured arm as she leans against the boulder, breathing hard as she peers up at Ritani. She managed to dodge the blow of the sword, but the witch is getting closer, murder in her gaze. No mercy or pity in her heart. Only a lust for the queen's blood.

For years, Bolara and his family underestimated Assyri. She may preach peace, but that doesn't mean she's weak.

With a scream, Assyri raises her hand and sends a blast of cosmic energy at the boulder behind her, smashing it into pieces. At the same time, she raises a shield behind her, protecting herself from the flying shrapnel. Unprepared, Ritani staggers, throwing an arm over her face to protect herself from the flying rock.

Assyri snatches up her sword, yanking her robes from the ruined rock, and tackles the blinded witch, throwing her to the ground. Ritani's eyes spread open, her mouth opening in a fierce snarl.

Assyri's blade enters Ritani's stomach. The queen pushes the blade deep, aiming up, ruining the woman's organs.

The half-witch lets out a scream. '*Aaahh.*' It is her last. The light dies from Ritani's eyes. Assyri lets out a relieved gasp.

'*Aargh!* ' a fierce growl sounds behind her. Before Assyri can turn, piercing pain flares in the back of her left shoulder, making her scream through gritted teeth. Blood spurts on her tongue.

In shock, Assyri rolls off the dead Ritani, agony burning in her shoulder as she stares behind her. Bolara stands tall, with a crossbow in his hands, all the rage and anger in his face as he glances down at his dead wife.

Ritani stares sightlessly up at the sky, her mouth open in an unsaid word, blood pooling around her limp body.

Assyri is drained. She's exhausted, her energy spent. The arrow tip is buried deep into her shoulder blade; her left arm flares with agony as she tries to move. Bolara is unstained, fresh for battle. No blood on his armour. She doesn't stand a chance against him.

'Always the coward,' Assyri snarls. 'You let others fight your battles for you.'

'Yet in the end, it is I who will end your miserable life,' her brother snaps, drawing his sword. The blade glimmers in the waning daylight. 'Prepare to meet the gods, Assyri.'

'I am ready,' she responds as her eyes close, thinking of her children. At least she got to see Arteo and Preeya. At least she played her part in saving the kingdom of Pendilor from evil.

They will avenge her death. She is sure of it. Bolara raises his sword to kill her and . . .

The ground gives a violent shudder, almost throwing the false king off his feet. His eyes narrow as a young, man, skin glowing in a blue flame, appears before them, standing between Assyri and Bolara.

'You will not touch her,' thunders Arteo. 'You will not harm her any more!'

'Ah, good, the lost prince has arrived.' Bolara sneers. 'I heard what you did to Thamios. Must have given you great pleasure.'

'You are a blight on this planet, Bolara.' Arteo glares hard. 'You are a disgrace to all demigods and mortals.'

Bolara curls his lips in anger. 'Once I finish with you, I will take the head from your mother.'

'Enough, Bolara,' roars Arteo. His voice is deeper, more resounding, somehow, as though the power of the sun god, Suriyar, is infused in his bones. 'It is over. Your armies are in ruin. Ristos and Syrana are dead. Everything is lost. Give up now, and my mother *may* show you mercy.'

Bolara is stunned for a moment, then shakes off Arteo's words as though he doesn't believe anything he's saying. He barks a laugh and withdraws a second sword. 'I will show you the true power a demigod can wield, little Arteo. You may have bettered Thamios, but you will find me a different proposition.'

Bolara clangs his swords together, and Assyri flinches as her brother's body lights up like Arteo's. His skin glowing blue, his eyes gleaming white. His swords are glowing and appear sharpened. Bolara grins at Arteo, cocking an eyebrow in challenge.

Arteo whips his arms across his body and withdraws his own two swords. Hands firmly planted on the grips. He does not feel the weariness of recent battles. He radiates the pure energy of the sun surging through his body, ready to battle for his life.

They circle each other as Assyri lays wounded, half-conscious. 'Be careful, my prince,' wails Assyri.

Bolara lunges forward with all his might.

CHAPTER 23

───────◎───────

SHAKTI UNLEASHED

The several dozen remaining troops of Bolara throw down their weapons and raise their hands in defeat. Without their leader, what little motivation they had to fight quickly dwindled away.

King Paraksha and King Ranakin, brothers in their fight, gather the surrendered soldiers in a circle, commanding them to drop all their weapons. The clatter of metal and wood rings out as soldiers throw down their maces, daggers, and bows, some unused, others covered in crusting, drying blood.

A healer, who joined the back of the jungle dwellers, is on his knees beside Preeya. The girl is unconscious but breathing; she is simply exhausted, with no fatal wounds. Her blonde hair spreads about her head, almost like a golden halo. Balin and Karina sit nearby, watching her chest rise and fall as the healer tends to her wounds, checking her pulse and reassuring the siblings that she is all right.

Nearby, the mother Tolverine growls something to her puppy and the smaller beasts and backs into Gazzadeil. The dragon's enormous head whips around to face her, smoke bursting from his nostrils as he bares his teeth. The Tolverine's hackles raise as she growls. Karina and Balin tense as they stare, some nearby soldiers glancing anxiously at the duo.

Then the great dragon lowers his head, acknowledging the enormous Tolverine. She mirrors his act, bowing, a mild snort coming from her, and they carry on.

'Look at that,' says Balin. He's hugging his legs, his chin resting on his knees. 'You ever seen anything like that?'

Karina is still uncomfortable at the sight of the dragon. He nearly burned her to death, after all. But he proved today that he's on their side now. She privately thinks that as long as he doesn't come too close to her, she can tolerate his presence.

'Karina', says her father, approaching them. He spares a glance for Preeya, still lying unconscious. 'Where is the queen of Pendilor?'

'She's in the cliffs,' she says, pointing to the rugged terrain. Worry runs through her. Arteo and his mother still aren't back yet. She's seen him fight, but is he strong enough to fight that evil man, Bolara, the false king? She prays nothing bad has happened to her future husband or Queen Assyri, but she can't do much more than monitor Preeya and wait for news. Very frustrating.

'I'm going,' says King Paraksha, tying his sword back around his waist. 'I need to see if they need any help.'

Karina lets out a groan, but better not to argue. 'Please be careful,' she whispers, and he pulls her into a hug, kissing her cheek.

'I'm always careful,' he says, making her smile weakly.

'Yeah, always, especially when you're hunting Burrintots.' She sighs and lightly pushes his shoulder. 'Go. I'll take care of Preeya and Balin.'

✳ ✳ ✳

Thunder cracks across the sky as though the gods themselves are witnessing this battle. Bolara, his eyes bright fire and wild, gives a shout of fury as he lunges forward, his swords flashing. Arteo dodges one swipe and blocks the other, steel clashing like loud claps of thunder.

Assyri watches in fear, hardly able to follow the two fast figures, shining like miniature suns as they zoom around, seemingly flying in the air, sending cosmic energy blasts and trading blows with their swords. Their attacks are aggressive, desperate; Arteo lunges out of the way, backflipping.

Bolara matches his acrobatic grace, moving with astonishing finesse. His age is no matter, here; he is drawing on his Shakti 5 powers like a well, using all his power.

Sweat pours down Arteo's brow, his muscles crying out in protest as he blocks, parries, and evades, trying to find a weakness. Neither of them is gaining any advantage over the other. Fighting his uncle, the false king, makes fighting General Thamios look almost easy. *How will I beat him?*

Exhaustion lingers on the horizon, threatening to approach and consume him, but he furiously pushes it away.

Bolara lands on the ground like a cat, using an energy blast to uproot a dead tree. He hurls it towards Arteo, dirt and rocks flying everywhere. Arteo jumps out of the way, nothing but a few pebbles scratching him. He counter-attacks by pulling a boulder off the ground, sending it rolling towards his uncle. With Bolara distracted, Arteo sends another cosmic blast, but Bolara leaps over the rock, deflecting the energy blast with a wave of his wrist.

They trade more blows, the sky crackling above, threatening rain. Bolara thrusts with both swords, and Arteo feels a burning pain; the blade slices through his armour, and though it has mostly absorbed the blow, a cut appears across his chest. Arteo reels back, breathing hard through his teeth. Bolara smirks, sensing he's gained the advantage.

'The mighty prince of Pendilor,' he sneers. His smirk turns to rage. 'After I'm done with you, I'm going to enjoy killing your mother. Slowly. She'll be begging for me to finish her life before the end.

Arteo screams his anger and his hate, fighting back with renewed vigour.

⁂

Assyri breathes hard, her shoulder still prickling from the crossbow bolt. Darkness clouds her vision, and she blinks, furiously trying to push away the oblivion trying to claim her. She witnesses Bolara slashing Arteo across the chest.

'No.' She moans, raising blood-soaked fingers. She wants desperately to help him, but she can barely move. When she tries to raise to her feet, nausea churns her belly, dizziness threatening to throw her to the ground. 'Arteo . . .'

The pain of losing her husband, Ranay, comes back in full force, burning her eyelids. If Bolara defeats Arteo, how will she possibly go on?

'May the gods protect you, my son,' she whispers, collapsing back to the ground with a pained wince.

✄ ✄ ✄

The cut burning across his skin dims his concentration, Arteo groans as Bolara pummels him without mercy. Arteo struggles to block the blows coming at full force. The edge of the cliff is at his back, the slashing of steel like foul music, sending up sparks and singing in their blood.

Arteo cries out in pain as another deep cut lands on his arm. His weakened fingers fumble, dropping a sword to the ground with a clatter. The other is slashed out of his hand by a vicious swipe from his uncle.

Bolara sends a mighty wave of cosmic energy which Arteo deflects with his good hand, teeth bared. He's teetering on the edge of the cliff now, the back of his foot already over the edge. Several stones fall down the cliff, falling and echoing.

Arteo tries to send a blast of his own, but Bolara grabs his wrist, their noses inches apart. 'I haven't forgotten about Preeya,' he snarls at him, spittle landing on Arteo's face. 'She will experience my full wrath too.'

He lunges his leg up, his knee smashing into Arteo's ribcage. The boy's lungs empty of air, making him wheeze, darkness prickling his vision. Then he fires a blast of energy, hitting Arteo in the chest. Weakened, the young man gives a pained grunt.

He falls off the edge of the cliff. '*No! Arteo!*' Assyri screams.

Bolara pants ever so slightly, armoured chest heaving as he turns towards Assyri. His blade gleams in his hand as he steps towards her, ready to finish the job. Murder in his eyes. A vicious victory curling on the corners of his mouth. He twirls his swords in his hands, savouring the victory.

Assyri tries to edge away, but every movement sends a knife-like pain slicing through her shoulder. She saves up her energy, planning to throw a blast at him. If she times it right, she may be able to throw him over the edge too. Her palm warms in her clenched fist as she forces herself not to weep. She holds more hatred for her brother now than she ever did.

Whoosh. Bolara whirls around, catching a dagger in his hand with lightning reflexes. He stares at the blade, somewhat amused, gripping the hilt. King Paraksha has arrived, throwing a dagger to try to save Assyri. He appears stunned when Bolara holds the dagger. The false king's demigod reflexes are just too fast to sneak up on him.

'Really?' Bolara sneers, his back to Assyri. 'A mortal trying to fight a demigod? What is this nonsense?' He throws the dagger away, ready to march over to king Paraksha and cut him down.

Ruummble.

The ground violently trembles, like hell itself is angered. There is another deep rumble, like an earthquake, and a howling wind picks up, blowing their hair and clothes. Bolara swirls around.

Arteo suddenly appears from the cliff, airborne, *his skin glowing like fire.*

He opens his hand. His sword flies into it, and he glares in fury at his uncle, shining like a miniature sun. King Paraksha shields his eyes, backing away. Assyri's heart lifts. She can barely dare to believe it.

'What madness is this?' Bolara gasps, stepping back. Only a level 6 Shakti, almost unheard of, can fly unassisted. *It is a power reserved for the gods.*

Arteo gives an angry yell, the frustration of years of torment ringing, as he surges towards his uncle. He deflects Bolara's energy blasts with ease. He raises his sword; Bolara blocks with one blade, but Arteo's sword slices right through. The useless pieces of metal fall to the ground.

Arteo is so bright Bolara drops the hilt of his broken blade and shields his eyes, attacking with his second sword. Arteo parries it, but instead of sending it back, he smashes the blade into thousands of pieces.

The sound shattering echoes throughout the cliffs, and the wind quietens. A lightning bolt, far away on the horizon, flashes in the cloud-ridden sky. Then silence descends, Bolara looking in horror at his ruined weapons.

King Paraksha is now at Assyri's side, helping her. They both glare, stunned, at Arteo's newfound power. Bolara is struggling to make a decision as he has never faced a demigod more powerful than himself before. He thought none existed!

Arteo gives a final roar, surging with his sword, cutting a deep gash across Bolara's body, shoulder to hip. The older man gasps, blood dribbling from his lips. The young prince spins and swipes, the blade cutting easily through his uncle's arm. Bolara screams, fury and fear mingling into something ugly as he raises his other arm in defence.

The planet seems to stop. Everything is in slow motion.

Arteo's body shines bright like a beacon as he jumps into the air and comes crashing down, his sword before him. He slices through the remaining raised arm and right through Bolara's body. The others stare in horror as the sword slices through Bolara's shoulder, cutting him in half.

For a moment, Bolara blinks in shock. Then both halves slide to the ground, separating and spilling blood and guts. Arteo's red-stained sword tip touches the ground as he breathes hard, kneeling on one leg.

The light fades from his skin, and the fire in his eyes dims as he returns to normal. Blood drips from the wound on his chest and his arm, but he's alive. When he peers up to meet his mother's eyes, there is nothing but victory in his gaze.

'By the gods,' mutters King Paraksha.

Arteo comes over to them, wiping his brow. Assyri is breathing slow, blood pooling from the arrow still stuck in her shoulder. King Paraksha gathers her into his arms, and she winces, red dripping on to his armour. 'Let's get back to the others,' he says, glancing at Arteo partly from fear and partly from admiration.

'Will she be all right?' asks Arteo in concern. With the thrill of battle wearing off, it is replaced by cold fear as he senses how shallow his mother's breathing is, how the skin around the crossbow bolt is paled and blued.

'If we get her to a healer, she may have a chance,' responds King Paraksha firmly. 'We just need to get her there quickly. Come on.'

They head back down the cliff path. The wind subsides, the storm a mere thought on the horizon. It appears like the rain will hold off, for now. The breeze is cool on their aching skin. Thoughts fly like a whirlwind through Arteo's mind.

A sudden shape materializes in the cloudy sky, and Arteo raises his sword in defence, his heart pounding. Is it Bolara, or Ristos, perhaps, somehow back from the dead?

As it gets closer, it takes the shape of a bird. 'Oh', he says in surprise as the shape gets closer; it's the Paraka which led him to Assyri's refugee village in the forest. The same markings adorn its eyes, the same quiet intelligence. 'What is this special bird?' He turns to the others as the Paraka lands before them. For a moment it stares at them all, its head cocking. Then before their eyes, the Paraka glows brightly as it starts to transform.

Its feathers fall away, and it manifests into the form of a man wearing a white robe. He is tall and muscular, with glowing, golden skin and hair the colour of the sun. He smiles down at them all as they gaze in awe.

Assyri's eyes flicker as the golden light bathing her from this new man warms her skin. 'F-Father?' she croaks. 'You've come?'

'Father?' asks Arteo, glancing between them all. 'You . . . you're Suriyar? The sun god? You're my grandfather?'

Suriyar smiles at them, his face full of fatherly love. When he speaks, his voice booms like thunder, sending goose pimples springing up on Arteo's skin. Even so, his voice is somehow both comforting and awe-inspiring. 'Arteo', he says. 'You have done well, my child. You have saved the kingdom, and now you must restore peace to the lands.'

Arteo lowers his sword. 'I . . . yes, Grandfather.'

'There will be others,' continues the sun god. The light radiates from him, a beacon in the night. 'In the future, more enemies will come. They aim to cause devastation and destruction to this beautiful planet. You must be ready to meet them.'

Arteo gives a nod, his face hard and determined. 'May I ask a question, Grandfather?'

'Of course, my son.'

'Was it you who saved me that day?' Arteo steps forward, staring in awe at such a resplendent sight. 'Did you give me my mask and wipe my memories?'

'I protected you until you found your true self,' Suriyar gently responds. 'You did so quickly and fulfilled your destiny. But next time, you will be on your own. Gods should not intervene in such matters.'

'Yes, sir,' says Arteo, stepping back. 'I understand.'

'Now go. Restore the kingdom of Pendilor.' Suriyar blows into the air, and something tiny and glowing, like a miniature star, comes out of his lips. It floats towards Assyri, and when it touches her, she's consumed in light.

They gasp and reel back as Assyri's bright-white silhouette lands slowly on her feet. The glow fades; the arrow is gone from her shoulder, and she's standing on her feet, healthy and bright-eyed as before the battle. The wound in her shoulder is gone. Smooth skin now exists.

Her eyes become glassy as she beholds her father with gratitude but says nothing and smiles.

'Goodbye, my children.' Another blinding light. Suriyar turns into the Paraka again and flies off into the sky with a squawk and several flaps of its wings. It disappears into the clouds; Arteo stares in awe.

On the horizon, the clouds are turning pink: nearly sunset. Although Assyri is on her feet, King Paraksha is so stunned from their encounter with a god that he's still holding her about the waist.

She gently clears her throat. 'Thank you, King Paraksha, but I can manage on my own now.'

'What? Oh!' His dark hands jolt from her like he's been struck by lightning. 'Forgive me, my queen.'

Her cheeks go pink as she straightens her armour. Arteo runs to her and hugs her, rubbing his cheek against hers. She holds him close, smiling. He will always be her little boy, even if he does have the almighty, godlike powers of a Shakti 6. When Arteo draws back, he gives King Paraksha a hug. 'Thank you for helping,' he says to the older man. 'You were brave to take on a demigod with your dagger.'

'King Paraksha starts to blush, his dark cheeks going a shade darker. 'Yes, well, it's nothing, but I'm glad I could help.'

'You saved my mother.' Arteo smiles. 'Now, shall we join the others?'

CHAPTER 24

PEACE IS RESTORED

Two weeks have passed since the bloody battle at the cliffs of Heldegar. The remaining troops who are loyal to Bolara are held in captivity; it will be decided what to do with them later.

Though some people call for their blood, insisting they be made examples of by being hanged in the gallows, the reinstated Queen Assyri reminds them that revenge is not their way. She will not spill one more drop of blood in the name of Bolara and his vile rule.

Queen Shyana is released from her own dungeon in Kyetin where Bolara's men imprisoned her, much to her townsfolk's delight. Her people rally to rebuild when the last of Bolara's soldiers are turfed out. Many of them desert by themselves, no longer having a reason to fight now that the false king is dead and the true queen of Pendilor is back on her rightful throne.

Those who were previously refugees can now rejoin their families in their hometowns, though many of them decide to help their neighbours rebuild their lost homes. As for Pendilor itself and its palace, people band together to restore its original beauty. People in hiding who were cooks, maids, ladies-in-waiting, and gardeners flock to return to their posts in the palace and are warmly welcomed.

Most of the training arenas, far too many for Queen Assyri's liking, are stripped away, new flowers, fences, and plants put down in their place. The gardens will return in time, and a new wildlife enclosure is built in the west corner.

Though Preeya has not taken care of animals for years, her eyes shine in delight at the new enclosure, remembering fondly her time of feeding birds and small animals here.

Queen Assyri's eyes fill with happy tears when a farmer and his family come to the palace with a familiar portrait they hid when Bolara took over. Their daughter, a maid in the palace, managed to sneak it out before Bolara ordered his soldiers to burn all the portraits and destroy the sculptures that ever showed Queen Assyri and her family resided there.

'We kept it under the floorboards for years,' says the farmer as he and his wife hand the portrait to some waiting servants. 'We knew you would return one day, my queen, and made sure it was safe. Bolara's soldiers never searched for it.' His skinny chest puffs up with pride at his words.

It is a beautiful painting portraying Queen Assyri and Ranay, looking happy and healthy, their children on either side of them back when they were small. She orders it to be hung on the wall in the dining room immediately. 'How can I ever thank you?' asks the queen. She turns to her guardsman. 'Thank you, Your Majesty. All I ask is that Aplera continues to work at the palace here. She loves working here, and your gratitude is more than enough.'

'You have done a wonderful service for this kingdom, my friend.'

Peace and harmony are returned to the kingdom, and the last of Bolara's followers put to work or imprisoned. Many of them serve a short time in the palace dungeons and come out reformed, seeing that his ways were cruel and that he was a usurper, not a true king.

'And if they change their minds and rebel?' asks Preeya as a bowing man, a former soldier, leaves the palace with the promise of full loyalty to the crown.

'We'll be ready,' says Queen Assyri, watching the man as he leaves through the heavy double doors.

⚒ ⚒ ⚒

Queen Assyri sits on a balcony overlooking the gardens. Many people are hard at work, combining their passions to create beautiful new rose beds, lilies, petunias, and even a new pond for frogs and goldfish. Much of the palace grounds are damaged; many months will be required to restore its original glory, but time is not an issue.

She sighs as she thinks back to what occurred between her brother and his family. The waste of innocent lives and the needless bloodshed.

King Paraksha sits beside her. He came claiming royal business, but they have not talked politics since his arrival here.

'Nice day', says King Paraksha. 'And, um, tasty ale'.

'Pendilor's specialty', she says, blushing at his words for a reason she can't explain. 'I'm . . . glad you like it.'

The doors open with a dull creak, and Preeya walks in. Her hair is getting longer, tied in a simple braid, and though she's wearing a modest gown, the sleeves are rolled up, rumpled like she impatiently pushed them over her elbows, the skirts slightly darkened from walking through dirt.

'Why are you still following me?' she snaps behind her. Balin is on her heels. Though they are the same age, he is half a head shorter than her, watching her like he's entranced.

'I'm here merely to offer assistance, my princess,' he says.

King Paraksha lets out a shout of laughter. 'He hasn't left your side since we arrived.'

'I am aware,' says Preeya, ice in her voice. 'He's like a little puppy.' Balin appears crestfallen at the reference.

'That isn't a way to woo a girl, my son.' King Paraksha chuckles, taking a sip of ale.

'Woo?' Preeya demands, her cheeks blushing pink. She swallows, approaching her mother. 'Enough about me. When are *you* two officially going to court?'

King Paraksha chokes on his drink as Queen Assyri gives a gasp, spilling her own all over her white gown. Dabbing herself with a nearby cloth, she says, a little too quickly, 'What in heaven's name are you talking about, Preeya?'

Her daughter smiles, her eyes sparkling. 'Come now, Mother. Are you two going to continue playing games then?'

Queen Assyri concentrates on cleaning her gown until a maid scurries in to help. Balin mumbles an excuse and dashes off.

⁂

Arteo sits beside Karina near the wildlife enclosure. The baby Tolverines, some injured, some purely there to play, are scampering around the grounds, play-fighting and growling to one another. It is quite a sight to behold, and Karina leans into Arteo as he wraps an arm around her.

After everything, he's so glad she is here with him. Seemed like a wild dream that they would end up back in their rightful place in Pendilor, and now his true love is by his side as well.

'I thought I'd lost you,' she says, seeming to be on the same wavelength of thoughts. 'All those times you ran off to fight, I thought it would be the last time I ever saw you. I felt so helpless, but I'm glad I was wrong.'

'I'm sorry I made you worry so,' he says, stroking her hair, soft and curly in his fingers, and she lets out a happy little sigh, closing her eyes. 'The memory of you kept me going. Whenever I thought all was lost, I remembered your face.'

'You don't mean that.' She laughs.

'Oh, I do,' he says, looking serious and drawing back. 'I imagined you screaming to me, "Don't you dare die, or I'll kill you!"'

She giggles and kisses him. 'Yes, if you died, I would be furious. I'd never have forgiven you, Arteo.'

'Good thing I'm not going anywhere then.' He grins. He glances around the gardens.

'Waiting for someone?' She cocks her head when he doesn't reply. 'Is everything okay, Arteo?'

He nods, then his eyebrows raise as Balin runs over. His legs move comically fast, and he's panting when he arrives, a bow clutched in his hand. 'You finally got here.' Arteo grins at him. 'Are you done following my sister around like a lovesick calf?'

'Don't know . . . what you're . . . talking . . . about.' Balin pants, passing him the bow and a quiver of several feathered arrows.

Arteo gets to his feet, nocking an arrow and aiming. Balin and Karina both stare as he fires the arrow. It curves around three trees, stabbing into something. Still attached, it travels with the arrow, weaving its way back, and pierces the tree nearby.

'How do you do that?' asks Balin, stunned. 'I can barely shoot an arrow straight.'

'One day, I'll teach you,' says Arteo, going to the tree and snagging the small pouch the arrow pierced. He sits beside Karina, opening the small bag.

In his fingers is a gorgeous diamond ring, glimmering in the sunlight. Karina's mouth opens, staring between Arteo and Balin; her little brother whistles to himself, looking away, though it is obvious he knows what's going on.

'Karina, I've been in love with you since the moment I laid eyes on you. Will you honour me by becoming my queen?'

'Oh, Arteo, of course I will!' she cries, throwing her arms around him. She tackles him to the ground, raining kisses on his face while Arteo laughs. He slips the ring over her delicate finger, and they hold hands, grinning at each other.

The three of them head over towards the palace to tell everyone the exciting news. Queen Assyri is ecstatic, hugging and kissing them both. King Paraksha gives a knowing smile, asking what took them so long to make it official as his eyes sparkle with mirth. Arteo shouts for wine, and the servants happily join them, toasting the young couple's happy announcement.

King Paraksha and Queen Assyri hug each other, laughing in delight, then jump away as though burned, avoiding each other's gaze. Arteo and Preeya smirk at each other. Many things have happened since their father was killed; why shouldn't she move on?

'Father, Balin, *look* at this ring!' Karina exclaims, showing them the fabulous sparkling diamond on her finger. 'It's beautiful?'

'Well done, big brother, you've got a good one there,' says Preeya, kissing Arteo on the cheek and squeezing Karina's hand. Karina squeezes back, happy tears in her dark eyes. 'And what a beautiful ring.' She hugs her close. 'Welcome to the family, sister.'

'Aww, yes, it is a beautiful ring,' babbles Balin, rushing in to hug Preeya. The princess politely evades, her nose wrinkling. Balin tries to go in for a kiss, but King Paraksha slaps the back of his head.

'Take a hint, boy.'

Preeya smirks, shaking her head.

✄ ✄ ✄

Arteo squeezes his mother in a one-armed hug as they peer out at the gardens. The sun is beginning to sink, casting an orange glow on the palace grounds and the mountains on the horizon. The delicious scent of Yackenhaus wafts in from the kitchens, Arteo's favourite.

Arteo is frowning, and the queen turns to see his expression. 'What is it, my prince?' she asks. 'Today is a day for celebration. Why so serious?'

Arteo gives a sigh, removing his arm from her waist to put his hands on the balcony rail. 'Something that Grandfather said, up on the cliffs. He said more forces would come? That it wasn't the end of the conflict. What was he referring to? Bolara and my cousins are gone.'

'It is yet unknown, Arteo,' says his mother, reaching to rub his back like she did when he was a child. 'For now, we mustn't worry about the future but enjoy the present. We will be ready to deal with such things, if and when they occur. I know it. You'll also make a terrific king.'

Arteo lets her warm words wash over him. He sighs through his nose, leaning back with a nod. 'You're right, Mother. If there is a next time, we'll be prepared. We will have our soldiers trained and be vigilant.'

'Yes, we will.' She smiles, slipping her hand into his. 'Now don't we have a glorious royal wedding to start preparing for?'

He hugs her again, closing his eyes as he inhales her familiar flowery scent, his heart aching for the years of memories he lost, for his perished father, and all those brave souls who died in defence of their freedoms.

They rejoin the rest of the group, who are pouring more wine and laughing. With everyone so happy and jovial, chattering at top speed about wedding plans and the future of Pendilor and its liberated people, it is easy to let the worries of the future slip away . . . for now.

EPILOGUE

R istos and Syrana fall down, down, deep into the heart of the earth. Their bodies tumble, hitting jagged cliff walls, rocks penetrating skin and gushing blood. Limbs snap and break against the harsh impact. Their bodies limp like rag dolls as they tumble further and deeper into the endless cavern.

It is limitless, endless, but then . . . a sudden jolt.

The impact is not as harsh as one might expect; their landing is soft and cushioned, as though hitting an enormous bed of feathers.

At first, nothing but silence, penetrating after the many hours of wind rushing through their ears. The sound of slow, heavy footsteps. More. Hundreds of heavy feet move towards them.

Syrana's eyes flicker open. Her left hand is cut off at the wrist, crusted blood on the stump. Ristos is lying nearby. His remaining eye is open, the other a gaping black hole. She can feel pulse in her neck, beating feverishly against the strange cushioning beneath their bodies. Unbelievably, miraculously, they are alive.

She tries to move, but her limbs are like heavyweights. She struggles to even blink. Suddenly, bumpy hands like stone roughly drag her up. In the distance, she sees Ristos pulled up too, though she can't get a good visual at the creatures holding him. They're swallowed by darkness. Dizziness overwhelms her, and she passes out.

She wakes to the sensation of drowning, her limbs heavy, helpless to do anything but choke. Her body convulses, trembling, trying to throw off whatever is filling her lungs and squeezing her throat.

Crack. Crack.

What is that? Am I dead?

Syrana's body gets some movement to it, like her body's starting to wake. She fights to reach the surface: no glimmer of light anywhere. She screams, mouth filling with water, when a heavy weight lands on top of her, forcing her back down.

When she regains consciousness again, a knife-like pain slices in her left arm, prickling and burning, like the whole limb is on fire. She tries to scream, but no sound comes out. She fights, but new weights are on her limbs, tying her down.

Tears burn on her eyelids as she fights through madness and agony, her arm burning like hell's fire itself. She slips back into the thankful blackness of death, or half-death, or whatever this bizarre darkness is, waiting for the nightmare to be over.

When Syrana opens her eyes, she's in a cell that reeks strongly of sulphur. The rock bed is hard beneath her back. She glances around, blinking, a single candle casting meagre light around her. No windows, and a solid door sits on the other side. A bowl of water beside it.

Damn hot in here. Her skin is drenched with perspiration. She gets up to a sitting position, and nausea and dizziness instantly hit her, making her groan. Surely, all her bones are broken, but when the pain subsides, she gets to her shaking feet. She steadies herself. No gashes, no broken bones. *Strange.* Whatever found them saved them.

She raises her hands. *Hands!* Her left hand is back, but not made of flesh.

She flexes the fingers. They're made of gravel, but they wriggle and flex at her wordless command.

She marches through the cell. Her breath comes out of her lips, finally making a sound. She bellows at the top of her voice, 'Ristos! Where are you?'

Though she expected it, the lack of response makes her heart sink.

The heavy door swings open with a scrape. Four creatures lumber inside. They're five feet tall, a head smaller than Syrana, and strange in appearance. They're wide, broad-shouldered, and made of rock. Hunched shoulders reveal round heads, red eyes, and small slits for breathing.

Their hands and feet are oversized and also made of rock. Syrana backs into the wall as they glare at her, steel prongs in each of their enormous granite hands. The nearest squints at her, gesturing for Syrana to follow them.

Syrana's fists clench, building up cosmic energy to blast these weirdos to pieces, but she recognizes a familiar voice on the other side of the door.

'Stop poking that thing at me, or I'll shove it down your throat.'

Ristos!

She follows the guards out of the door. Ristos is there, looking worse for wear but alive, being poked by more of the rock-people guards. Syrana shoots one of them with a cosmic blast.

'Wait, don't! It won't—'

The rock man plants its weapon on the ground; the forked point absorbs Syrana's cosmic blast. She gapes in shock as he turns it towards her. She falls to the ground with a grunt, thrown back by her own energy.

Ristos yanks her to her feet. 'I was going to say that won't work.' He smiles at her.

'Your eye,' she says. 'It's made of glass.'

'Courtesy of Arteo'. He spits the name. 'And the handiwork of these . . . creatures. I see your hand is different.'

She glares at it, flexing the new, strange fingers. She quickly hugs him. They don't show affection often, but they almost died down here. Strangely, she feels a little vulnerable, perhaps a little afraid.

'What's going on here?' she asks him. 'Why aren't we dead? And just what are those?' She gestures to the rock men, who prod them both. They lead them down a rock-laden corridor, much to the siblings' disgust. Red dust adorns the hard floor, and the walls are of granite. They reach a thick door, which opens at a prod of their steel rods, opening to a larger chamber.

Hard to believe a chamber this size can fit down here. Thousands of the rock soldiers stand in formation, surrounding the demigods. Guided forward by their captors, they step slowly into the room. Lanterns of fire illuminate the massive stone hall, as massive as a cathedral.

In the centre is a wooden dining table bearing plates of bread, jugs of water, and a bowl of fruit. It is unbearably hot down here, and Syrana's throat is like sandpaper; the sight of the food makes her groan in longing.

They're guided to the table, and the rock people gesture for them to eat. They don't need telling twice; the brother and sister stuff bread in their mouths, taking long, blissful gulps of water and attacking the fruit, closing their eyes in bliss as they chew.

How do they grow food down here? Where are we? What do they want?

As they're eating, a sudden loud rumble erupts. The rock men around them cower in fear. Ristos's eyes widen as they meet Syrana's. Thunderous footsteps approach. They drop the food, anticipating the worst.

'What in the gods is that?' Ristos mutters.

An enormous creature appears in the doorway. At least eight feet of pure granite, carved into a muscular shape, made of rock and blade-shaped horns spiking from its head and arms. At the ends of its enormous arms are huge hands with claws that appear like they could rip you open with a thought.

Its head is the most frightening: rows and rows of endless, jagged teeth and green eyes that fix upon the siblings.

With rumbling footsteps, the monster stomps towards the table, pausing to glare at them both. Syrana is not frightened. She stands defiant, by her brother. Her hands curl into fists, ready to fight.

'Welcome, demigods.' The beast's voice is deep and coarse. 'My name is Drogard. I've been expecting you!'